Highland Solution

Duncurra Book 1

By
Ceci Giltenan

This is a work of fiction. The characters, incidents and dialogues in this book are of the author's imagination and are not to be construed as real. Any resemblance to actual events or persons, living or dead, is completely coincidental.

Duncurra LLC
www.duncurra.com
Copyright 2013 by Ceci Giltenan
ISBN-10:0990487636
ISBN-13:978-0-9904876-3-0
June 2014
Cover Art by Earthly Charms
Produced in the USA

Praise for Highland Solution

Highland Solution is a RomCon Reader's Crown Finalist
with a score of 9.5 out of 10!

From the first page to the last, this is a beautiful story of love,
strength and devotion. The characters are believable, lovable
and well developed. This story captivated me from the first
page. I can't wait to read more from this author.
—Suzan Tisdale, Bestselling Author of Scottish romance

One of the best books I've ever read! Amazing this is a debut
book, I can' praise it enough
—Barb, Amazon reader review

"This book is exactly what I look for in romances. Great plot,
amazing characters and good drama. I'm really hoping this
author writes many more books like this one. I'm waiting!
—Amy, Amazon reader review

"I recommend this book ... You will experience every
emotion while enjoying these characters. I have laughed with
them and also cried - you will wish the story never ended."
—Diane Geibel, Amazon reader review

"This book was wonderful. ... Ceci Giltenan impressed me
with her well rounded characters, her descriptive passages,
and her realistic dialogue."
—Gramma Catalano, Amazon reader review

I love romance and adventure and this story had both. It was
not too steamy but steamy enough and, in my opinion, it had
a great story line and lots of action/adventure.
—R. Williams, Amazon reader review

Other Books by Ceci Giltenan

Highland Courage, Duncurra Book 2

Highland Solution Audio Book

Coming Soon:

Highland Courage Audio Book

Highland Intrigue, Duncurra Book 3

Highland Revenge, a novella

Dedications

To my beloved husband and children, thank you for your love and support.

To the incomparable Kathryn Lynn Davis, thank you for jumping in and helping me reedit this me at a moment's notice. I am looking forward to great collaborations in the future.

To my dear friends and sisters in heart, Lily Baldwin, Kathryn Lynn Davis, Kate Robbins, Tarah Scott, Suzan Tisdale and Sue-Ellen Welfonder—I will never be able to thank you enough for your kindness and support over this rocky road. I feel incredibly blessed to have you and your combined magic in my life.

Chapter 1

"Lady Katherine, oh! Lady Katherine, there you are," said an ashen-faced chambermaid as she rushed into the kitchen. "You must come quick. There are two Highlanders in the great hall with your uncle. Sir Ruthven bid me fetch you there now."

Hot, flushed, and certainly not prepared to receive visitors or face her uncle again so soon, Katherine sighed. "You stay here. I'll go to the great hall alone. It never pays to keep Uncle Ambrose waiting." At the look of panic on the girl's face, Katherine added, "I'm sure it's nothing. Don't worry."

Katherine froze when she saw at least a dozen rather imposing Highland warriors waiting in the courtyard. An even larger group of Ruthven soldiers kept their distance, observing the strangers cautiously. Knowing she'd pay for it later, she stepped back into the kitchen and asked Moyna to offer them food and ale. Then, fearing she had already kept her uncle waiting too long, she hurried into the great hall.

She entered with her head down. Sometimes a show of subservience tempered his anger. He read from an unfurled scroll and didn't acknowledge her immediately so, with her eyes still downcast, she took a quick look to her right.

Two sets of feet in the open leather shoes Highlanders wore caught her attention. Unbidden, her eyes followed the nearest thickly muscled bare legs up the length of the man's tall, powerfully built body. He wore typical Highland clothing, a belted linen tunic that barely reached his knees, with a plaid fastened by a brooch around his massive shoulders. She had to tilt her head back to see his face. The grim expression he wore startled her. Clearly this man was not happy, and she suspected Uncle Ambrose had something to do with it.

Katherine realized eventually that her uncle didn't intend to acknowledge her. Unable to stand the tension any longer, she said, "Uncle Ambrose, you sent for me?" Chancing another quick glance at the Highlander, she saw his grim expression replaced first by confusion, followed very quickly by anger.

When she turned her attention back to her uncle, his barely concealed glee worried her. Finally he replied, "Yes, Katherine, my darling, we have received a missive from the king and it concerns you."

This is definitely not good. She carefully kept her emotions masked. "Me?" she asked calmly.

"Yes, my sweet. This is Niall MacIan, Laird of Clan MacIan." He gestured to the angry warrior she had eyed. "And the commander of his guard, Diarmad. Our king has requested that you become Laird MacIan's wife."

Katherine took a breath and, with supreme will, continued to appear calm and emotionless.

"Requested that I become his wife?" she asked slowly.

"Of course it is a request."

"I can decline this request?

"Certainly you can, Katherine. However, His Majesty says if you choose to decline, it is in your best interest, and the best interests of Clan Ruthven, for me to be named Lord Ruthven and for you to enter the religious life."

"And what happens to Cotharach and my people if I accept the proposal?" she asked, a note of panic creeping into her voice.

A look of smug satisfaction crossed her uncle's face, and he spoke to her as if she were a very dull child.

"Oh, my dear, I have bungled this badly. I will start over and try to help you understand. His Majesty feels it is in the best interests of Clan Ruthven for me to assume control as Lord Ruthven and rule Cotharach. He is giving you two options. The one His Majesty prefers is for you to marry Laird MacIan and go with him to his home in the Highlands. As your husband, Laird MacIan will renounce his claim to your title and lands. In return, he will receive an exceedingly generous dowry. However, if this is not acceptable, you may choose to enter the religious life. The good sisters will receive a modest dowry, but His Majesty has determined that Laird MacIan will still receive the bulk of your dowry, because of his willingness to aid his king in this matter. Does that make it clear, my dear?"

Katherine trembled, feeling as if she had descended into swirling chaos. Trying not to reveal her inner turmoil, which would only add to his pleasure, she bowed her head and whispered, "Aye, Uncle. I understand."

After a moment, she looked directly into the eyes of each of the three men staring at her. In Uncle Ambrose's expression she read joy, in Diarmad's pity, and in Laird MacIan's iron determination. She wanted to run—she needed to think.

Her uncle prodded, "Well, my dearest Katherine, which will it be?"

"You want a decision now? Am I to be given no time to consider?"

In a colder, less unctuous voice, her uncle declared, "You must choose now. You can leave for the convent within the hour or, if you choose marriage, we will summon Father James and you can be married as soon as he arrives. Laird MacIan is anxious to return to the Highlands, so he wishes to depart immediately after you plight your troth to one another. Either way, you leave today."

Katherine knew her uncle had won, she just didn't know how he had done it. From the day her father died, Ambrose had wanted the title and lands that were to be held in reserve for her husband. How had this Highlander been convinced to marry her and relinquish all but a portion of her wealth? But the convent? She didn't relish either option. Finally she said flatly, "I will marry."

"Very well, I will send for Father James."

As Katherine turned to leave, her uncle demanded, "Where are you going?"

She glanced down at the old gown she generally wore when working and realized the absurdity of this situation. She lifted her head and stared at him. "For the next few minutes at least, Uncle, I am Lady Katherine Ruthven. This is my keep. I am going to pack my things and dress for my wedding."

She turned again to leave the great hall, and for the first time, she heard her betrothed's voice. "Lass, one bag is all ye'll be bringing."

She nodded and quietly said, "Aye, Laird," before leaving. Katherine paused at the bottom of the steps and waited for the messenger Uncle Ambrose would be sending to the priest. Stopping him before he left the keep, she asked him to deliver an additional message on his way. Then she climbed the stairs to her chambers.

~ * ~

Being already in a foul mood by the time he arrived at Cotharach Castle, Niall MacIan's temperament only worsened at the enforced wait for the Lady Katherine to appear where he stood with her unpleasant uncle. When MacIan saw a servant enter the great hall instead of Lady Katherine, he reached his breaking point. He could not believe his ears when this servant addressed Ruthven as Uncle Ambrose. The lovely lass couldn't be the one whispered about in Edinburgh Castle. Yet Sir Ruthven's response indicated that this, indeed, was she. He stared boldly at her, taking in her honey-colored hair and small, willowy frame. The faded gown she wore revealed softly curving hips and full breasts.

Niall could only watch, speechless, as her uncle toyed with her like a cat with a mouse. At first she had appeared poised and impassive, but it didn't take long for her mask to slip. He heard the panic rise in her voice, but surely she didn't expect him to believe she was only concerned for her people? If she intended to manipulate his feelings by faking compassion, she would soon realize her folly.

Still, when she captured his gaze for a moment, it shocked Niall to see the fear and confusion in the green depths of her eyes. From out of nowhere, he felt a powerful urge to take her in his arms and comfort her, but he refused to give in to that weakness. Still, while Lady Katherine was likely the same faithless, self-absorbed creature he believed all women to be, at that moment he wanted to crush Ruthven for being an insensitive, manipulative cur.

Feeling it necessary to shake his unwelcome response towards her apparent vulnerability, and also determined to clearly establish his authority after her momentary show of spirit as she turned to leave them behind and 'dress for her wedding.' Before she disappeared, he spoke. "Lass, one bag is all ye'll be bringing." She immediately became the meek, subservient lass who had first walked into the hall. Although it was what he intended, for some reason he found it disconcerting.

~ * ~

Upon entering her chamber, Katherine found her maid, Emma, waiting. "I guess good news travels fast," she said bitterly,

"Oh, my lady, what is going to happen to ye? Those Highlanders are huge. Ye'll be killed for sure." With that dire prediction, Emma burst into tears.

Katherine put her arm around the girl's shoulders. "Don't worry so, Emma. This is what the king wants and I will do it. Everything will be fine." Dear God, she hoped with every fiber of her being that everything would be fine, but she doubted it herself.

"There isn't much time and I need your help to get ready," she said, hoping to get her distraught maid to concentrate. Even with the unusually warm day, Katherine would have given anything to slip into a warm, relaxing bath and attempt to come to terms with things, but she didn't have time. Instead, with a few buckets of cold water, she refreshed herself with a quick wash. Emma helped her dress in a fresh white linen kirtle under her best deep blue linen gown, the neck, cuffs, and sleeves of which Katherine had embroidered with delicate, pale blue forget-me-nots like those growing near the loch by which Cotharach stood. Around her waist she fastened a gold belt that dropped low on her hips and she slipped on soft leather shoes. Emma unbraided and combed her lady's hair, letting the mass of honey colored curls fall down Katherine's back.

"I always thought your wedding would be a great event," Emma said as she gathered Katherine's things to pack. "We would have two things to celebrate—not only your wedding, but being well rid of your uncle, too."

Funny, thought Katherine, at almost twenty, well past the age most noblewomen married, she had never given her wedding any thought. However, even if she had given in to such musings, she never would have imagined the one that awaited her. She smiled at her maid and said, "Well, at least we haven't had ages to worry about it," at which Emma burst into fresh tears.

When Emma's tears stopped, Katherine helped her finish the packing. "I am to only bring one bag," she said with mock sternness, making the maid giggle.

"Oh, my," Emma said, in the same mocking tone. "How will you ever decide what to pack?"

Although very wealthy, Katherine had few belongings worth taking. Uncle Ambrose had confiscated all her jewelry and anything else of real value, ostensibly to safe-guard it. He only provided her with necessities—"to protect her from the sin of vanity"—so she took very good care of the few worn, faded garments she owned. She selected two white linen kirtles and the two least shabby of her gowns: a gold one made of soft light wool and a heavier, dark green one. Although the summer days had been very warm, she knew they were traveling north to the Highlands, where even in summer the nights might be cold, so she packed a woolen mantle, too. She removed the most important items from her sewing basket, rolled them in a short length of linen, and tucked it into the bag. This left room for several shifts; some linen toweling; the leather bag containing a small supply of healing herbs and other ingredients for potions, balms, and poultices; and her one luxury, a cake of sweet smelling soap imported from Spain. Finally she packed the only belongings holding any sentimental significance to her: her mother's ivory comb and her father's jeweled dagger.

"I suppose I'm ready," she said to Emma.

"Go on, then. I'll carry your things down."

"Emma, I might not get to see you again before I leave. I may not be able to say farewell to anybody. Please tell everyone I will miss them and I will keep you all in my prayers. Take care of yourself, Emma, and stay out of my uncle's way." Before Emma had a chance to burst into tears again, Katherine gave her a quick hug and left.

~ * ~

After finalizing the business agreements relating to the marriage, Niall and Diarmad waited in the great hall with Ambrose Ruthven while Lady Katherine readied herself. Eventually Niall had to turn his back to stare into the cold hearth because he couldn't stand seeing Ruthven's barely contained joy. The greedy bastard's pleasure sickened Niall, yet he couldn't deny feeling a certain amount of disgust at himself as well. It took a very desperate man to accept this betrothal. Niall had been beyond desperate. He had no funds to pay even the interest on the crushing debt Clan MacIan held. He had journeyed to Edinburgh to request financial help from the king, only to learn King David II had a significant debt of his own. He owed King Edward III of England a colossal ransom—one hundred thousand marks sterling, with ten thousand marks due yearly on the nativity of St. John the Baptist. Apparently he had no compunction about bartering royal favor for coin, and clearly Ruthven had purchased such favor, inadvertently providing the solution to Niall's problem as well.

Niall had to admit Ruthven's attempts to deter his niece's suitors were particularly effective. He remembered his stepmother's unpleasant reaction when she learned of his pending marriage.

"Niall," she had said, "I have heard about this creature you plan to wed. My poor boy, it must be humiliating to know this is the best you can do. Why I have heard, from people who know, mind you, not only is she brainless, but she is practically an ogre. They say she even has fits, and is a hunchback." When he failed to respond to Eithne's barbs, she added, "Well, hopefully your brother will find a more suitable wife. He is so good-natured and handsome, we will be able to have a proper wedding. Perhaps he will give me grandchildren of whom I can be proud."

Even the king believed he might be saving Katherine from the humiliation of remaining unattached if he ordered her to enter a convent, leaving Ambrose with everything. He had all but agreed to do so until Niall approached him for aid. Niall assumed after seven years in exile and eleven more held captive for ransom, albeit not in depravation, the king would have some qualms about forcing a young woman into a cloister. Evidently, he had no qualms about marrying her to a financially desperate Highland Laird, who would trade her title and lands for a larger dowry in coin. Why was it, for men like Ruthven, problems had a way of disappearing if the man threw enough money at them?

As the silence grew heavy, Niall turned back around. He was pleased to see the happiness originally written on Ruthven's face replaced with consternation. Perhaps he was questioning the wisdom of giving his niece away to a complete stranger.

With Niall's attention on him once again, Ruthven cleared his throat a little to break the silence, then said, "Ahem...uh, Laird MacIan, it occurs to me that you and my sweet, gentle niece will be traveling for several days to reach your home, and will likely be sleeping out of doors."

Niall arched an eyebrow and gave a slight nod, disdain etched on his features. "Yes. Well, you understand that my dear Katherine is of course innocent and might appreciate privacy." A wiser man would have taken heed of the rising fury on the Highlander's face, but Ambrose charged on. "I think it would be best if you wait until you reach your home to...consummate your marriage."

"Sir, would ye willingly marry your niece to a man without honor?" Laird MacIan said with menace.

"N—no, of course not," Ruthven stammered.

"Then ye can be assured I do not need ye to school me in decency!" he roared.

~ * ~

When she returned to the great hall, Katherine saw her uncle sitting in his upholstered chair looking oddly uncomfortable. Both Highlanders stood silently by the hearth. Father James had arrived and even his chatter about the weather and crops didn't lessen the tension in the room. He was the first to notice her as she slipped quietly into the large room. He stopped mid-sentence, proclaiming, "My lady, you are radiant."

Laird MacIan looked up and practically gawked at the sight of her. Katherine had dressed like the noblewoman she was, instead of as a servant. The gown she wore clung to her, revealing her womanly curves, and her hair, released from its braid, shimmered around her shoulders like a golden brown cloud.

After registering Laird MacIan's look of awe, she kept her eyes cast down so he couldn't read the fear on her face, but she was sure no one could miss the way her hands trembled.

"Well, we have a wedding to perform," Father James said, motioning to the door of the great hall "Shall we go to the chapel?"

News of the wedding had spread through Cotharach and its village like a brushfire. Now, in addition to the Highland warriors, the staff at Cotharach and many villagers gathered in the courtyard to witness Lady Ruthven's marriage. The ceremony began outside the chapel with Father James asking the assembly if anyone knew of any reason why Laird Niall and Lady Katherine could not be married. Although no one spoke, a million reasons flew through Katherine's mind. The priest continued, "Niall MacIan, wilt thou have this woman to thy wedded wife? Wilt thou love her, and honor her, keep her and guard her, in health and in sickness, as a husband should a wife, and forsaking all others on account of her, keep thee only unto her, so long as you both shall live?"

She heard Niall answer, "I will," his voice deep and melodic.

Katherine felt strangely detached as she heard the priest ask for her assent. "I will," she answered, the reality of the situation finally sinking in. *This isn't a nightmare, it's really happening, and it is forever.*

"Who gives this woman to be married to this man?"

"I do," answered Ambrose as he stepped away.

Katherine could all but hear him thinking *and good riddance.*

The couple then made their vows of marriage. After Katherine said, "And thereto I plight thee my troth," Father James took the ring Niall gave him, blessed it, and returned it to Niall, who placed it on the third finger of Katherine's left hand. She had always heard a vein ran directly from this finger to the heart and for this reason a wedding band was worn there as a symbol of love. It seemed slightly ridiculous to Katherine, given she had only just met the man who placed it there.

Father blessed the couple and led them into the chapel, followed by Diarmad and Ambrose. The bride and groom knelt before the altar while the priest prayed again.

Kneeling beside her new husband, Katherine felt very small; the top of her head didn't reach his shoulder.

There would not be a nuptial Mass, so after the prayers, Father James gave them a final blessing. When he had finished, he beamed warmly and said, "You may kiss the bride." Niall tipped her chin up and kissed her. She had expected he would give her only a chaste peck, but once he started, she was amazed by how warm and soft his lips felt and that he held her there, deepening the kiss for a moment before pulling away. Stunned, she raised her hands to touch her lips. They tingled where his had touched her, and she hadn't wanted him to stop.

He looked momentarily stunned as well, but rapidly recovered. "Say your goodbyes quickly," he told her. "We are leaving."

Her uncle approached and kissed Katherine on both cheeks. "Goodbye, my dear. I can't tell you how much we will miss you." He spoke blandly with an insipid expression on his face.

That is because you won't miss me. She didn't know why he bothered with the farce, because Laird MacIan had already left the chapel. She managed to say, "Goodbye, Uncle," civilly.

Lord Ruthven returned to the keep, not bothering to see them off. Father James gave her a hug and Katherine couldn't suppress a wince.

Father looked concerned and asked, "Katherine, dear, will you be all right? Perhaps you should tell your new husband about your back. You have a long journey ahead."

"No Father. Please don't say anything. Nothing good can come from telling him that now. I'll be fine."

He shook his head but didn't argue, and taking her arm, walked with her into the courtyard, saying, "Katherine, I'm certain you will be a wonderful wife and mother."

She loved the old priest, so she smiled and teased, "How do you know I'll be a wonderful wife; you've never been married."

He chuckled and took both her hands in his. "My sweet girl, this world is full of people whose first concern is usually their own needs or desires. You're one of the few who always considers the needs of others before your own. You have learned the surest way to open yourself to hurt is to love, and yet you love anyway. How could one so full of love and compassion not be a wonderful wife and mother?" He smiled, traced a cross on her forehead with his thumb, and kissed her on the cheek, saying, "Go with God, my dear one."

Katherine squeezed his hands and smiled at him, blinking back tears. It could be the last time she would ever see this gentle man. She couldn't speak. She took a deep breath to muster her courage, and walked toward the gray mare the stable master led. Before she reached them, Laird MacIan waved the stable master away. "Lady Katherine will ride with me."

~ * ~

Her vehement and panic-stricken, "Nay!" surprised Niall.

She hurried towards him. "I can ride very well, my lord. Stormy is mine. My father gave her to me years ago."

Perhaps for the first time since he'd met her, she wasn't trying to hide the emotion she felt. While he expected to see defiance, fitting his expectations of a pampered noblewoman, instead he saw fear. On the verge of barking at her for publically challenging him, when he caught that glimpse of raw fear he hesitated.

"I'm sure ye do ride well, for a woman, but the journey will be hard, over very rough terrain. Your mare is not sturdy enough. It would be cruel."

She laid a hand on his arm, stopping him before he turned away. Looking him in the eye, she leaned close, saying in a voice so low only he could hear it, "It will be cruel to leave her."

Unable to ignore the beseeching look she gave him, after a moment he said, "We will take her without a rider."

The sudden warmth he felt when he saw the tension leave her body and heard her sigh of relief, surprised him. He helped her into the saddle of his huge warhorse. She put her right knee over the pommel and he mounted behind her, pulling her close. He inhaled her sweet, clean scent and her soft, round bottom pressed intimately against his groin, fanning the warmth he'd felt before into full flame. He frowned as Katherine stiffened and leaned forward ever so slightly, holding herself away from him.

Having removed Stormy's saddle, the stable master handed the reins to one of Niall's men and they set out. After they cleared the castle gate, Katherine said quietly, "Thank you for bringing my mare, but you don't plan to take her the whole way, do you."

She hadn't asked it as a question; she simply made the statement. Her accurate assessment of the situation surprised him. In fact, this day and his new wife seemed to be full of surprises. "Nay, I don't," he agreed. "Our pace and the terrain really will be too hard on her. I assume there is some reason why ye were afraid to leave her behind?"

"Aye. My uncle is...cruel."

The brief pause in her comment made Niall wonder what other description of her uncle she had censored before arriving at "cruel."

"Tomorrow we will be passing through a holding belonging to one of my allies. The mare will be well-treated there."

Katherine gave a slight nod of her head. Then her brow furrowed and she appeared worried about something else. Looking as if she was about to confess some mortal sin, she said, "My lord—"

"I am your husband now, call me Niall."

"Niall," she said and took a breath as if steeling herself before launching into her confession. "I have done something, and I hope you won't be angry, but I really saw no other option." She felt his body become tense, but she went on. "When you arrived, did you see Tomas, the young stable boy?"

"I remember a small lad," he said cautiously.

"Tomas' parents are dead. He lived with his grandfather, our former stable master, but that kind, old man passed away a few months ago. Tomas continued to work in the stables, under my uncle's new stable master, but he is as bad as my uncle. So you see, I was worried about Tomas. Without me, there really is no one in any position to protect him." She paused, biting her lower lip.

"Are ye coming to the part where ye are going to tell me what ye did?" Niall asked, not attempting to cover the frustration he felt.

Katherine cringed a little at his tone. "Aye. Well, when my uncle summoned Father James to marry us, I sent a message to Tomas, telling him to follow the northwest road from the village until he reached the tree line and to wait there for us—so we could bring him with us."

"Bring him with us?" Niall said, completely dumbfounded by her audacity. "Bring him with us?" he repeated incredulously, "Are ye asking me to steal another man's serf?"

"Tomas isn't a serf. His father and grandfather were hired freemen," she assured him hurriedly.

"And why do ye think he will fare better with me as his laird?"

She leaned a little, turned, and tilted her head up so she could look him in the eyes. "My Lord—" She paused at his stern expression and corrected herself. "Niall. If I didn't think life with you would be a vast improvement over that with my uncle, I would not have agreed to marry you." At his look of doubt, she added, "I know King David ordered this marriage, but I would have joined the nuns at St. Oda's before consenting to marry a man like Ambrose Ruthven."

Although surprised by the intensity of her statement, he knew it didn't take much to be a better man than Ruthven.

Still, he took some bit of pleasure in hearing his new wife say it.

"Diarmad," he called to his commander, riding in the lead.

"Aye, Laird?"

"There will be a lad waiting for us as we reach the tree line."

"Aye, Laird. I've already seen a lad ducking in and out from behind the trees. He looks to be the stable-boy from Cotharach."

"He'll be going with us."

"Aye, Laird." Diarmad quietly chuckled.

Niall glanced at Katherine. Almost undone by the brilliant smile she gave him, he could do nothing but stare. She blushed, dropped her head, and turned away from his gaze to face front, but that brush with delight unsettled him. He did not need a wife, he reminded himself. He believed a wife could only be a distracting nuisance. He certainly did not need a wife whose smile made him forget everything except thinking of ways to make her smile again. He had learned the hard way that a soft body and pretty face can blind a man to treachery.

When they reached Tomas, another of Niall's guard, a young man, whom she had heard addressed as "Fingal," called to him and pulled the lad up onto his saddle.

It didn't take Tomas long to begin asking Fingal a never-ending stream of questions.

Chapter 2

Katherine could hear Tomas' chattering, but couldn't concentrate on his words. Niall hadn't exaggerated—they were traveling at a brutal pace. Katherine's back became extremely painful as the day wore on. She couldn't stand the friction created by resting against her new husband's rock hard chest, yet holding her body forward made her muscles ache unbearably.

She wondered if Niall noticed the white-knuckled grip she had on the edge of the saddle, or if she appeared as stiff and uncomfortable as she felt. She had told him earlier that she could ride "very well," but he was probably questioning the truth of that now.

Stopping once, only briefly, to water the horses, they travelled for hours. Finally, shortly before sunset, they stopped for the night in a clearing near a small loch. Niall lifted her off the horse and looked at her, apparently startled.

"Lass, ye look pale and exhausted. How can riding for a few hours drain ye so profoundly? Go rest," he said, dismissing her. Then he turned back to his horse to settle him for the night.

Katherine ignored his rude assessment of her; she was used to worse. Tired and sore, she needed to move a bit to loosen her stiff joints. She looked around and, seeing Stormy, walked over to her. Her pet whinnied and tossed her head as Katherine approached. It had clearly been a hard day for the mare, too, even without a rider. She stroked Stormy's velvet nose and leaned her head against the horse's strong neck. Her father had given her the beautiful grey and Katherine had adored Stormy immediately. After her father's death, her beloved horse became a refuge. When things became too difficult, she could escape, and, even if only briefly, forget her grief while flying across a meadow on Stormy's back.

How would she be able to bear giving her away tomorrow? Her throat felt tight while unwanted tears welled in her eyes. Forcing the tears back, she whispered, "It's for the best, my pretty girl," as if the horse had been the one about to cry. In an effort to regain control, Katherine walked a short distance into the clearing, pulled up a large handful of grass with which to rub Stormy down, and returned to the mare. She enjoyed grooming the animal and found the simple, mindless action calming. She had barely started when she heard Niall bellow, "Katherine, I said rest! Tomas, see to your lady's horse."

The abrupt order startled Katherine and she lost the last little bit of her remaining control. Tomas rushed to her and took over the task. She walked to the edge of the clearing, determined not to let anyone see her cry. She had learned years ago that tears not only gave her uncle power over her, but also delighted him. In an effort to deny him this pleasure, she had learned how to control her emotions. Sometimes she couldn't hold the tears back altogether, but she could usually master them until she found a place to be alone. Keeping her back to the Highlanders, she took a few steps into the trees and sat down on the roots of a great oak, pulling her knees to her chest. In pain, exhausted, and with an aching heart, she buried her face on her knees and wept.

She cried out her pain and the fear until her tears were spent. Then, once again in control, she sat there in the deepening gloom with her head resting on her knees, allowing the evening breeze to cool her cheeks and dry her tears. She took stock of the day. Aye, her king had all but forced her to marry a stranger. In fact, the rather large man she had married frightened her a bit, but, as she had boldly admitted to him earlier, she believed him to be a vast improvement over her uncle. Tomorrow she would lose her beloved Stormy, but Niall had assured her the gentle grey would be well cared for. She worried about those of her father's people left under her uncle's tyrannical rule, but she had managed to keep Tomas safe, and he the most vulnerable of them all. All things considered, she told herself she had every reason to feel hopeful.

She knew she needed to rejoin the rest, but hadn't quite found the courage yet when Tomas slipped up beside her. "Are ye done crying?" he asked.

Horrorstruck, she said, "Do they all know I was crying?"

"Nay, just me, cuz I know ye."

Relieved, she nodded. "Aye. I'm done crying. You won't tell them?" she asked, smiling at him conspiratorially.

"Nay, I won't. I know ye don't like people to see when ye cry. Since ye aren't crying now though, why don't ye come back? Moyna packed supper and she put in the nut bread ye love."

Katherine laughed, "You can't fool me, Tomas. You love that nut bread almost more than I do."

Tomas grinned and took her hand as they walked back to the campsite. When Katherine noticed Niall watching her, she blushed, wondering if, in the twilight, he could see her red, swollen eyes.

~ * ~

Niall had been watching Katherine discreetly from the time they dismounted. Her pallid appearance when they stopped had him convinced she bordered on collapse, but she had defied his order to rest. He watched her walk into the edge of the forest. He could just see her sitting on the other side of a large oak, finally resting as he had ordered. He hoped her earlier obstinacy did not indicate things to come. He would not tolerate defiance.

When the men had settled their horses, they opened the package of food sent with them from Cotharach, while Niall continued to watch her. Although she sat upright, she didn't move. Her stillness made him wonder if she had fallen asleep. He started to cross the clearing to get her when

Tomas hopped up in front of him. "I'll get Lady Katherine, she loves nut bread."

Niall nodded slightly, letting the lad go. When Tomas returned with her, Niall was struck again by her beauty. The priest had called her radiant when she appeared in the great hall just before their wedding, and he had silently agreed. He found her stunning. Seeing her now, holding the lad's hand and laughing with him, took his breath away once more. He had overheard the priest's words to her earlier, and now they echoed in his mind: *My dear, I am certain you will be a wonderful wife and mother.* He frowned, chiding himself silently for being a fool. He knew very well what master manipulators women could be. Would he never learn? He only *wanted* this illusion to be true, so the sooner he drove out these romantic notions, the better.

His men spread the food Moyna had sent on a low, flat rock, appearing to fully enjoy the change from the oatcakes and dried meat they usually ate while traveling. After selecting some food for herself and Tomas, Katherine moved to sit where Niall indicated, on a plaid spread on the ground. Tomas plopped down beside her, chattering about all the exciting things he had learned from Fingal. "Fingal says he and the other men are not just ordinary soldiers."

"Nay?" she responded.

"Nay," he said firmly. "They are the laird's eeleet guard. Do ye know what eeleet means?" Without waiting for an answer, he went on, "I asked Fingal and he told me it means they are special. They are the best warriors in the clan. Ye know what else Fingal told me? The laird's castle is called Duncurra and Fingal said it is in the middle of a loch. Cotharach is by a loch, but I wonder how ye build a castle in a loch?"

Although everything in his head screamed at Niall to keep his distance from the enticing woman, he brought his food and sat on the plaid with Katherine and Tomas.

"Laird MacIan, how can a castle be built in water?" asked Tomas boldly.

"It isn't built in the water, Tomas. Duncurra is built on a crag that juts into the loch, so it has water on three sides," Niall explained. Tomas continued to chatter and ask questions until they had finished eating. It seemed for every answer the boy received, he had at least two more questions, but like Fingal had all afternoon, Niall patiently answered them all.

The lad amused Niall, and Tomas' excitement about his new home pleased him. After they had finished eating, Fingal approached. "Excuse me, Laird. It has not escaped my notice that there might be a lad hiding under the wee mound of dirt there beside ye. I thought perhaps it would be a good idea to give it a rinse in the loch and see."

Niall smiled. "Ah, Fingal, ye might be right, because now that ye mention it, I have never heard a mound of dirt talk as much as this one." Katherine laughed and for the second time that day she rewarded Niall with a heart-stopping smile. Raw desire rose unbidden, and once more he forced himself to remember he did not want this marriage, no matter how bonny a smile his new wife had. "In fact," he added, "I think I will join ye." Niall rose and walked toward the loch, accompanied by Diarmad and two other guardsmen, Alan and Keith.

Fingal scooped a squirming Tomas up under his arm and followed. "But I don't need a bath," moaned Tomas.

"Trust me, ye do," Fingal said firmly.

Katherine laughed again. "Behave, Tomas," she admonished with mock severity. The enchanting sound of her laughter followed Niall. He could not deny he desired his lovely little wife, but his wedding night would have to wait until they reached Duncurra. Niall suspected the chilly loch water would do little to cool his desire. Suddenly, he realized he had one more excellent reason to hurry home. While he didn't need or want a wife, having his bed warmed by this lass might prove to be an unexpected boon.

~ * ~

When they reached the loch, the other men stripped and dove in, leaving Fingal to deal with Tomas. Determined to scrub off a layer of dirt and the accompanying aroma, Fingal had to wrestle Tomas out of his tunic, much to the amusement of the other men. Finally able to pull it over Tomas' head, he stopped, looking very serious. Even in the low light, Fingal saw old, dark bruises on Tomas' thin frame, as well as two fresh, angry lash marks on his back. With a casual calm he didn't feel, he asked, "Lad, who took a whip to your back?"

The other men fell silent as Tomas answered quietly, "Sir Ruthven."

Niall clenched his jaw and Fingal recognized the furious expression.

"What happened?" Fingal asked, trying to keep his voice nonchalant.

Tomas looked down, embarrassed. "He was out until very late last night. Berty, the stable master, went to bed and made me wait in the stables until Sir Ruthven returned. Sir Ruthven was still out when the storm hit, and when he got back to Cotharach he was drenched and the horse was winded and lathered. I met him like I was supposed to and took the horse into the stable. He followed me, telling me he wanted me to take special care of his new saddle because it was very valuable. I said I would and I took it off the horse. I—I—I thought he would want me to take care of the horse first. Honest, I did. The horse looked bad, so I started to rub him down, but Sir Ruthven screamed at me, saying I was too stupid to live, and hadn't he just told me to take care of his new saddle."

"He wanted ye to take care of the saddle before the beast?" Diarmad asked in disbelief.

"Aye, he grabbed a whip from the wall and started to beat me."

"Ye must have gotten away, ye only have two stripes on your back," Alan said.

"Nay, I didn't run. He would be sure to kill me then," Tomas said seriously, "He only hit me twice because Lady Katherine got there."

"Lady Katherine?" Niall asked, his voice deadly calm. "She stopped him from whipping ye?"

"Not exactly," said Tomas in almost a whisper. "Lady Katherine put herself between us and Sir Ruthven beat her instead."

Fingal glanced at Niall, who appeared to be barely able control himself as he got out of the water and pulled on his clothes. Waves of white hot anger practically rolled off him.

Tomas continued, "I tried to get her to move away, but she had her arms around me tight to keep the whip from hitting me. He must have hit her eight or nine times before the steward came into the stable and told Sir Ruthven his bath was ready. Sir Ruthven threw the whip down, screamed at me to tend to his saddle, and left. Lady Katherine let go of me and tried to get up, but she was shaking. Her dress was torn and her back was bleeding. The steward woke Berty, telling him to see to the horse, and I took care of Sir Ruthven's saddle like he ordered. The steward helped Lady Katherine into the keep."

Fingal asked Tomas one last question. "As we rode today, ye told me Lady Katherine was the healer at Cotharach. Who tended her wounds?"

"Lady Katherine tells her maid, Emma, what to do when she is hurt herself. She sent Emma out to the stable to put a balm on my back, too, 'cept I didn't need it as much as my lady, cuz he only hit me twice this time."

Tomas had said *this time*. Those two words spoke volumes. Not only had Ambrose Ruthven beaten Tomas before, but that Lady Katherine's maid had experience tending her injuries suggested Ruthven had very likely beaten Katherine before as well. It also explained why she had unilaterally arranged for Tomas to accompany them.

Niall strode away without speaking. Tomas looked up at Fingal and said timidly, "Is the laird mad at me?"

"Nay, Tomas."

"Is he mad at Lady Katherine?"

"Not really. He is angry at her uncle." Fingal thought, judging by the other men's expressions, Niall wasn't alone in that. Determined to give Tomas the much needed bath and, in an attempt to break the somber mood, Fingal looked at him squarely and said, "I still have to find the lad under this talking mound of dirt." Tomas giggled and Fingal gently scooped him up again and carried him squealing with glee into the loch.

~ * ~

Katherine looked up from where she sat on the plaid and saw her husband stride angrily into camp. The men whom he had left at the camp immediately became alert, but he waved them away, telling them to go to the loch. Stopping at the edge of the plaid, he asked, "Why did ye not tell me ye were injured?"

Wary, Katherine looked away and tried to school her expression, but as his words sank in, she became angry. "Tell you? When exactly would I have told you? When you rode into my home with a small army and a missive from King David requiring my uncle to give me to you in marriage? Or perhaps when the priest was summoned so we could be wed immediately because you were anxious to leave?" At this she rose to her feet, no longer the image of perfect submission, her anger clearly rising. "Mayhap I should have mentioned it as my dear uncle gave me away. That would have made a lovely addition to the wedding ceremony, 'Aye my lord, I will marry you because my doting uncle thinks less of me than he does his cursed saddle!' Perhaps I should have said something as we were riding out of my home, which had just been handed over to my uncle in exchange for my hand and a bag of gold." A sob escaped her lips as tears threatened for the second time that day.

She turned away, not wanting him to see. "Perhaps I should have said, 'Oh, by the way, the beast who just bought my birthright from you laid my back open with a whip last night. That isn't a problem for you, is it?'"

She choked on another sob and turned to look at him again, at his eyes black with fury. She knew she should stop, but exhaustion and pain pushed her past the point of caution. "And what if I had told you? What would you have done then? Wrought vengeance on him for doing something he had every legal right to do? I don't think starting a war over a bit of chattel would have pleased our king, do you?" As the horrible image passed before her eyes of her new husband's lifeless body cut down in the courtyard at Cotharach, she could no longer hold back the tears. Her anger spent, she sobbed, sank to her knees, and said with a note of desperation in her voice, "You would have been killed."

~ * ~

Niall had seen women cry before, usually when all other forms of manipulation had failed. His stepmother's tears had stopped having any effect on him years ago. He realized then that he had never seen a woman cry genuine tears of sorrow and pain. His heart began to ache for her, for everything she had suffered, and for the first time in his adult life he felt completely helpless. He knelt beside her, taking her gently in his arms so as not to cause her further pain, and pulled her onto his lap, holding her while she cried. "Wheesht, lass," he crooned, kissing her head while rocking her gently. Eventually she stopped crying, giving in to her exhaustion. She fell asleep in his arms, but for reasons he didn't fully understand, he continued to hold her.

He thought about what had just happened. Walking away from the loch, he had nursed a hot rage. As Tomas told his story, images of Katherine throughout the day flashed through Niall's mind: her white knuckles, her tenseness in the saddle, an occasional wince, the drawn expression on her face when they had finally stopped—all things he had blamed on her weakness. He had unwittingly added to her pain throughout the day by the brutal pace he set. As he headed back to the camp to confront her, he hadn't known who angered him most: himself, her insane uncle, or Katherine, for not telling him about her injuries from the start. If she had only told him, he began to rationalize to himself…but he knew better. The signs were there and he had simply failed to heed them.

He wanted to kill Ambrose Ruthven. Only a man who was completely without honor abused women or children. Niall now understood why Ruthven suggested that they wait to consummate the marriage. *The bastard was worried about how I might react when I learned of his abuse, and wanted to make damn sure that didn't happen until I was too far away to do anything about it.*

His guilt made him angry at himself, and his sense of honor fueled his rage for Ruthven, but why had he been angry with Katherine as well? *Because she didn't give me the opportunity to murder the abhorrent bastard.* Then the last words she said before collapsing into tears penetrated his thick head. *You would have been killed.* Shaking his head slightly, he realized Katherine had been worried about him. She sought to protect him by not revealing her injuries. When he heard the priest tell her, *you are one of the few who always considers the needs of others before your own*, he hadn't believed it, couldn't believe it.

Maybe she is different, he thought. *The surest way to open yourself to hurt is to love, and yet you love anyway*, the old man had said. Niall knew risking that kind of pain took a strength he didn't have. Maybe the fragile lass, who clung to him in her sleep, did.

~ * ~

When her tears stopped, Katherine became aware he was holding her. With his arms snugly around her, she felt secure. I'm safe, she thought, as she drifted asleep.

~ * ~

After bathing Tomas, Fingal wrapped him in a plaid and washed his dirty tunic. The boy looked up at him seriously and said, "I have never heard my lady yell like that."

"That doesn't surprise me."

After a moment Tomas said "It would have made Sir Ruthven mad. Will it make the laird mad?"

Fingal knew Niall would have flattened any man who dared to speak to him that way, but he would never hurt a woman intentionally. He said, "Tomas, there is no need to worry about Lady Katherine. Our laird takes care of his own."

"Am I 'his own' now, too?" Tomas asked.

"Aye, Tomas, ye are," Fingal answered.

The boy seemed relieved. He turned onto his side, curled into a ball and went to sleep.

Chapter 3

When the men returned from the lake, Niall eased the sleeping Katherine onto the ground and wrapped the plaid around her. Rising, he told Diarmad they'd have to set an easier pace.

"I thought as much," Diarmad replied.

Niall shook his head. "The problem is, we carry a small fortune, and half of Edinburgh knows about it. I had hoped that by moving quickly, we would stay ahead of any threat, but we need a contingency plan now. I want ye to go ahead with half the men and most of the dowry. Travel as fast as ye can. We shouldn't be more than a day or so behind ye."

"Do ye want your brother to ride ahead with us?"

Niall gave him a dark look. "Nay, he'll stay with me. I'm beginning to question the wisdom of bringing him back from Laird Chisholm's. Perhaps I should have considered making Rowan MacKenzie a guardsman instead."

Diarmad laughed. "Prying one of his sons away from Cathal MacKenzie would have been a challenge. Besides, I thought ye wanted to keep your brother close."

"That may not have been the best idea. I'm not sure he can be trusted."

"All the more reason to keep him close, but I don't understand why ye think that. For what it is worth, I think ye made the right choice."

"I suppose ye are right, Diarmad, and what's done is done. Nevertheless, I don't want Fingal guarding the coin." Looking across the camp, he watched as Fingal laid a sleeping Tomas near where the other men were bedding down. "Besides, I'm not sure I want to inflict Tomas' endless chatter on anyone else for the moment."

Diarmad chuckled, "Ye aren't worried ye are punishing Fingal unfairly?"

"I'm only paying him back for years of the same treatment from him," Niall said lightly. But the fact remained that he didn't trust Fingal and had no intention of sending him ahead.

~ * ~

During the night Katherine woke once to find Niall sleeping beside her with an arm thrown over her protectively. It felt so very good. When she woke the next day alone, she missed him. She stretched, groaning a bit at her soreness, and rose, glancing around the camp for him. He stood with his back to her, talking with a few of his men, and she got her first real chance to stare appreciatively at her very attractive husband.

She took in his lean, powerful build and blushed slightly as she remembered how good those strong arms felt wrapped around her. She bent to gather up the plaid on which she had been sleeping and shook it out. Yesterday she had agreed to marry him because she didn't want to become a nun. That was a good decision, she thought wickedly, and blushed again as she folded the plaid.

Niall walked towards her almost cautiously. Taking the folded plaid from her, he asked, "How are ye feeling this morning?"

"I am well, thank you," she said, blushing furiously. Suddenly she felt very shy after last night's outburst and her bold thoughts moments ago. Looking around, she realized many of the men and horses were gone. "Where are the rest of your men?"

"I sent half of them ahead with the bulk of your dowry. I suspect ye have never been to the royal court, but ye can imagine very little remains secret there. The news of our betrothal became widely known, as did the size of your dowry. Having a large portion of it with us makes us a target for thieves. I wanted to travel fast, to stay well ahead of trouble."

"And you are slowing down because of me?" she asked, feeling a little ashamed.

At the worried look on her face, he said, "We are only slowing down a little. I have to think of our safety as well as the dowry, but it also makes sense to divide it and transport it separately." She nodded and he added, "Still, we need to move as fast as is reasonable, so will ye be ready to go soon?"

"I only need a few minutes to wash up."

"Gather what ye need and we will go to the loch."

"You don't need to go with me, I—I really won't be long," she stammered.

"I would not let ye go alone, unprotected, but I have another reason as well. I need to see the extent of your injuries," he said seriously.

"Really, Niall, it isn't that bad and—"

He cut her off with a wave of his hand. "Don't argue with me about this. I need to know. I don't want to cause ye any additional pain, and I can't avoid hurting ye if I don't know what your injuries are."

Katherine nodded. His stern demeanor brooked no further argument, so opening her bag, she removed what she needed and they went to the loch. She laid a towel and a jar of balm on a large rock and took the rest to the water's edge. Niall sat on the rock and waited for her as she washed up, then combed and braided her hair. She still wore her wedding clothes and, although a bit wrinkled and dusty, they would do. She brushed herself off and smoothed out the wrinkles as best she could. When she turned around, the intensity of his gaze took her breath away. His eyes were the same deep blue as the summer sky.

~ * ~

Niall enjoyed watching her and realized again how much he desired her. He wondered what those small hands would feel like caressing him. As she combed her wild curls, he longed to run his fingers through them and felt more than a little disappointment when she captured them in a braid. He imagined what she would look like naked, with her beautiful hair cascading around her, and became so aroused he had to force those musings away and think of something else.

When she had completed her ablutions, she joined him and said brightly, "Are you ready to go?"

He leveled a stare at her. "Ah, my little wife, ye will find my memory is not that fleeting." He motioned for her to turn around.

Sighing, she turned her back to him and undid the laces on the side of her gown, pulling her arms out and allowing it to bunch at her waist. Then she reached behind her neck and untied the ribbons at the back of her kirtle. Again she pulled her arms out of the garment but held it to her chest, blushing profusely.

Niall opened the back of her kirtle a little wider, enjoying a glimpse of her creamy white shoulders. He untied the linen strips holding the bandage in place, lifted it away, and cursed. Dark bruises and open lash marks crisscrossed her slender back. As he suspected, older scars marred her pale skin as well: evidence Ruthven had beaten her many times before. The new wounds looked angry but clean. Hopefully a fever would not set in. Taking up the jar of balm, he applied it to her lacerations, causing her to wince. He paused. "Does this sting?"

"Just a little when it first goes on, but it really does make them heal better."

It tore at his heart to know she had firsthand knowledge of this. He finished applying the balm as gently as he could, placed the clean towel on her back, and retied the linen strips.

"Thank you," she said quietly. She slipped her arms back into her garments and made to step away.

He put his hand on her shoulder, holding her where she stood. He refastened her laces before turning her to him. He had a powerful urge to taste her sweet lips again and, lifting her chin, kissed her gently. Surprised but pleased by her response, he kissed her more deeply as she leaned into him.

With a pang of regret, he forced himself to break the kiss, knowing if he didn't, they would never leave. Pulling away slightly, but leaving his hand on her chin, he said firmly but gently, "Don't ever hide anything from me again. Promise me." She didn't answer for a moment. "Promise me," he said again, more gruffly this time.

"I won't hide anything from you," she said. "I promise."

It only took a few more minutes to be prepared to leave. Niall insisted she eat something before they go while his men readied the horses. When Niall had his horse saddled, he motioned for Katherine to come to him, lifted her into the saddle, and mounted behind her. Niall stopped her before she turned forward, pulling her onto his lap. "If ye ride like this and put your left arm around me, twill be easier on your back and ye won't be jarred as much."

Katherine did as he suggested. Her shoulder fit snuggly under his right arm while her cheek rested on his chest with her head under his chin.

"Better?" he asked.

"Aye," she agreed.

"Ye will tell me if ye need to rest?"

"Niall, I am stronger than you think."

"That's not an answer. Can I trust ye to tell me if ye need to rest?"

"Aye. I will tell you if I need to rest."

"See that ye do."

They set out at swift pace, though still much slower than they had ridden the day before. In the middle of the day, they crossed a river before stopping to water the horses and give them a rest. While there, they finished the remainder of the food Moyna had sent. Katherine ate sitting under a tree slightly apart from the group of men. Once she finished she pulled her knees to her chest and rested her head on them. Niall came to sit beside her. "Are ye all right? I wanted to head out again in a few minutes, but if ye need to rest longer..."

"Nay, I'm fine," she said. He arched an eyebrow at her in doubt. "Really. I told you, I'm stronger than you think." she assured him.

He nodded but didn't stand up to leave. He dreaded what he had to tell her. He had no patience for tears and pleading.

"Katherine, there is something else. I told ye yesterday we would be passing near the holding of one of my allies, Laird Carr." She nodded grimly. "It will be somewhat out of our way for all of us to ride to his keep and we are already going slower than I had planned. I have asked Keith to take Stormy to Laird Carr, and join back with us this evening. He is ready to leave." Niall braced himself for the tantrum he anticipated, but it didn't come.

Katherine nodded. Standing up, she walked over to Stormy, put her arms around the horse's neck, and leaned her head against it. She didn't cry or plead, but after a few moments, she simply whispered her goodbye. Untethering Stormy, she walked the mare to where Keith stood, giving him the reins. He appeared at a loss for what to say. He just clicked to his horse and rode away.

Tomas came to her, his brow knitted. "Where is he taking your Stormy?"

Niall remembered Tomas hadn't been at Cotharach as they left yesterday so he didn't understand what was happening now. He watched as she knelt down beside the boy and put an arm around him. "Stormy has to go and live somewhere else now."

"But why?" he asked, his lip trembling.

"Tomas, have you noticed the land around us is hillier and rougher than it was at Cotharach?"

He nodded.

"As we get closer to Duncurra, it will get even more rugged. It would be very hard for Stormy because she isn't used to it."

"Why isn't it hard for the other horses?" he asked, still looking as if he might cry.

"Well, look at them," Katherine said. "They are all a lot bigger and stronger than Stormy is. Besides, this is their home. They're used to it."

"But ye love Stormy," he said.

Katherine bit her lower lip, appearing to blink back her own tears. "Aye, I do," she said finally. "I love her so much, I don't want her to get hurt. That is why I didn't leave her at Cotharach, and why I am giving her to someone else now who will love her."

He put his arms around her ,whispering "Is that why ye were crying yesterday?"

"Partly," she whispered back.

"It's going to be all right," he said, this time not whispering, "cuz ye know why?"

"Why?"

"Cuz Fingal says Laird MacIan takes care of his own, and you're 'his own.'" Leaning in and whispering again, he said with a little smile, "So am I."

Although she hugged him and said, "I'm sure it will be all right," Niall thought the expression on her face suggested she might not be all that confident. She looked around, seeming to realize for the first time that both Niall and Fingal had heard the exchange. Blushing, she let go of Tomas, stood up, and without making eye contact with anyone, brushed the dirt off her gown. When she finally looked up again, her mask of self-control was once more in place. She asked Niall, "Shall we go now?"

He nodded. No begging, no tears, no pouting. Once again he was impressed with her. Katherine only showed concern for the well-being of her horse and the feelings of a wee peasant lad. Puzzled, Niall lifted her onto his horse, mounted behind her, again positioning her sideways on his lap. She put her arm around him and they rode this way in silence for the rest of the afternoon.

~ * ~

Although their pace was easier and Niall took care to protect her back from further injury, Katherine became more uncomfortable as the day progressed. She didn't want to tell him she needed to rest. She knew she was already slowing their progress, but she didn't think she could take much more. She was pulling together the courage to tell him, when he finally announced they would halt for the evening. She sighed with relief. Her backed ached incredibly and she didn't think she had ever felt so tired. She didn't argue when Niall told her to rest, but sank to the plaid he spread on the ground, watching as he and his men made camp. Tomas energetically helped where he could.

By the time the men had settled the horses for the night, Keith had rejoined them bearing gifts. "My lady," Keith said, bowing to Lady Katherine, "Laird Carr sends his sincere thanks for the fine mare. He also said although it is a very small offering, he wanted ye to have something in return." Keith handed her a soft bundle. Inside she found a silver brooch and a length of soft cream-colored wool woven with stripes of green and blue.

"This is beautiful," she said, genuinely pleased as she ran her hands over the soft fabric.

"That is called an *airisaidh*," Niall explained. "It is like the plaid men wear but it is usually made of a lighter wool. It is held on with a brooch and worn over a garment like your kirtle that we call a *léine*."

"It is very thoughtful of Laird Carr," said Katherine.

"Laird Carr has four daughters. I suspect they had a hand in this," Niall said.

"Aye, they did," said Keith, laughing. "His oldest daughter, Anna, insisted on it. Laird Carr gave Stormy to her. She was overjoyed."

Katherine knew it had been the right thing to do, but the confirmation that her beloved mare would not only be well treated, but loved, lightened her mood a great deal.

"Laird, he also sent a small gift to ye with his congratulations on your wedding," Keith added.

Niall arched an eyebrow at that. "I'll bet he did. For the last few years, every time I have seen him, Laird Carr has needled me about marriage. I have always assured him I had no intention of getting married. I am confident he found this new situation very amusing."

Katherine wondered why Niall was so set against marriage but didn't ask.

Keith produced two small casks of mead, a jug of excellent whisky, meat pies, cheese, brown bread, and small sugared buns.

After the meal, Tomas curled up beside Katherine with his head in her lap and went to sleep, sugar from the buns still circling his mouth. Niall's men talked and joked throughout dinner, but Niall remained as quiet as he had been all day. After hearing his comments about marriage, Katherine thought to herself that she really knew nothing about this man, or any of them, really. She had managed to figure out their names over the course of the day, but other than that, the only bits of information she had had came from Tomas the previous evening. She smiled to herself when she remembered how he thought Duncurra was built in a loch.

"What amuses ye?" Niall asked.

She laughed a little. "I was thinking about how little I know of you all. I know these men are your 'eeleet' guard," she said, emphasizing both syllables of the word as Tomas had the previous evening, "and Tomas thought Duncurra was built in the middle of a loch."

Niall, too, chuckled at that memory, "To be fair, I know very little about ye, either."

"I'm sure you know most of it."

"Frankly, everything I thought I knew about you has been wrong."

Confused, she said, "I don't understand."

"Never mind, it isn't important. Tell me, how long has Ambrose Ruthven acted as your guardian?"

"Five years. He and my father were hunting. Apparently something spooked my father's horse. He was thrown and killed instantly."

"Your mother died before him?"

"Aye, she died when I was ten. The plague swept through Scotland that year." She paused for a moment. "So many people died then, entire families in some cases. At least my father and I had each other." She sighed, stroking Tomas' head. "Things changed so much after he died." She took a deep breath, looking away for a moment before saying, "So, I became an orphan, an heiress, and ward to a cruel uncle at fourteen. There isn't much more to the story."

Niall's expression grew dark at the mention of her uncle's cruelty.

Fingal broke the silence by saying, "Gentleman, our lady would like to learn a little bit about us. Shall I tell her?"

"Just don't damn us with faint praise," said Keith.

"It is much more likely he will simply damn us," Alan added.

Fingal glared mockingly at Alan, then glanced around. "Hmm, where shall I start?" he considered the other men. "With the three old men at the top, I think. Diarmad is Niall's second in command. As ye know, he left today with six other men. There are two captains under Diarmad, Cairbre, who remained behind in charge of Duncurra, and Alan here. As we have established, Alan is old," Fingal teased. Alan did appear to be older than the others, but while lines creased his weathered face, his dark brown hair didn't have any gray in it.

Alan frowned, "Mind who ye are calling 'old,' Fingal. Any of the three of us can still best ye."

The men laughed and Fingal went on, undaunted.

"Alan is married to the lovely Effie, who is one of the clan's midwives. She is a very good midwife, probably because she has had a lot of practice."

Again, the men laughed, and for the first time all day, Niall joined in, explaining, "Alan and Effie have been blessed with eight children. I would ask him to tell ye about them, but he is a very proud father. His children are his favorite topic of conversation. If I give him an opening, he might still be talking about them as the sun rises."

More laughter erupted, but Alan replied, "I will remind ye of this someday, Laird, when ye are bending my ear about your own brood."

Katherine blushed, realizing the "brood" to which Alan referred would be hers as well.

Fingal continued, "Then we have Muir." Shorter than Niall and with a leaner build, Muir had sandy brown hair. "Muir, too, is married, but no one understands how that happened." It was Muir's turn to glare as Fingal went on. "His wife, Shona, is one of our finest weavers. They have two sons, one of whom is training with one of our allies, Fearghas Chisholm. The other is now training with Niall's men."

"How many men do you have?" Katherine asked.

"There are twenty in my elite guard, who not only guard my back, but are leaders and trainers of my other men. There are roughly one hundred more warriors who see to the clan's protection full time," Niall answered. "In addition to Cairbre, six other guardsmen remained at Duncurra."

Ruthven had more than twice that many soldiers, she thought, but if Niall's elite guard was any indicator, she doubted the Ruthven men were half as well trained.

"Next is Turcuil," said Fingal. Huge didn't begin to describe Turcuil.

Katherine suspected people believed in giants because of men like him. At least a head taller than and half again as wide as Niall, he had to be the biggest man she had ever seen. His size, coupled with his black bushy hair and beard, gave him a fearsome appearance.

Fingal's eyes twinkled with mischief as he continued to introduce the giant. "Ye mustn't tell anyone, but ye should be warned because once we get to Duncurra, ye are bound to notice," said Fingal, glancing around as if checking for eavesdroppers. "Turcuil is a changling."

Confused, Katherine cocked her head to one side.

"Oh, aye, he is," Niall said dryly.

Deciding to play along, she asked, "What, pray tell, does he change into?"

"A lovesick swain," answered Niall, and the men chuckled.

"Ye see," Fingal explained, "Turcuil is rather fond of Edna, who is in charge of the staff at the keep. Edna is a widow and most of us think she has a soft spot for Turcuil, too, although it's hard to know why." This elicited more chuckles. "The problem is whenever Turcuil is near Edna, he forgets how to form words, so he has never actually done more than grunt at her. It is no wonder she doesn't know of his affection."

The other men roared with laughter.

Katherine suspected the huge man could put the fear of God into anyone, but when she glanced at him, he blushed like a maid.

"Since I am going by age, I have to tell ye about Keith and Keavy together."

"They are the same age?" Katherine asked, glancing at the two men. Keith had pale blond hair and was shorter and slighter than the other guardsmen. He laughed a lot and looked youthful. But tall and stocky with shaggy brown hair, Keavy appeared quiet, almost sullen.

"I guess technically Keith is older by a few minutes. They are twins, though ye have probably noticed they are not identical. They are, in fact, as different as the night is from the day, but they are as close as two brothers could possibly be."

"That they are," said Alan. "If Keith eats too much, Keavy gets the indigestion."

The men laughed but Fingal interjected, "Alan must have cleaned that joke up out of respect for ye, Lady

Katherine. As I recall, it is normally a much bawdier comment."

The men laughed harder.

When the laughter died, Fingal went on, "Now we come to Rab." Fingal indicated a tall slender man with a head of shocking red hair. "Most people refer to him as 'Rab the Red.' I trust I don't have to explain why; that isn't a fire burning on his head."

Rab grinned and ruffled his own hair. "Fingal, ye know it makes me a fierce warrior."

"It only makes ye easy to see from a distance," Fingal countered to the amusement of the other men. "And finally, ye have me, the more charming and handsome of the MacIan brothers."

"Brothers?" said Katherine.

"Brothers," answered Niall. "And the one who is going to die young if he doesn't watch himself," he added. Although he appeared to be teasing, Katherine thought she heard a serious undertone that surprised her.

Niall rose, offering his hand to her. "Now that ye have been properly introduced, I think it is time ye rested. We have another long day ahead of us."

Somewhat reluctantly, Katherine kissed Tomas' cheek and slid his head off her lap before taking Niall's hand. Moving away from the rest of the men, she lay down with him on a plaid. He wrapped it around them and she fell asleep within the safety of his arms, thinking she could get very   used   to   this.

Chapter 4

Their third day of travel went much the same as the first. Niall changed the dressing on Katherine's back again before they left. The lacerations still looked very angry. He knew no matter how he tried to cushion her as they rode, the constant motion was irritating them. Then, late in the afternoon, the skies grew dark and a wind whipped up, signaling a brewing summer storm. Well into the Highlands now, Niall knew they really must have shelter this evening.

If he pushed their pace once again, they might be able to reach the protection of some caves he knew of. As much as he hated to do it, he reasoned sleeping in the rain would be considerably worse on Katherine than a couple of hours of hard riding. Niall wrapped his plaid around her as the storm hit, but it didn't prevent her from getting drenched and cold before they reached the shelter of the caves. The previous evenings had not been cold, so Niall had chosen not to risk drawing unwanted attention by starting a fire. Tonight he would have welcomed the warmth of a fire, but there was nothing dry with which to build one.

Looking chilled to the bone and trembling, Katherine stepped deeper into the dark cave. When she returned, she had changed into dry garments. She still shivered slightly, holding a heavy mantle around her shoulders.

"Ye are still cold."

"Not as cold as I was. Everything is still a bit damp, but I'm a little warmer."

Niall pulled her close to him, wrapping her in his plaid, hoping that his heat would further banish the chill while they slept. He held her close throughout the night, but she slept fitfully, waking with dark circles under her eyes.

"Katherine, ye don't look well," he observed.

"I am just a bit tired and achy. I'm sure I'll feel better soon."

"Just a bit?" he asked skeptically. He hadn't known her very long, but he suspected that if she was admitting to feeling "a bit tired and achy", she actually felt much worse than that. Still, there wasn't much he could do, so he didn't push her. "Come, let me change your dressing."

Katherine turned her back to him with no argument. Niall opened her kirtle to find her back was not healing and one particularly deep lash showed signs of festering. Following her directions, he cleansed it as best he could. Her clenched teeth and fisted hands told him that it caused her pain, but there was nothing else to be done. When he finished, she looked as pale and drawn as she had the evening before.

Once again they set out with Niall cradling his wife on his lap. The storm had blown itself out during the night. The day grew fine and warm, but by midmorning she was shivering in his arms. Closing her eyes against the bright sun, she snuggled closer to him, seeking his warmth. Her flushed face felt hot and dry to his touch. He realized that, in spite of all his efforts, fever had set in; she was desperately ill. When they stopped at midday, he tried with little success to get her to eat or at least drink something. Instead she curled up on a plaid and slept. He said to his men, "If we ride hard, we can reach Brathanead by this evening."

Alan asked, "Do ye think she can tolerate traveling any faster?"

"I think if I don't get her into the hands of a healer soon, I might lose her," Niall answered, his voice unable to hide the anxiety he felt.

Niall pushed as hard as the horses could tolerate, Katherine burning up in his arms. They reached Laird Malcolm MacLennan's keep, Brathanead, at dusk. The MacLennans had been staunch allies of the MacIans for as long as Niall could remember. He had trained under

Malcolm's father and he had enormous respect for the old laird.

Malcolm and Niall's father, Alastair, had been good friends. Niall and Fingal thought of him as an uncle. Now, just as his father had, Niall considered him to be his most trusted ally.

Malcolm met them in the courtyard. A flicker of surprise crossed his face when he saw the limp, feverish lass in Niall's arms. He issued orders to see to their comfort and sent for the clan's healer. "Give her to me, lad." Malcolm reached up to lift Katherine off Niall's lap.

Niall hesitated.

"Lad, I won't break her. Ye have to get off that horse."

Hesitantly, Niall lowered her into Malcolm's waiting arms and dismounted.

"God's teeth, lad, where did ye find this waif and what in the hell happened to her?"

"She is my wife, Malcolm." At his shocked expression, Niall added, "It's a long story." He took Katherine back into his arms, and they entered the keep.

Fingal followed, carrying a sleepy Tomas.

"Who is the other urchin?" Malcolm asked lightly as he led them up the stairs into one of the towers containing bedchambers.

"A clansman," answered Fingal, without offering any further information.

Katherine mumbled feverishly. "I promised I wouldn't hide anything from you."

"Wheesht, lass."

"Niall, I'm ill."

"Aye, lass, I know, but ye will get better now," Niall answered, willing it to be true.

Then, in a more panicked voice, she asked, "Where is Tomas?"

"Tomas is fine; he's with Fingal," Niall assured her.

She still seemed agitated, begging, "Niall, Tomas needs you. I need you, please don't leave me."

"I won't," he said.

Katherine calmed, slipping back into the oblivion she had been lost in for hours.

Malcolm opened the door to one of the larger chambers on the second floor. Niall entered and laid her on the bed. Two maid servants helped remove her garments. When the MacLennan healer arrived, she turned Katherine on her side before removing the bandage. She sucked a breath in through her teeth and said, "Well, I have some work to do. Lairds, it will be best if ye leave so I can get to it."

"I'll stay," said Niall.

The healer gave an entreating look to her laird and stared at Niall. "I know ye mean well, but there is nothing ye can do here but get in the way."

Malcolm took the cue and said firmly, "Niall, ye need food and rest, and Agnes doesn't need a worried husband under foot."

"I promised her I wouldn't leave."

"Lad, she was delirious, and ye aren't leaving her. She's unconscious now and ye will be just downstairs. Agnes will call if she needs ye."

Niall still hesitated.

Malcolm put his hand on the younger man's shoulder, gently pushing him towards the door. "Ye need food and rest, too, lad. I must insist. Ye will make yourself ill, then what good can ye be to her? I promise ye, she is in good hands."

Niall gave in and left the chamber, followed by his host.

Descending to the great hall, Malcolm motioned to a screened area behind which servants prepared a bath. "A meal will be served soon. I thought ye might want to have a bath in the meantime."

Niall ran his hand through his hair distractedly, glancing back at the stairs to the tower.

"At the risk of sounding discourteous, lad, ye smell of sweat and horses. Stop worrying and bathe."

Niall obliged, taking a quick bath before joining Malcolm and Duncan, Malcolm's second in command, at the table. Gratefully he accepted the tankard of ale offered by a serving maid, taking a long drink of it.

"Now," began his host, "tell me how ye, of all people, find yourself married to a lass who looks as if she has been horsewhipped."

"Ye know the MacIans have never been wealthy. I knew my father worried incessantly about money over the last year or so, but I didn't know how little we had until after he died in the spring. We literally had nothing left. Even less than nothing. Eithne managed to run up a huge debt while living at court."

"Yes, your stepmother enjoys her comfort."

"Her comfort? God's teeth, Malcolm, her extravagance knows no bounds. She accrued more than half of the total debt in the last year alone. She owed something to practically everyone in Edinburgh. I had no way to cover the debt. To make matters worse, Matheson raided our western border several times just before Da died. I couldn't afford to lose a chicken, much less cattle and sheep."

"I'm sorry to hear about your financial problems, Niall, but what has the lass got to do with them?"

"I went to Edinburgh to try to negotiate with my father's creditors and to put a halt to Eithne's spending, but nothing could be done. I finally appealed to King David for help."

"He has financial woes of his own."

"So I learned. He suggested I marry an heiress. I thought he jested, but he had one in mind. He needed to find someone who would be willing to forfeit her title and lands in exchange for a larger dowry, so he could give everything but her wealth to her uncle."

"There must be plenty of men who would do that."

"One would think, but the rumors about her discouraged most men."

"What rumors?"

"They are lies not worth repeating. I suspect Ruthven started them himself."

"Ruthven? Ambrose Ruthven?" asked Malcolm.

"Aye, Ambrose Ruthven," spat Niall.

"That lass is Katherine Ruthven?" Duncan asked.

"That lass is Katherine MacIan now," said Niall.

Malcolm looked shocked, "Her hand was sought by quite a few men who desired her wealth, but the rumors—"

"All lies," Niall said irritably. "He clearly intended to avoid a betrothal, hoping to gain everything for himself. He is the bastard who beat her."

"Perhaps she is willful," suggested Malcolm.

"She did nothing to earn a beating but protect a lad who was equally innocent," Niall snapped. "Ye haven't lived at court for years. How is it ye know the rumors about her?"

Malcolm chuckled. "I haven't lived there, but I still visit occasionally. There are many would-be matchmakers who would like to see me chained to a bride, but even they discouraged me from pursuing the Lady Ruthven. Ah, what folly it is to listen to rumors."

"Ye are old enough to be her father," Niall admonished him. The thought of Katherine married to anyone else, much less a man as old as Malcolm, turned his mood even darker.

"Don't get your hackles up, lad, I certainly wasn't the oldest man considering her hand, nor would I be the first old man to take a young, wealthy bride."

His response didn't soothe Niall's temper.

"The lad Fingal toted upstairs," Duncan asked, "is he the one she was protecting?"

Glad that he was changing the subject, Niall nodded, taking another long pull of ale from his tankard.

"Who is he to her?" Malcolm asked.

"The orphan of one of her clansmen," Niall said simply. "Katherine is fond of him. She treats him like a little brother. He seems to have attached himself to Fingal."

~ * ~

When the lairds finally left the chamber where Katherine lay, the old healer turned back to her charge. She knew she had to draw the poison out of the wounds on the lass's back. She added some salt, a large handful of shredded wych elm root, and several other herbs to a kettle of water before putting it on the fire to bring it to boil. She washed Katherine's back with a solution of soapwort while the herbs stewed. Then she poured the boiling liquid into a bowl to cool briefly. Tearing strips of linen, she dipped them into the solution. When she could handle them without burning her hands, she wrung most of the liquid out and placed the linen strips on the purulent wounds crisscrossing the lass's back.

Agnes had hoped the lady would remain unconscious while she worked, but Katherine awakened at the first touch of the hot cloth. The healer knew the solution stung, but it had to be done. Agitated and writhing, the lass cried out, but soon oblivion reclaimed her, releasing her from the agony. Once she had slipped back into her fevered sleep, Agnes concentrated on finishing cleansing her wounds. She worked as quickly as she could, replacing cool strips with hot ones until the cool strips she pulled away had no more yellow drainage on them and the wounds looked clean. She allowed Katherine's back to dry and cool before applying a soothing balm, which she covered with clean linen.

~ * ~

When Malcolm and Niall stopped at the room on the second floor, where they laid Katherine on the bed and met with the healer, Fingal passed them. He continued up the stairs to a chamber on the third floor. Initially thrilled to see Fingal, the maid who had readied his room pouted when she saw Tomas.

Fingal chuckled, the reason for her chagrin obvious to him. "Another time, lass." He stayed with Tomas until the lad had eaten and fallen asleep on a pallet. Knowing the exhausted boy wouldn't awaken until morning, Fingal left the chamber and descended the stairs. As he passed Lady Katherine's room, he heard her distressed cries. Upon reaching the great hall, Fingal became infuriated when he saw Niall sitting at the long refectory table with his hosts. "What are ye doing down here?" Fingal demanded.

Niall glared at him and asked in a low, menacing voice, "Ye dare address your laird with that tone?"

"I beg your pardon, Laird," Fingal said mockingly. "I thought I was addressing my brother."

"Do ye need to be reminded they are one and the same?" asked Niall, rising to his feet.

"Do ye need to be reminded that less than an hour ago, your wife begged ye not to leave her? Now she is crying out for ye, and ye are not there," Fingal responded, without backing down.

Niall appeared stunned for a moment, but then he turned toward the tower stairs.

Malcolm clamped a hand on his shoulder. "Niall, sit down," he commanded. "This is why Agnes wanted ye out of the room. We must allow her to do what is necessary, and ye can't interfere. Fingal, I know ye mean well, son, but it will not help Katherine to have Niall there. She is delirious anyway and Niall will only be in the way. Let the healer finish."

Both young men looked murderous until Malcolm roared. "Sit down. Both of ye!"

~ * ~

Agnes told Niall she had done everything she could to stop the source of the fever, but it still raged. Now they could only wait. She finally allowed him to return to his wife's side, although she stayed to keep watch.

Niall watched Katherine's restless sleep helplessly. She moaned, occasionally, crying out incoherently. He felt consumed by guilt. When faced with the forced marriage, he had actually welcomed the possibility that she might be weak and slow-witted. He had thought of her as a little broken doll he could put away on a shelf and ignore. He had planned to settle her in Duncurra, assign a clanswoman to tend her, and go on with his life. He only needed her money.

But he couldn't set this bride aside, and he didn't want to. That was reasonable, he told himself. She was clearly bright; she'd evidently managed Cotharach. She had the skills to run a household—the most basic requirement of a wife. If he had to have one, she would do as well as any other.

He also had to admit he felt a strong attraction for her. *What man wouldn't?* He didn't think he had ever seen a more beautiful woman, and he stirred even now, remembering her passionate response to his kisses. He relished the thought of bedding her.

How had he let this happen? After Ceana, he had sworn he would never again allow a woman to have the power to hurt him. Words of her devotion for him slid easily off her tongue, even as she loved and freely gave herself to another man. Ceana had wanted to be "Lady MacIan" someday, so she had charmed and manipulated Niall into asking for her hand. He was a fool. After eight years, the bitterness of his pain and humiliation still remained.

He must not confuse desire with love. He did not love Katherine and, while he doubted he could ever love any woman, he would still remain vigilant and guard his heart. Perhaps simply having no delusions of love would be enough to ensure he wouldn't lose his heart again. Yet even now he felt a crushing pain. The thought of losing her terrified him. Surely his admiration of her skills and beauty did not justify this feeling.

This is not love, he tried to assure himself once again. *It is...appreciation.* That must explain his despair. On top of being skilled and attractive, she provided the means by which he could save his clan. Only a heartless cur would feel nothing for her. Surely this was why his heart ached at the thought of losing her.

Chapter 5

Early in the morning, just before dawn, Katherine's fever broke and she sweated profusely. Agnes dried her gently and changed the linens. Katherine finally slipped into a still, natural sleep. Telling Niall the worst was over, Agnes left with instructions to send for her if anything changed. Drained, Niall lay down on the bed beside Katherine and, giving in to his exhaustion, fell asleep.

He slept for several hours, awaking late in the morning. Lying on his side, on top of the bed linens, he put his arm around Katherine. She had turned off her stomach during the night and had curled up against him with her back to his chest. The dark bluish shadows under her eyes gave witness to the ordeal of the last few days, but her pale skin felt cool and no longer looked flushed with fever. The linen towel with which the healer had covered her back the evening before, slid off when Katherine turned to her side, leaving the lacerations on her back in view. Niall breathed a sigh of relief when he saw the open lash marks looked clean and less angry.

He had been married to her for four days and now, for the first time, he gazed on his wife's naked form. After assuring himself she would recover, he enjoyed perusing her charms at his leisure. Her thick braid hung over her shoulder, disappearing into the cleft between her breasts. Although her arms partially shielded them from view, he could see the upper curve of the creamy mounds, barely glimpsing the edge of the pale pink nipples. He found them delightfully enticing. His gaze continued down her slender body to where his hand lay on her flat stomach. The rest of her enchanting body disappeared under the sheet. Although he thoroughly enjoyed the sight, it came at a price—he grew hard, aching for release. He knew he would have to wait a little longer until she had fully recovered, but he reveled in the thought that this lovely creature belonged to him.

With a sigh, he rose and slipped from the room. He sought out Alan and instructed him to return to Duncurra with the rest of his guard, taking the remainder of the dowry. Only Fingal would remain behind. Niall thought it better not to send Tomas away from Katherine, so the lad would continue to be Fingal's responsibility until they returned to the seat of the MacIans.

Because he did not yet know whether the six other men led by Diarmad had reached Duncurra unscathed, Niall still worried about the target they posed to raiders. Cnocreidh, the large Matheson holding, bordered the western edges of MacLennan and MacIan land, and could be reached in less than half a day from both Brathanead and Duncurra. Niall believed a small contingent of MacIan warriors, known to be traveling with a treasure, would make a tempting target to the thieving bastard. For the same reason, Niall would not risk travelling to Duncurra with Katherine unless a full contingent of guards accompanied them. He sent instructions to Diarmad to return with ten men in five days time. He wasn't sure if Katherine would be ready to travel by then, but he wanted to be prepared to leave as soon as she recovered sufficiently.

~ * ~

The healer, Agnes, came to inspect her injuries shortly before noon, accompanied by a serving maid. Chivying Niall out of the room again, she woke Katherine, who felt as weak as a kitten. They helped her wash quickly, trying not to tire her, and Agnes dressed her wounds. After helping her don fresh clothing, Agnes made her drink some broth and eat a little bread. The brief activity exhausted Katherine and she fell asleep before they left. Niall stayed with her through the afternoon and evening, and slept beside her as he had the night before.

~ * ~

The next several days proceeded in much the same way. Well out of the woods now, Katherine slept less and less and her strength returned steadily. Once convinced of this, Niall left for longer stretches during the day, but always returned in the evening to dine with her. During these evenings she finally learned a bit more about him and his clan. His mother had died in childbirth when he was six. His distraught father, wanting to ensure his small son had a mother, married Eithne Chisholm almost immediately. After Fingal was born, Eithne visited court frequently, preferring the intrigues there to life in the Highlands. Niall didn't seem comfortable discussing his stepmother, so she didn't pursue the topic further.

Tomas visited several times a day. Niall had given strict orders not to allow Tomas to tire her by staying too long, so Fingal had the job of marshaling him. On the afternoon of the fifth day, during one of Tomas' visits, Laird MacLennan tapped on the open chamber door as Tomas animatedly described the wooden sword Fingal had given him while the man himself stood quietly near the door.

Malcolm cleared his throat.

"Lady Katherine," he said, "I think it is time for us to formally meet. I am Laird Malcolm MacLennan, your host." He made a small bow. A tall, lean man who looked to be about two score and ten years old, Malcolm had jet black hair with grey temples and hazel green eyes. He wore a well-trimmed graying beard and mustache.

Katherine sat in one of the two chairs by the hearth, and Tomas, suddenly quiet, crawled into her lap. "Laird MacLennan, I am very pleased to meet you. I am so sorry to have been such a nuisance."

"My dear," he smiled warmly, "ye are certainly not a nuisance. I considered Laird Alastair MacIan to be my closest friend, as close as a brother, really. His family is always welcome in my home. Niall and Fingal are like nephews to me. Isn't that right, Fingal?"

"Aye, Laird, ye always make us most welcome here."

Katherine thought she heard a coolness in Fingal's response.

"Not still arguing with Niall, are ye?" Malcolm said, then to Katherine, "these lads." He shook his head in mock frustration. "Have ye ever known two brothers to be so different?"

Malcolm walked farther into the room and stood near the chair in which Katherine sat. It meant she had to look up at a rather sharp angle to see him. Katherine felt momentarily wary, but Malcolm was a close friend of Niall's and she realized she was being silly. She answered, "I really couldn't say, Laird. I met them for the first time barely a week ago, and it seems I have slept most of that time away."

"Of course, how could I have forgotten? Are ye feeling quite well now?"

"Aye, Laird, thank you, Agnes is a very skilled healer."

"Ye see, Fingal, even Katherine agrees that Agnes knew what she was doing that night."

Confused by his comment, Katherine glanced at Fingal, whose expression was inscrutable. Had Fingal argued with Niall about the healer?

Malcolm went on, "Fingal, son, ye really need to let it go. Ye see, Katherine, when ye arrived, ye had a raging fever and in your delirium, ye begged Niall to stay with ye."

Katherine remembered and knew she had not been delirious then. Although a bit foggy, she recalled feeling terribly ill and afraid. She hadn't wanted Niall to leave her.

"Agnes has been a healer for quite some time and knows anxious husbands can do more harm than good."

Although she respected Agnes, Katherine silently disagreed. In her experience, patients benefited from having loved ones close. Unless someone became a problem, she did not insist they leave, but many healers held Agnes's opinion .Clearly Laird MacLennan respected her.

"Niall very wisely stayed downstairs with me while Agnes was working. Fingal became indignant when he realized Niall had left ye and ye called out for him. But, ye see, Fingal, it was simply the delirium. Niall made the right decision in leaving Katherine in Agnes's care to spend the evening in the hall with us." Turning back to Katherine, he said with a laugh and a shake of his head, "Young men can have such romantic ideas. Katherine, I can tell ye are a wise, practical young woman."

Katherine wasn't sure why Malcolm was telling her this, but Fingal appeared to be both angry and embarrassed. Malcolm must have been trying to smooth over whatever had happened between Niall and Fingal, but it wasn't working very well.

Tired of looking up and thinking to change the subject, she motioned to the other chair by the hearth, saying, "Laird, I am terribly sorry, I have been rude. Please, sit down."

"Oh, nay, thank ye, lass, I won't tire ye any longer. Ye have been through a terrible ordeal." He glanced at Tomas, who still sat on her lap. "I just wanted to ask if ye would feel up to joining us in the great hall for dinner this evening?"

"Aye, Laird, I am feeling much better. I would be delighted to dine in the great hall tonight," she responded.

"Well, until later then,." He bowed, then looked pointedly at Fingal, inclining his head towards Tomas before leaving.

When his footsteps had retreated down the hall, Fingal said, with the humor back in his voice, "I think I have just been told to remove Tomas and allow ye to rest."

Katherine smiled. "Tomas, why don't you and Fingal go see if there are any dragons to slay with that fine sword of yours?"

Tomas scooted off her lap to leave, but before he did, he asked, "Are there really dragons in the Highlands?"

"It would seem so," answered Fingal.

Katherine smiled at his obvious reference to their host, but before they reached the door she said, "Fingal, I'm sure Agnes meant well the other night. Please don't be angry with Niall over this."

"Don't worry, my lady, it is past. Malcolm has indeed always been like an uncle to us. I'm sure he thought my argument with Niall meant more than it did."

Chapter 6

Diarmad arrived with ten guardsmen late that afternoon. Niall was relieved to learn the dowry was secure at Duncurra. However, his second-in-command reported that while they were in Edinburgh, Matheson had raided again near the southwest border of the MacIan lands and spirited away ten head of cattle. The MacIans retaliated, but returned with fewer beasts than they lost.

"God's teeth, why is Matheson doing this?" swore Niall, as Malcolm entered the great room.

"What is Matheson doing now?" he asked.

"He can't keep his hands off my stock. We have been plagued with his raids for months now, as if he needs any of our meager stock."

Malcolm answered, "Why does this surprise ye? The Mathesons have never been particular about the way they gain their wealth. Their feud with the MacIans has been long standing, has it not?"

"The MacIans and the Mathesons have never been allies," Niall said, "but the argument between our grandfathers about our borders was resolved without a full-scale feud. Neither laird liked the compromise, which resulted in little squabbles erupting from time to time over the years. However, until this last year, they were only a minor annoyance. Now he is relentless and the losses are crippling. Your land borders his; has he pilfered your stock?"

"Nay," said Malcolm. "Perhaps Laird Matheson has his eyes on expansion? Certainly one way of defeating an opponent is to critically weaken him first. Now you have sufficient funds, maybe your best option is to go on the offensive."

"That really isn't an option at the moment. A full-scale feud with Matheson would critically weaken us, regardless of our current financial state. I simply can't risk it."

"I'm sure ye know what is best for your clan. On a more pleasant note, I just had a nice visit with your lovely wife and Fingal. She appears to be recovering well from her ordeal. I thought perhaps ye would both join us in the great hall for the evening meal."

"Certainly," said Niall absently, but he wondered what the hell Fingal was doing visiting with his wife. Moments later, his brother appeared with Tomas, who wielded a wooden sword. Niall's jealously cooled when he realized Tomas had been visiting Katherine. Fingal had merely accompanied him as ordered.

~ * ~

Agnes declared Katherine sufficiently recovered to make the trip to Duncurra. Since his guard had returned, Niall planned to leave the next morning. Therefore dinner would be something of a farewell feast. After bathing in the loch, Niall returned to their chamber to escort his wife to dinner. The effects of the cold loch water vanished instantly when he laid eyes on his lovely wife. A bath had been brought up for her and she sat drying her honey-colored silk hair by the fire. She wore a pale gold gown that hugged her figure provocatively. He hadn't paid much attention to his lovely wife's green eyes before, but now they mesmerized him. He wondered if the gold flecks had always been there, or if her eyes simply reflected the gold gown she wore. Once again, Niall remembered Father James had called her radiant; he couldn't find a better word to describe her.

~ * ~

Laird MacLennan spared nothing for the feast. His staff served an endless variety of delicacies and wine flowed freely. Malcolm could not have been a more charming host. It warmed Katherine's heart to see the love and respect Niall had for Malcolm. After years under her uncle's cruel control, she had forgotten what it meant to be loved as part of a family. Malcolm certainly had made her feel welcome and she realized how much she'd missed that. She wondered if Niall's clansmen would accept her as easily when she reached Duncurra.

Until that evening, she had not left their bedchamber and she enjoyed herself immensely. The evening would have been perfect except she had the impression many of the women disapproved of her. She felt this most acutely from Duncan's wife, Lana, who sat at the laird's table with them. Lana made no attempt to hide her disdain. She barely spoke to Katherine during the meal, pointedly turning away from her and not engaging in conversation. Occasionally, Katherine caught Lana staring at her with contempt. Katherine couldn't imagine what she had done, but assumed it might be because she wasn't a Highlander, so she tried to ignore it.

~ * ~

Although the feast showed signs of lasting well into the night, Niall told Malcolm he wanted to make sure Katherine rested well before they began their journey, so they retired early.

When they reached their chamber, the beautiful man she had married finally kissed her in a way he had only hinted at before. She shyly responded, opening her lips, and he deepened the kiss, exploring her mouth with his tongue. She put her arms around his neck, giving in to the wonderful sensations, returning his kiss with abandon. He stroked her back lightly and, with the pain from her injuries gone, she shivered with delight. He cupped one breast through the fabric of her gown, rubbing the nipple lightly. Awed, she felt it harden at his touch and was surprised to realize the throaty moan of pleasure she heard was her own. As he trailed kisses down her neck, she arched her head back, giving him greater access.

"Lass," he whispered roughly, "I was going to wait," claiming her mouth again, "until we were home... Ye need to rest."

"I don't want to rest." As he continued to caress her nipple, the warmth kindled by his kiss became a liquid fire spreading through her. The feeling of his tongue exploring her mouth, together with his hand on her breast, made her knees weak. She didn't know exactly what she wanted, she only knew she wanted more. She needed more.

She felt him remove her belt before he stopped kissing her to turn her away. She had a moment of panic as she thought she might have done something wrong, but then he unlaced her gown and pulled it off her shoulders. He turned her back to face him again before continuing the tender onslaught of her mouth. He removed the rest of her clothes, letting them fall to the floor. He stopped kissing her for a moment and simply looked at her. Realizing for the first time she stood naked in front of him, she raised her hands nervously to cover herself.

He grasped her hands and held them away from her. "Nay, lass, ye are lovely. Let me look at ye." She flushed under his perusal and, although she couldn't quite look at him, she didn't cover herself when he released her hands.

Leaning down, he captured one pert nipple in his mouth, suckling on it. This new sensation fed the fire building in her core until it became almost unbearable. Returning once again to her lips, he gave his kisses more urgency and she put her hands around his neck again.

"My sweet lass, I have wanted ye from the moment I saw ye." He pulled her hair free from its braid, running his fingers gently through her tresses.

Stepping away from her, Niall quickly removed his plaid and belt, dropping them with her garments on the floor. He scooped her into his arms, carried her to the bed, and laid her gingerly upon it. He stepped back, gazing at her again for a moment, sobering slightly. "Lass, are ye sure? Ye have been so ill, and I don't want to hurt ye. We will wait if ye need time."

"Please, Niall, don't make me wait." She wasn't sure what she was asking for, but she knew she didn't want to stop.

He pulled his tunic over his head. She gasped and heard him chuckle when she saw the full length of his naked body.

Although Katherine had the general idea of how men and women coupled, she had never seen a completely naked, very much aroused man. She felt a hot blush flood her cheeks, but before she had too much time to think about it, he lowered himself onto the bed beside her. He captured her lips again, and caressed her breasts, teasing the nipples until they were taut. "Ye are so sweet, lass," he whispered before trailing kisses down her neck. He fondled one soft breast, taking the nipple in his mouth to suckle.

She had never felt anything like this. What was happening to her? As his caresses inflamed her, she became bolder, her hands roaming over his back and shoulders.

He slid one hand down her waist to her hip. Slipping it between her thighs, he nudged them apart, stroking them lightly. He caressed the curls at the apex of her legs, slipping one finger between the moist lips.

"Nay," she said, stiffening as she tried to push his hand away.

"Wheest, lass," he whispered, capturing both her hands in his free one and kissing her lips again. His finger found the sensitive nub at her core and gently circled it, eliciting a moan. Instead of pulling away she arched into his hand. He replaced his finger with his thumb, continuing the circular movement, while sliding one finger inside her. She was momentarily startled by the intimate caress, but while one tiny corner of her consciousness thought perhaps she shouldn't allow it, she enjoyed his touch too much to stop him. Lost in sensation, she barely noticed as he nudged her legs farther apart and positioned himself between them, continuing to pleasure her with his hand.

She had never felt so powerless and yet so completely free. She pushed against him, wanting more. When she thought she would surely die if the intense sensation building at her core continued, she exploded in ecstasy. It was unlike anything she had ever experienced. She felt as if the world shimmered around her.

While she still felt dazed, before she knew quite what was happening, he penetrated her with one swift thrust. The sharp pain breached the blissful fog enveloping her. It was sobering. She squeezed her eyes shut, clenching her teeth to keep from crying out. For a moment she trembled and tried to pull away, but she felt him gently caress her face, soothing her.

"It will pass, sweetling," he assured her, remaining perfectly motionless while still sheathed in her. Opening her eyes to look into his, she plainly saw both his concern for her as well as rigid tension.

Just as he said it would, the sharp pain subsided and she relaxed. He slipped his hand between her legs, gently stroking her again. When his finger once more rubbed the sensitive spot, the heat in her belly stirred for a second time. That same indescribable need built, only, if possible, even more profoundly than before.

"Katherine, my beautiful lass, ye feel so good." He began to gently move slowly in and out of her, but she could feel the supreme tension in his body.

She writhed under the movements of his hand and body, becoming almost frenzied. "I need you, Niall," she cried out, meeting his thrusts.

Responding to her abandon, he plunged into her again and again until she felt the heat of his seed within her. She arched against him and cried out as she reached another shuddering climax. She was astounded by her powerful reaction to his love-making and was vaguely aware that even her fingers and toes tingled. She had never imagined this bliss was possible.

He shifted his weight off her, but they remained joined as they lay there for what may have been a moment or an eternity. Finally, he eased out and moved beside her, pulling her close against him. He lightly caressed her hair and face, kissing her softly.

Finally he asked, "Did I hurt ye very much?"

"Aye," she answered honestly, "but not for long."

He laughed and said, "I did make ye promise never to hide anything from me."

"Aye, ye did."

"It won't hurt like that again," he reassured her.

"I hope not, because I liked everything else," she admitted boldly.

He chuckled and whispered, "I know," kissing her again.

Chapter 7

Katherine slept soundly that night in Niall's arms.

Niall slept less soundly. He woke up during the night with her enticing round bottom tucked up against his groin and he stiffened in response. He would have happily made love to her again, but he knew the ride to Duncurra in the morning might be uncomfortable for her, so he gritted his teeth while trying to go back to sleep.

Just after dawn they left Brathanead keep and Niall walked with her to where the men prepared their horses. He took Katherine's hand before saying, "I sent word for Diarmad to bring ye something." He winked at her. "Tomas, ye can bring your lady her mount now," he called.

Grinning from ear to ear at being part of the surprise, Tomas, led a strong brown gelding out of the stable.

Katherine was thrilled and threw her arms around Niall, hugging him.

A little taken aback, he looked down at her. "It isn't that I don't enjoy having ye ride on my lap and, if ye get tired ye can ride with me, but he is yours. I know your father gave Stormy to ye and nothing can replace her, but I thought having this brown beast as your own might help."

"He is beautiful, Niall, thank you. He isn't the horse my father gave me, but he is the horse my husband gave me," she said, hugging him again. "Does he have a name?"

"Not that he told me. Tomas, did he tell ye his name?"

"Nay," said Tomas seriously, "But Diarmad did. Diarmad said his name is Eachann."

"Hello, Eachann," she said, stroking his neck in greeting.

Niall helped her mount and, at last, they headed home. In spite of his worries, they completed the journey without incident. By early afternoon, still several miles away, they could see Duncurra.

"It *is* in the middle of a loch," Tomas cried in awe.

"It certainly looks that way from here," Katherine agreed.

"This is Loch Craos. As we ride along the western edge, ye will begin to see the tail of the crag behind Duncurra. There is a wall built across the bottom of the tail that extends around the whole crag. It encircles the castle and most of the village. It makes Duncurra easy to defend." Niall couldn't keep the note of pride out of his voice.

"If there is a wall, how do ye get into it?" Tomas asked.

"Tomas, don't be silly. There will be a gate in the wall, just like at Cotharach." Katherine laughed.

"But Duncurra isn't built out of wood like Cotharach," Tomas observed.

"Nay, it isn't. It is built from stone, but when we get close enough to see it better, ye will see a low tower built into the wall. That tower is called a 'barbican'," Niall explained. "In the middle of the barbican is a heavy iron gate that can be raised and lowered. It is called a portcullis."

"Port-cull-iss," Tomas tried the word.

The boy was enthralled, but to his surprise Katherine was, too, so Niall continued to describe the fortress. "The wall is very tall and thick near the bottom, but it becomes lower as the crag rises."

"If it is low, couldn't someone just climb over it?" Tomas asked.

"Where the wall is lower, the edge of the crag drops straight into the water. It would be very hard to climb out of the water, up the crag, and over the wall."

"Why do you need a wall there, then?"

"To keep wee lads and other people from falling off the edge of the crag. Ye are never to climb on that wall, Tomas, it is very dangerous. Do ye understand?"

"Aye, I understand," Tomas replied seriously.

Niall went on. "Do you see the two tall towers?"

"Aye."

"Well, the men in those towers can see us, too, even though we are still quite a long way from Duncurra. What do ye think they would do if we were an enemy?"

"Close the port-cull-iss?" Tomas asked, wide-eyed.

"Aye, they would do that, but they would also have plenty of time to prepare for a fight to defend the castle. It is very hard to sneak up on Duncurra without being seen."

~ * ~

Katherine realized how true those words were as they reached the village. Word of their approach must have spread, because it seemed that the whole clan had turned out to meet them. As Niall's clan called words of welcome to them, Katherine smiled at them, quietly taking in her surroundings. She realized painfully that Duncurra was impoverished. Everything was well cared for but she saw signs of disrepair. Many of the cottages needed roof or wall repairs and the wall circling the crag was crumbling in places. Most distressing, however, was seeing the villagers themselves. They were thin, their clothes threadbare, and none of them wore shoes.

During the ride from Cotharach, she had given a lot of thought as to how Niall had become involved in her uncle's scheme to seize her lands and the leadership of her clan. Not completely naïve, she knew Niall wanted her wealth badly enough to agree to marry her sight unseen, relinquishing his other rights, but she hadn't known why. She understood many men measured their success by their financial worth. Still, although she knew very little about Niall, after spending the last ten days with him, she had trouble believing he fell into this category. Now his reasons stood all around her. He had married her because he needed her dowry for his clan. She fully understood and respected that decision and she knew, in the same circumstances, she would have made a similar choice for the sake of her own people.

~ * ~

As Niall rode through the village with his new wife, he couldn't help but wonder what she was thinking when she saw the poor conditions. Her warm smile and graciousness towards his clansmen appeared genuine. He hadn't warned her about the rundown state of Duncurra. She had asked him about his home and clan during the evenings they spent together at Brathanead, but she never pushed for more detail than he gave, and he never revealed their desperate circumstances. He expected her condemnation now, but she gave no hint of disapproval. If anything, she appeared concerned.

When they reached the courtyard, he helped her dismount. He led her up the stairs, through a set of large double doors, and into the great hall. The great hall connected the keep's two large towers. Normally a flurry of activity, it was even more crowded than usual because of all of the people who came to greet them.

"Welcome to Duncurra, Katherine," he said.

~ * ~

Katherine looked around the great hall with interest. The most impressive feature was a massive hearth standing directly across the room from the entry doors. She noticed four doorways, one in each corner of the hall. "Where do those doors lead?"

"These two in the front lead to the two towers. The left rear door goes through to the kitchen and the other one leads to the buttery."

"The floors are timber," she noticed.

"Aye, there is a level below this one, mostly used for storage."

Katherine noticed a large refectory table surrounded by wooden chairs, standing near the far end of the hall by the hearth. Although it wasn't on a raised dais, she assumed it was the laird's table. Benches and trestle tables were stacked against the side walls, but she saw no other furniture. The room's only adornment, a frayed tapestry, hung over the hearth. While not as richly appointed as Cotharach, everything was clean, and fresh, and sweet rushes covered the floor.

Niall introduced her to Edna, the widow in charge of his household staff. Edna, a tiny ball of efficiency, was shorter than Katherine by several inches. Katherine admired her no-nonsense air. She remembered with amusement that Edna was the object of Turcuil the giant's affection. Having met her now, Katherine understood why the energetic little woman left him tongue-tied when she was near. She had no doubt Edna could be every bit as fierce as any giant.

Niall also introduced her to an older couple, perhaps close to three score in years. Small, balding, and bookish Hendry, the steward, had an air of authority as palpable as Edna's. His strong, sturdy wife, Bridie, managed the kitchens, and while she was courteous, Katherine felt stark disapproval from the older woman.

Excited about finally reaching Duncurra, Katherine looked around eagerly. Just as Niall had described to her, the women wore a full belted *léine* under an *airisaidh*. Additionally, Bridie, Edna, and many of the other women wore a triangular white veil. She wanted to ask them about it and generally learn more about her new home and clan. Therefore, she felt profoundly disappointed when Niall said, "Edna will introduce ye to the rest of the staff over the next few days. I have been away now for almost a month and I must attend to some business that can wait no longer. She will show ye to our chamber now. I want ye to rest."

Katherine hesitated; she didn't need to rest, and there was so much she wanted to know. Her primary concern was what would happen to Tomas. She realized that when she had made the decision to bring the lad, she had not been thinking beyond his immediate safety. She wanted to ask Niall about it now.

When she didn't leave immediately, Niall arched an eyebrow at her and asked in a chilly tone, "Did ye misunderstand me?"

Surprised by his obvious displeasure, she answered, "Nay, Laird, I was going to ask you a question, but it will wait."

The look on his face told her the formal address irritated him. His voice was clipped when he responded, "Very well. I will join ye soon."

Edna cringed and a quick glance around told Katherine others, too, noted the laird's annoyance.

She nodded, embarrassed, before following Edna to the east tower. As they walked, Edna explained that the ground floors of both towers contained armories and some store rooms. The laird's family occupied the upper floors of the east tower, where there were rooms for guests as well.

"Laird MacIan's chamber is on the second floor and Fingal's is on the third. Although Diarmad isn't family strictly speaking, he also has a room on the third floor," she explained. "The unmarried members of the laird's elite guard have rooms in the west tower. Hendry and Bridie also live in the west tower, as do my children and I. Some of the servants and unmarried men-at-arms sleep on the floor of the great hall, but many live in the village."

Edna showed her into Niall's sparsely furnished chamber. It contained a large bed, a chest, a wardrobe, two wooden chairs, a small table, and a washstand. The faded green bed hangings looked threadbare but clean, and a woolen counterpane covered the coarse linen sheets. Katherine walked over to the one window to look out. "Oh, my, the view of the loch is beautiful."

"Is there anything else ye need, my lady?" Edna asked.

"Nay, not really. I would like to learn more about Duncurra." Katherine attempted a warm smile, but she felt a little lost. She wished Edna would stay and chat with her a bit.

Edna herself seemed reluctant to go, but said gently, "My lady, there will be plenty of time for that later. Ye have just arrived after a long journey, and ye have been very ill. The laird wishes ye to rest, and so ye should. He would not be happy with either of us if we ignore his order."

"I suppose he wouldn't. I am just not in the habit of spending so much time resting."

"Well, then, take advantage of it while ye can. When ye are fully recovered, I'm sure ye'll find there is never a shortage of work."

Katherine laughed. "I'm sure there isn't."

"If there is nothing ye need, I'll leave ye to rest now." Edna left, closing the door behind her.

~ * ~

Fingal was concerned when he saw the clan's response to Lady Katherine. Highland clans tended to be very insular; even if Lady Katherine had been from another Highland clan, it would take her a while to fit in. However, being an outsider made it much worse. Niall's callous dismissal of her as soon as they entered the keep did nothing to alleviate the problem. If anything, it was a signal to the clan that he was less than pleased with his new bride.

According to Diarmad, the clan was ecstatic because of the financial security resulting from the union, and they considered Lady Katherine lucky to wed their laird. *Lucky?* Fingal thought no one who truly knew Niall would consider the lass lucky. The snatches of conversation he heard were impossible to ignore.

"Can ye believe she has the nerve to show herself like that?"

"Lowlanders must all be hussies."

"She is obviously an embarrassment to the laird."

Although he hadn't given it much thought until then, he knew what the women were gossiping about. No decent, married Highland woman would appear in public without covering her hair. For them, the linen *brèid*, or kertch, was similar to wearing a wedding band. He shook his head in disgust at their reaction. Rather than thinking Lady Katherine might be unaware of the custom, the women saw it as an insult to the laird. Sadly, he realized this would be the first of many "mistakes" the women of the clan would tally against their laird's new wife.

As he pondered this, he saw Edna reenter the hall. She appeared angry and strode toward the back door leading to the kitchens. Curious, Fingal followed her. He stopped outside the kitchen and was not surprised to find the women had gathered there to gossip, making no effort to keep their voices down. Although overseeing the preparation of the evening meal, Bridie led the charge, saying "A brazen thing she is, walking in here on the laird's arm like that."

"Aye," said another woman, "then it's off to bed with her for a nap. Weak she is."

"Or plain lazy," added another.

Then to his surprise he heard banging on the table, and in a manner befitting the laird, Edna yelled, "Enough!"

The women fell silent.

"The 'brazen thing' about whom ye are speaking is our laird's wife. Can any of ye holy women tell me how that lass was supposed to know our traditions? Do ye think the MacLennan women would have been more gracious than ye, or did ye expect our laird or the other big eejits who brought her here, worried about whether she covered her hair or not?"

There was only guilty silence.

"Bridie, who tied your kertch on ye and asked for God's blessing the day after your wedding? Caolan, Seanna, who did yours?"

The women didn't answer.

"My mother did and I suspect your mothers, or another woman who loved ye, did the same for each of ye.

Who blessed this child? The uncle who beat her half to death? She has no mother, nor, it seems, any compassionate clanswoman to guide her."

Fingal smiled. The silence told him the women were sufficiently embarrassed, but Edna continued. "What other choice words did I hear? 'Weak?' Was it 'lazy' ye called her, Caolan? The laird ordered her to rest and he was right to do so. Alan said he didn't think she was going to live through the night when they arrived at Brathanead less than a sennight ago. Do ye begrudge a lass who has been that ill a rest after a long day's journey?"

Again her indictment was met with ringing silence. "Perhaps none of ye have stopped to think about this, but it seems to me the king, the lass's uncle, and our laird have all benefitted in one way or another by this marriage, but I am hard pressed to see any benefit to the lass herself. And don't tell me being wed to him is benefit enough. If ye are honest, most of ye know as well as I do marriage to him will not be easy."

Well, trust Edna to be blunt, thought Fingal with a grin, but her last weapon was clearly meant to lay them low.

"I suspect Lady Katherine will do many things over the next few months that all of ye might find odd or even insulting, but before ye decide to spew any more venom, remember Lady Katherine's wealth saved this clan, and see if ye can find a bit of compassion in your hearts for her."

Chapter 8

Niall intended only to address the most urgent issues, but as usual they were all urgent and it took longer than he thought it would. Just before the evening meal, he finally joined Katherine in his chamber, expecting to find her asleep. Instead, she stood looking out the window and the bed hadn't been disturbed. "I am fairly certain I told ye to rest," he said, more than slightly irritated.

"I did rest," she answered. "You didn't say sleep, but I couldn't have anyway. I rested in the chair and now I'm resting looking out the window," she said with a smile.

He was not amused. "Katherine, ye knew what I meant. If I ask ye to do something, I want no argument. I expect ye to do it."

Katherine considered that statement for a moment before replying with a slightly cheeky grin. "Perhaps then, you will be more specific with your next order."

He couldn't help but chuckle. "Let me try again. Come here and kiss me, wife," he commanded.

She crossed the room into his arms and gave him a chaste kiss on the lips.

"That is not at all what I had in mind," he said, and lowered his lips to hers, giving her a passionate, soul-stirring kiss. "That, my sweet little wife, is a kiss."

"Do you see how important details are?" she said audaciously.

He gave a low growl, "I would be happy to give ye plenty of details on this subject, but it will have to wait until after dinner." He kissed her again before asking, "Ye had a question earlier?"

"Aye," she answered, her expression turning serious. "I was wondering what is to be done with Tomas?"

He, too, had been trying to determine what would be best for Tomas. She seemed fond of the lad and she obviously wanted to protect him from her uncle. However, in general, Lowlanders were as class-conscious as the English. Therefore, as a peasant, the son of a stable hand, Tomas' social status was only slightly higher than a serf's. He did not want the lad growing up without a mother's love. He had warm memories of his own mother and bitter memories of Eithne. Although she hadn't revealed the harsh side of her personality to her husband, it was evident to nearly everyone else, but perhaps most evident to her stepson. Even after she had a son of her own, nothing changed; she treated Fingal no better than she did Niall. In the lad's best interest, he thought perhaps it would be better for Tomas to live with the family of one of his clansmen, but he didn't want to discuss this now. He finally answered, "I haven't decided yet. For tonight he will stay with Fingal as he has been. We will discuss it in the morning."

Although Katherine didn't appear happy about it, she said no more.

Wanting to banish the solemn look from her face, Niall kissed her again. Her warm response pleased him immeasurably, and the kiss had its desired effect; she no longer looked troubled. "Ye're distracting me again, lass. My clan will starve if ye don't desist."

"I'm distracting you?"

"Well, the details on who is distracting whom may be a bit fuzzy. We will have to work them out later," he said with a wink and, taking her elbow, led her downstairs for the evening meal.

Niall walked to the refectory table in the great hall with Katherine on his arm. Generally, everyone who lived or worked in and around the keep ate their meals on the trestle tables, while the laird's family and invited guests dined at his table. Diarmad and Fingal were seated there, as well as Alan. Niall introduced their other guests, Cairbre, his other captain, Cairbre's wife, Maude, and Alan's wife, Effie. Katherine appeared thrilled to see Tomas at the table too, and gave the lad a quick hug before taking her seat.

She seemed to enjoy the company of the two women. Effie and Maude told her stories about their families and the clan and kept Katherine laughing through the meal. Niall conversed with his men, but Katherine's voice or her musical laughter frequently distracted him and he often caught himself gazing at her.

"Laird, are ye listening?" he heard Cairbre ask.

"Listening? My apologies, I was preoccupied for a moment."

"A moment? Ye have been preoccupied all evening," Cairbre answered. "Ye can't take your eyes off her. Has she captured your heart, lad?"

Momentarily taken aback, Niall recovered quickly. "Make no mistake, Cairbre," he said soberly, "she is lovely and she pleases me. I am glad she is my wife, but my heart was never part of this bargain."

The Laird retired with his wife as soon as the evening meal ended. It had been a very long day and his yearning to taste her charms once again had only intensified during the meal. This surely was what Cairbre had perceived. Once they reached their chamber, Niall pulled her into his arms and kissed her. She was so sweet and responsive. He wondered how he had been able to think of anything other than kissing her since he first captured her lips in the chapel at Cotharach. If he thought giving in to into those desires the previous evening at Brathanead would quench his need, he realized now he was sorely mistaken. He explored her mouth zealously with his tongue as she responded eagerly.

He pulled her hair loose from the braid, running his fingers through it. Clutching the silky lengths, he sought her mouth, finding her kisses and mewling responses intoxicating. He undressed her as he had the night before, but tonight she returned the favor, removing his plaid and belt.

"Ye are too tall, bend down. I can't get your tunic off."

Bending forward he said, "It is also called a *léine*, but ye can call it anything ye wish, as long as ye remove it. I love the feel of your hands on me."

Obliging, she removed the garment, rubbing his shoulders. She ran her hands lightly through the sandy hair on his chest before clasping them behind his neck and boldly pulling him into another kiss. He gave a low growl of pure pleasure, as her delicate touch made him shudder with desire. He had never wanted anyone as much as he did this sweet little morsel in his arms. He lifted and carried her to the bed.

As he had the night before, he took a moment to savor the exquisitely beautiful lass lying naked in his bed with her shimmering hair spread beneath her. She blushed shyly, but it pleased him that she didn't attempt to cover herself.

"I don't think I will ever tire of looking at you, sweetling." He lowered himself onto the bed beside her, kissed her forehead, and rubbed his cheek against her hair. "You are sweet enough to eat," he said, burying his face in her neck, kissing and nibbling at it until she giggled. That musical sound, which had distracted him all evening, was now his alone to enjoy.

She appeared to lose herself in the sensations, responding to his touch and exploring his hard muscled body with her hands. He teased her nipples into hard peaks, flicking them lightly with his tongue. He grinned when he heard her swift intake of air and he continued suckling one breast while he rubbed the firm peak of the other. He slid his hand down her body, finding the spot that had driven her mad the evening before. Moaning, she pushed into his touch, seeking more. "I love your touch, too," she whispered, her blush deepening.

Her uninhibited response thrilled him. All conscious thought fled and he became aware only of the fire growing within him. As she writhed against him, the almost unbearably intense sensations overwhelmed him. Her unrestrained response increased his own desire until he ached to possess her completely. He pushed her legs apart and entered her with as much restraint as he could muster. He did not want to risk hurting her, but she crushed his good intentions. She was like a wild thing rising to meet him. She drove him deep within her, over and over again, until he felt her muscles contract around him as she reached her climax moments before he exploded with his own release.

He panted as, his head dropped to her forehead. He eased his weight off her, lying at her side, his hands still caressing her silken skin.

Breathless, she looked up at him, her green eyes dark with passion. As he ran his hand lightly down her body, she shivered.

"Lass, ye delight me," he said huskily.

She smiled. "I haven't quite figured out what it is you do to me."

He laughed and pulled her to him so her back was to his chest and his arms encircled her. "Well, I guess I'll just have to keep doing it then, at least until you get it sorted out," he said, and kissed her head.

~ * ~

In moments his breathing had become slow and regular and she knew he had drifted off to sleep. She found that a little astonishing because she felt energized. As she listened to his deep steady breaths, she enjoyed feeling the weight of his arms around her.

She had never really imagined what it might be like to fall in love, or to feel loved by a man. Smiling to herself, she supposed that as a young lass she might have had some romantic notions about love. She couldn't really remember too much about her parents' relationship. As in her marriage, her parents barely knew each other when they wed, but they had seemed affectionate. She remembered her father's sorrow when her mother died. Maybe they had grown to love each other.

After her father died, she'd had precious little time to think of much else other than protecting her clan and herself from her vicious uncle. The fear of who her uncle might choose for her accompanied any thought of marriage, so she avoided romantic thoughts at all costs.

Now she found herself in the arms of a husband who, by all accounts, was a good man who was respected by his clan. She enjoyed his company and she reveled in his love-making. She knew she could love Niall, but she feared he could not love her in return. She had heard him tell Cairbre, "My heart was never part of this bargain." A voice inside told her to tread carefully; there would be pain on this road. It would be best to accept what Niall could offer, but at all costs protect her heart.

Then Father James' words came back to her. *You have learned the surest way to open yourself to hurt is to love, and yet you love anyway.* She realized it was too late. Not only *could* she love him, but she feared she had already lost her heart. *If you can't love me back, Niall, please, please, don't hurt me too badly.*

~ * ~

The sun had risen when Niall woke in the morning with the beautiful nymph from last night still in his arms. The lacerations on her back had mostly healed, leaving red scars. He knew eventually they would fade, joining the other fine white lines there, but he wondered if he would ever be able to look at them without a murderous rage building. He leaned down to kiss her white shoulder.

She stirred and rolled over to face him. Smiling sleepily, she said, "Good morning."

"Good morning, my sweet," he said and kissed her.

She stretched like a cat as she wrapped her arms around him, returning his kiss full measure. He wanted nothing more than to make love to her again as he had last night, but he knew he should give her a little time. He pulled away, saying, "Ah, temptress, we will have to pick this up later, or nothing will ever be accomplished at Duncurra again."

"Well, then, get off me, ye brute," she said, laughing. As he rolled to his side, she hopped out of bed, washed quickly, and dressed. After watching her for a bit, he, too, rose to dress and as he did, she asked, "Niall, have you given any more thought to Tomas?"

He really didn't want to start the morning out with this, but he knew he had to address the issue. Resigned to it he answered, "Some. Tell me, why was Tomas living in the stable at Cotharach?"

"Because I was fond of him and my uncle is cruel."

He frowned and said, "I was looking for a bit more information than that."

She sighed, "It isn't just that Uncle Ambrose is cruel, it is almost as if he enjoys causing pain. He takes pleasure in his victim's reaction to it."

The anger Niall felt earlier, when looking at her scarred back, rose again.

Katherine paced as she explained. "I learned if I controlled my emotions and didn't let him see he was hurting me, he soon lost interest in trying. Then he discovered he could hurt me through other people. If he saw me show someone a kindness, causing that person pain became another way to punish me. When Tomas' grandfather died a few months ago, Uncle Ambrose found a new target in the boy. He said he was being very generous to let Tomas live in the stable and if anyone interfered, they would be punished. I interfered a bit."

Niall arched an eyebrow. "The scars on your back suggest ye interfered more than a bit."

"All right, I interfered a lot, but no one else dared."

Niall thought about this for a moment. "So you feel responsible for him?"

"Partially, I suppose." Her brow furrowed as she appeared to consider her feelings about the little boy.

"I have clansmen with families who would take him in."

She looked stricken. "Do you think that is best? I was hoping—I was just hoping..." she stammered. "Niall, please, can he not just stay with us?"

Niall reached for her to stop her pacing. With his hands on her shoulders, he said, "As what Katherine—a stable boy? He needs parents."

"Can we not be his parents?"

"Ye are asking me to claim a Lowland peasant child as my foster son?"

"It doesn't matter to me that he was a peasant. I—I'm sorry, I didn't think it would matter to you. I love him," she finished somewhat helplessly.

She had finally said the words he wanted to hear. "That doesn't matter to me. I want him to have parents who love him." He paused again, considering the decision he was about to make. "I think he will. He is ours."

She rewarded him with a heart-stopping smile and, to his surprise, threw her arms around him and kissed him soundly.

~ * ~

When they arrived in the great hall they found a number of people there breaking their fast. Fingal, Diarmad, and Tomas sat at the laird's table.

Before Niall and Katherine joined them, Edna, Bridie, and several other women approached. Edna said, "Laird, there is something the women of the clan would like to give Lady Katherine."

He nodded to her and she turned to Katherine.

"My lady, it is a Highland tradition that when a woman is married, she covers her hair with a kertch." She indicated the covering on her own head. "It is a triangle of pure white linen and represents the Holy Trinity, under whose guidance the bride will walk. By custom, the bride's mother or another clanswoman ties it on her head the morning after her wedding, asking for God's blessing on the new bride."

Bridie stepped forward and said, "We became your clanswomen when ye married our laird and, although a few mornings have passed since your wedding, we would like to give ye a kertch now." She tied the kertch on Katherine's head. Together the women said the prayer for God's blessing and each one gave her a kiss on the cheek.

Overcome by the gesture, Katherine let several tears slipped down her cheeks before she could blink them back. "Thank you," she whispered.

Edna gave her a quick hug, and the other women curtsied before excusing themselves.

Niall hadn't thought much about it, frankly, but the fact that his clanswomen had welcomed her in this way pleased him. Even though it was not a custom in the Lowlands, the gracious way in which Katherine had accepted it also pleased him. Smiling, he took her hand, guiding her to the table. She wiped away her tears as they sat down. Tomas looked at her seriously and said in a loud whisper to Fingal, "Lady Katherine doesn't like people to see her cry."

"It's all right, Tomas," she said, embarrassed. "These are happy tears."

"Tomas," Niall said, his voice sounding very serious.

"Aye, Laird?" Tomas answered in a small voice.

"Lady Katherine and I have decided ye need to have a family; ye need parents."

"But I don't know how to get a family." Tomas sounded concerned.

"That's all right, you don't need to worry about that." Katherine knelt beside him. "We thought maybe you would like for us to be your parents."

"Really? Can I call you Mama?"

"Aye, sweetheart," she said, and he flung himself into her arms, nearly knocking her over with his fierce hug. Then he looked shyly up at Niall and asked in another loud whisper, "What do I call the laird?"

"I think 'Da' will be fine." Niall said and Tomas threw his arms around Niall's legs.

Fingal laughed, saying, "Before ye ask, Tomas, ye can call me Uncle Fingal."

Chapter 9

With Edna's help, Katherine slipped easily into life at Duncurra during the next several weeks. Her days fell into a comfortable rhythm. Although she was in the habit of waking very early, Niall generally arose before her. He had usually dressed and gone by the time she woke. He spent much of the day away from the keep, seeing to the needs of the clan and the training of his men, while she managed the keep.

Katherine looked forward to the evenings when they sat together by the hearth in the great hall before retiring. While no one could ever forget Niall was their laird, he seemed more relaxed and at his ease during this time. Fingal and Diarmad nearly always joined them, as did other guardsmen occasionally. Tomas also liked to stay with them at least long enough to hear several stories before Katherine put him to bed. During these relaxed evenings, she began to see the man she married more clearly.

When they did retire, she found joy with him she had never dared to hope for. One evening as they lay in each other's arms, savoring the afterglow of their love-making, the gold ring on her left hand caught her eye. She smiled to herself as she remembered her thoughts about it on her wedding day. As each day passed she recognized that the stranger to whom the king had given her hand now very firmly held her heart.

Happier than she had been in many years, Katherine embraced her Highland clansmen and their culture without reserve. She found the women of her new clan more than willing to help her adjust. She hadn't had a woman in her life to guide and help her since her mother's death, and it pleased her when every matron in the clan, most particularly Bridie, treated her like a daughter. It was not uncommon to hear,

"Och, lass, let me show ye now, if ye do that this way...," She was genuinely happy to learn from them. She didn't mind the familiarity. It also wasn't uncommon to hear her say to an older woman, "Och, Ana, that is much too heavy for ye to lift. Let me get it." Truthfully, she knew exactly how to run a castle and she worked as hard as her clanswomen did, which earned her their respect.

Learning how to live with the man she had married proved to be a bit more difficult. As laird, he ruled the clan without question. The words he said to her on her first evening at Duncurra, *Katherine, if I ask ye to do something, I want no argument. I expect ye to do it,* came back to her over and over again.

Katherine had no idea how difficult that seemingly simple request would be for her. It seemed odd in a way because her uncle had certainly been demanding. If he gave her a specific order, she followed it, or at least her interpretation of it. However, other than the things he needed to ensure his own personal comfort, he didn't really care about much else. She found Niall much more demanding in many ways, and while he would never raise a hand to her, she managed to raise his ire frequently. More often than not this happened because she broke a rule she either didn't know or didn't understand. In some cases she didn't quite realize something he said was an order.

On one of these occasions Katherine was working in one of the kitchens preparing an infusion of wych elm. When it came to preparing the plants and herbs she used in medicines, she preferred to complete the tasks herself to ensure the best results. Although time for the midday meal approached, she didn't expect Niall back at Duncurra until evening. She planned to finish her task and, if necessary, give orders to serve the meal without her. One of the serving maids found her in the kitchen.

"Lady Katherine, the laird has just arrived."

"He's back already? I didn't expect him until much later."

"He said he is ready for the meal to be served."

Intent on her work, Katherine said cheerily, "Oh, please begin without me, then."

In a few minutes the maid was back, saying, "My lady, the laird asks ye to join him for the meal."

"Well, please tell him I can't leave just at the moment. I need to finish this. Go ahead and serve the meal, and I will be along in a bit."

Moments later a white-faced Bridie found her and said, "Och, lass, the laird's in a fine temper. I will finish this for ye. Go."

"What is he in a temper over?" Katherine asked, thoroughly confused.

"Lass, did Seanna not just come and tell ye the laird wants ye to join him for the meal?"

"Aye, but—"

"If he wants ye to join him, ye'd best not keep him waiting," she said, shooing her away from the kettle.

Exasperated, Katherine went into the hall. It was unusually quiet and the glare with which he pierced her as she entered would have put the fear of God into most people. When she reached the table, she said matter-of-factly "You're angry."

"Aye. I'm angry."

Glancing at the table, she saw Diarmad suddenly rubbing his brow, looking as if he was trying desperately not to laugh.

"Why?" she asked.

"Why?" he repeated incredulously. "Ye defied me."

"Defied you?" She sounded astonished. "I'm terribly sorry. I certainly didn't intend to defy you."

"Ye didn't intend—Katherine, sit down," he growled and motioned for the meal to be served.

When the noise in the hall rose to normal levels, Katherine leaned over and said sweetly, "Niall, how did I defy you?"

Diarmad shook in silent laughter.

Now it was Niall who looked astonished. "Were ye not told that I wanted ye to join me 1?"

"Aye."

"And did ye not say me nay?"

"Not exactly, I didn't realize it was a command, and I just couldn't leave what I was doing at that moment."

"Katherine, if I ask ye to do something, I expect ye to do it. I don't care what else ye are doing at the time. I will not tolerate defiance. Don't do it again."

His anger seemed diffused and she ate in silence for a few minutes before asking, "Just so I understand, what do you mean by 'defiance'?"

Looking even more astounded, he asked, "Do ye truly not understand what the word means?"

"Oh, nay," Katherine said lightly, "I understand what it means. I am just wondering if it means the same thing to both of us."

A muscle in Niall's jaw twitched. "Defiance means willful disobedience. Do we understand each other?"

"Aye, I think we do. So you agree I didn't defy you and your anger is misplaced."

"Ye didn't—I—what?"

"Well, I didn't realize I had been given a command, thus I couldn't have made a conscious or willful choice not to follow it. So based on your definition, I didn't defy you; I was simply confused and you shouldn't be angry." She calmly turned her attention back to her trencher.

Niall stared blankly at her for a moment. He chuckled softly, but soon his chuckles evolved to uproarious laughter. When he finally had control of himself again he said, "My lady, I apologize. In the future I will try to make my wishes clearer."

"It will certainly save you a tremendous amount of upset if you do," she said imperiously, and he laughed again.

When he had stopped laughing and they were no longer the center of attention, she put her hand on his arm, leaned towards him again, and said in a voice only he could hear, "Niall, please don't always assume the worst of me. It was a misunderstanding. I would never intentionally defy you."

Katherine had no idea how difficult that simple request was for him.

Chapter 10

Fingal had said Niall "protects his own," but it took Katherine a while to really understand what that meant. She loved to go riding, but she had been so focused on the management of Duncurra, she hadn't been on Eachann's back since the day she arrived. On one late summer day, the open heath outside of Duncurra's walls practically called to her. She needed to replenish some of her herbs, so she gathered the supplies required for collecting them and headed to the stables. When she asked a stable hand to saddle Eachann for her, he seemed confused and asked, "Are ye riding to the village?"

"I need to gather some medicinal herbs," she answered by way of explanation.

"In the village?"

She laughed. "Nay, lad, there are not many herbs growing in the village."

The boy looked uncomfortable and asked, "So ye are planning to ride outside the walls?"

She laughed again. "Aye, lad. I will need to if I want to gather herbs."

"Then where is your escort, my lady?"

"My escort? I don't need any help."

Looking even more uncomfortable, he said, "My lady, ye can't ride outside the walls of Duncurra without an escort. It wouldn't be safe. The laird would never allow it. If ye will wait a bit, I will find the laird or Diarmad so an escort can be arranged."

She smiled at him and said, "Nay, lad. Thank you, but I don't wish to pull anyone away from more important work."

Disappointed, she left the stables. It seemed silly to tie up manpower with an escort, especially since she didn't really need to ride. She just wanted to for the enjoyment of it. She could gather much of what she required just beyond the village, so she strolled down the sloping crag through the crofts. When she reached the barbican, the watch there stopped her. "My lady, I can't let ye pass."

"Excuse me?" she asked, not quite believing what she heard. "I'm just going to gather some herbs in the heath beyond the village."

"I'm sorry, my lady, if ye will just wait a moment, I will send for a guardsman to go with ye."

"That really won't be necessary," said Katherine, feeling a bit irritated. "I'm not going far."

"I'm sorry, my lady, but the laird would not want ye to go outside Duncurra's walls without an escort. It will only take a few minutes to fetch one of the guardsmen," he said, motioning to another of the men-at-arms to go and do just that.

Katherine put her hand up to stop him. "Nay, thank you, but it isn't necessary." She turned to walk back through the village and up the hill to the keep. *This is completely ridiculous.* How was she supposed to gather the supplies she needed? She certainly had no intention of arguing with a stable boy or men-at-arms when they only followed orders, but she would have a discussion about it with Niall as soon as she could be alone with him.

The discussion didn't wait that long. Katherine had barely swallowed her first bite of the evening meal when Niall asked, "Where were ye going today that ye didn't want an escort?"

His voice sounded very nonchalant, but when she looked at him she could see the displeasure written plainly on his face. She wanted to tell him how she felt about being little more than a prisoner in her home. Instead she said, "Niall, can we talk about this later, when we are alone?"

"I asked ye a question, Katherine, and I want an answer," he pressed, his annoyance now clearly expressed in his tone.

"I wanted to go to the heath to gather some herbs I need for medicines." She hoped that answer would do for now.

"Why couldn't you do that with an escort?"

"It wasn't that I couldn't gather herbs with an escort; I didn't think it was necessary to pull someone away from their work for something as ridiculous as watching me gather herbs." Now Katherine was getting angry, too. "Please, can we discuss this later?"

"There is nothing more to discuss. If ye need to leave the walls of Duncurra, ye will have an escort." Niall said this loudly enough that those sitting closest to them stared.

Katherine nodded but said nothing. There was more to discuss but she wouldn't do it here. She shifted her attention back to her trencher.

"Do ye understand me?"

Raising her head slowly, she leveled a glare at him and said very quietly, "Neither my hearing nor my intellect are impaired. I understand you perfectly."

"Are ye angry with me?" he asked, sounding surprised.

She pulled the reins of her temper back in and adopted an unconcerned expression, before saying calmly, "It doesn't matter. I understand there is nothing more to discuss."

"Ye disagree?" Again he seemed astounded.

Of course, she disagreed, she thought angrily. She would not have asked to discuss it later if she felt there was nothing to discuss. She wanted to yell that at him but to do so would only raise his ire further and make everyone around them painfully uncomfortable. "I would never disagree with you in public."

This seemed to appease him and soon Diarmad drew him into conversation. She picked at the meal in front of her, but she had no appetite left for it. When a sufficient amount of time had passed and Tomas had finished eating, she excused herself to take him for a bath and ready him for bed.

Generally only the laird and the lady or their honored guests had a bath prepared for them in an upstairs chamber. Most everyone else bathed behind a screened area in one of the kitchens, where they could heat the water and fill the bath with much less effort. Katherine sent Fineen, one of Duncurra's chamber maids, to get a fresh *léine* for Tomas while she led him to the kitchen. Never happy about having to stop playing and wash, Tomas grumbled and complained through the entire bath.

She felt hot and tired, not to mention still very angry, by the time she finally had him tucked in bed. The last thing she wanted to do was go back down to the great hall. She retired to their chamber to spend the rest of the evening alone, sewing.

~ * ~

After the meal, Niall sat brooding by the hearth with Diarmad and Fingal.

"What ails ye, brother?" Fingal asked.

Niall shook his head, took a long pull of ale from his tankard, and didn't answer.

"If I had to guess," offered Diarmad, "I would say it was the argument he had with his wee wife at the table."

"That isn't your concern."

"Nay, Laird, it probably isn't. But then I am not the one who brought the issue up during the meal for all to hear, am I?"

Niall just glared.

"What issue?" asked Fingal, who hadn't heard the discussion.

"According to the watch, Lady Katherine wanted to go walking beyond the village this afternoon, but did not seem to think she needed an escort. She wouldn't let him call one for her and she returned to the keep."

"Why would she do that?" asked Fingal.

"That's what I asked her," growled Niall.

"What did she say?"

Niall shook his head again, and took another drink from his tankard.

"She said she would prefer to talk about it privately," answered Diarmad.

"Then go talk to her," said Fingal reasonably. "Surely the lad is in bed by now."

"Now, ye see, Fingal, that is where the problem started," said Diarmad.

"There is nothing to discuss. There is no reason for her to leave the walls alone and I told her that," said Niall angrily. "Why would she want to?" The suspicion in his tone was clear.

Fingal sighed. "It always comes back to that, Niall."

Niall gave Fingal a murderous glare, but his brother was not dissuaded. "Can't ye see ye married a guileless lass? Do ye truly believe Katherine set out to deceive ye?"

"Why would she shun an escort otherwise?" Niall demanded.

"I don't know. Perhaps she doesn't understand why she needs one. Did ye ask her why?"

"How could she possibly think she doesn't need one? And aye, I did ask her why, but her answer didn't make any sense," Niall said dismissively.

"She said she didn't think it was necessary to pull someone away from other duties," Diarmad explained.

Fingal laughed. "Niall, she doesn't understand."

"How could she not understand? She is a noblewoman. Surely she has been guarded her whole life. Why would she think it different here?" Niall's anger was rising. He yelled, "What does she think I have a guard for anyway, if not to protect what is important to me?"

Fingal asked, "Is it possible her loving uncle did not assure she was guarded, and so she doesn't expect to be guarded here?"

"That is ridiculous."

"Is it?" asked Fingal. "We are talking about the lass who looked like a servant when you first met her, are we not? The same one whose uncle not only laid her back open with a whip, but happily married her to an impoverished stranger for his own gain? Ambrose Ruthven had absolutely nothing to lose by risking her life."

Diarmad swore and said, "It's a wonder she lived long enough for the king to marry her off. There should be a special place in hell for beasts like Ruthven."

"Aye, and I would love to be the one to send him there," Niall growled.

"Go talk to her, Niall," Fingal urged.

Niall shook head in exasperation, rose, and walked toward the entrance to the tower.

Just before leaving the hall he overheard Diarmad say to Fingal, "Do you suppose he will ever learn all women are not apples from the same tree?" He ignored the comment and climbed the stairs to his chamber. Entering, he found Katherine sitting in a chair, sewing by the light of a candle. She was a vision with her cloud of hair floating softly around her shoulders, wearing only a shift. She didn't look up as he entered the room. He took off his plaid then sat in the other chair before speaking.

"Katherine, how many men did your uncle set to guard ye at Cotharach?"

"I required no guard at Cotharach," she said in a slightly defensive tone.

Niall arched an eyebrow, "Ye have never had guards charged with your safety?"

"Not since I was a little girl."

"Just exactly when did ye stop needing protection?"

"I don't know. After my father died, I guess, when the Ruthven holdings became mine."

"Why would ye stop needing protection then?"

"Because—it was my home, they were my people."

"So when your father was alive, he travelled around his lands with no guard?"

Katherine thought for a moment. "I don't remember. Nay, I think he was usually accompanied by at least one of his men."

"Katherine, ye were four and ten when your father died. If he never traveled around his holdings alone, why would it be safe for ye to?"

"I don't know. I didn't go very far and there were more important things for the guards to do."

"Sweetling, what could possibly be more important than the safety of their lady?"

She looked at him as if she was trying to come up with a logical answer but couldn't.

"Come here," he said.

She lay her sewing aside with a frustrated sigh and crossed to where he sat. He pulled her gently onto his lap and put his arms around her. "I can only guess at why your uncle didn't ensure your protection, and it is probably only by the grace of God ye came to no harm. The country abounds with thieves and banished clansmen. I suspect your uncle has his share of enemies, too. I'm sure your father knew the dangers, because he secured your safety as well as his own. Why would ye expect me to do less than that?"

"That's not what I—you misunderstood—I—I can't waste your guards' time just to gather herbs," she said, as if it made perfect sense to her.

"What do ye suppose my guards do, if not protect what I value?"

"But what harm could come to me just beyond the village?"

"I don't ever want to find out," he said, kissing her head. "And I won't because ye won't leave the walls without an escort," he said firmly. Before she could argue more, he added, "Katherine, guarding ye is an honor, not a chore, and nothing the members of my guard do is more important."

Still sounding miffed, Katherine asked, "If I wasn't allowed outside of the walls without an escort, why did you not tell me that?"

"I didn't think I had to."

"But you had to tell your men."

"Nay, I didn't. Sweetling, like your father, I rarely leave Duncurra alone. My men know the dangers and would certainly not let ye venture out without a guard, whether I had given an order or not."

She sighed and after a moment said, "I guess I can't stay angry with you, then."

"Nay, ye cannot. I won't allow it." He buried his face in her neck, kissing her until she giggled. Then he captured her lips in a kiss intended to make her forget she was ever angry in the first place.

He carried her gently to the bed, removed her shift, and made slow tender love to her. Later, as she lay sleeping in his arms, he marveled once again at his good fortune in gaining such a sweet bride. The thought of what might have happened to her in the years under her uncle's control made him shudder. The thought of losing her now chilled his very soul. He finally admitted to himself it was neither admiration nor gratitude giving rise to these feelings. He was fond of her. Perhaps he was more than fond.

Chapter 11

The next morning, Niall waited for Katherine at the breakfast table. "This is a surprise," she said happily as she joined him.

"It is the first of several I have planned today," he said mysteriously.

"Who else do you plan to surprise?" she asked, laughing.

"Oh, my sweet little wife, the surprises are all for ye." She gave him the brilliant smile he adored. "I realize I have spent very little time getting to know ye since we were wed."

She blushed and said very softly, "My dear husband, if we spent any more time 'knowing' each other, I fear nothing would ever be accomplished here."

He laughed. "Aren't ye the cheeky little wench this morning?"

She blushed even deeper.

"Now that ye mention it, I may have to allow a bit of time for that particular pursuit, but I had something else in mind. It looks to be a fine day, and I thought perhaps ye would like to go out riding with me. Ye can see more of the MacIan lands than Duncurra and its village, and we can spend some time alone."

"I would love to go riding with you," she answered, overjoyed.

When they finished eating, he took her hand. "Shall we go?"

"I will meet you in the stable. There are some things I need Edna to take care of today. I will only be a few minutes." When she arrived at the stable, Cairbre, Muir, and Turcuil were also preparing mounts. She whispered to Niall, "I thought you said we were spending the day alone?"

He whispered back, "I thought I told ye I rarely left Duncurra without guardsmen, and ye were never to leave without them. But don't worry, they will keep their distance." Then in a normal voice, he said, "What have ye brought there?"

"The supplies required to collect the odd herb or plant I might find."

"Lass, this is not a day for work. Ye can gather herbs tomorrow—with an escort."

She laughed and grinned. "I won't gather common herbs, but if I see something rarer to come by, it would be foolish to leave it behind, would it not?"

"I suppose," he agreed, feigning disappointment.

She laughed again.

He helped her mount Eachann and they headed out. "Niall, what about Tomas?" she asked in alarm before they reached the barbican.

"Taken care of," he said smugly. "I have assigned Uncle Fingal to keep an eye on him today. Later Alan or Keith will go with them to the loch to fish and swim." At the look of surprise on her face, he said, "My foster son doesn't leave Duncurra without a sufficient escort, either."

"Aye, husband, I'm beginning to see a pattern. You've made your point."

When they reached the heath, as Niall had promised, the guardsmen fell back to a discreet distance. Katherine was suddenly and inexplicably shy. Finally breaking the silence, she asked, "Where are we going?"

"I thought we would ride around the northern side of Loch Craos, then east a bit. The raids have occurred at the western edge of my holding and, while none were during the day, I don't want you anywhere near Matheson land."

At midmorning they came to a marshy area on the northeastern side of the loch and she asked, "Niall, can we stop here for a bit? Marshes harbor many useful plants and herbs."

"I did not intend for ye to work on this excursion."

"It isn't work. Please, I just want to see what might be growing here."

Her eyes shown with excitement and he couldn't refuse her. He handed their horses off to Muir and walked with her towards the marsh. To his surprise, his wife removed her shoes and *airisaidh* before pulling the hem of her *léine* between her legs and tucking it into her belt in the front. This pulled the bottom of the garment up to just below her knees. "What are ye doing?" he asked.

"I have to wade in a bit to see everything and I don't want my clothes to get wet."

"Can't ye just look from the edge?"

Katherine's musical laughter enveloped him. "Can ye hunt without going into the forest? All I can see from the edge is the tall purple loosestrife and that is easy to find close to Duncurra. Come with me. I'll show you what the marsh hides." She beckoned, holding her hand out to him.

How could he resist? Taking her hand, he waded in with her.

She pointed out a variety of common plants. She was pleased when she found bog bean, but became positively delighted when she discovered something she called marsh mallow.

"I wasn't sure I would find it this far north. It grew in the marshes near Cotharach, but it isn't very common in colder areas. It's an amazing plant; the flowers, the leaves, even the roots, are useful. Late summer is the perfect time of year to harvest it, too." She gathered some, saying, "You'll thank me the next time you get a sore throat."

"I'll thank ye to leave the muck of this marsh behind," he said. At her look of dismay, he softened his tone and caressed her cheek. "I'm teasing, pet, but ye needn't gather it all now. I will send men to harvest a larger quantity on another day."

"All right, if ye promise," she said with a shy smile.

They waded back out of the marsh, but she continued to talk about the plants they passed and their uses. This completely enthralled Niall. In the last few weeks he had seen several sides of his bride. There was the quiet, submissive maid he first met at Cotharach, who kept a firm check on her emotions but who, when pushed too hard, could unleash her anger with a vengeance. There was also the strong and compassionate lady of the castle, whom so many of his clansmen and women already respected and loved, as well as the gentle mother who cared very deeply for Tomas. Of course, one of his favorite sides was the uninhibited lover whose passion never failed to delight him. However, the woman he walked with now brimmed with knowledge, and had a confidence and self-assurance he had never seen in any woman. She impressed him and he felt oddly proud of her.

After their brief stop at the marsh, they rode east and entered the forest, where they soon arrived at a beautiful glade. His guard positioned themselves in the forest around the glade, again at a discreet distance, leaving Niall and Katherine quite alone. He spread a plaid on the ground before producing a packet of food and a wineskin from the bag on his saddle. They chatted as they ate.

"I am having a wonderful time," she said.

"So am I," he answered with a smile.

"I was just wondering..."

"Mmm?"

"Well, with so much to do, why did you decide to waste the day with me?"

He chuckled. "That is one of the reasons right there."

"What?" she asked, confused.

"A day spent with ye is not wasted, sweetling."

"Oh, I didn't mean—I—"

He put his finger to her lips. "I know what ye meant even if ye don't," he said gently. "I realized last night ye don't recognize your own value. On the day we married, ye said your uncle cared less for ye than he did his saddle."

She blushed and looked away. "I'm sorry, I was— upset."

"I know, and ye had every right to be. But even after hearing ye say that and knowing how cruel your uncle was, I still thought of ye as a noblewoman. As the head of your clan, I assumed ye would have been treated that way. Last night I learned, at least where ye are concerned, my assumptions are frequently wrong.

"Katherine, ye are dear to me, and I realized that since our marriage I have done very little to show ye that. I was immensely irritated with myself when it finally occurred to me this issue hadn't arisen before yesterday because ye haven't been outside the walls of Duncurra since ye arrived."

She blushed and shook her head. "It's not important—there were things—I—," she stammered.

"Wheest, lass, I'm not humbled often, let me suffer a moment."

She laughed, her embarrassment subsiding. "Will you at least try not to assume the worst in the future?"

"Aye, lass, I will try," he said with a grin, "but I fear I am a very flawed man, and set in my ways. It may take a few tries before I get the knack of it."

"Och, laddie, I fear I'll be giving ye plenty of practice at that particular skill," she said, adopting Bridie's manner of speaking.

"Will ye now?" he asked, all humility forgotten. "Then perhaps I shall give ye some practice at a different skill? It is, after all, the least I can do in anticipation of your kind tutelage."

She giggled as he captured her lips and lowered her gently to the ground. The giggles transformed rapidly to moans of carnal pleasure as he plundered her mouth with his tongue and caressed her lush breasts. He gloried in her sensual response to every kiss and caress and she returned his attention in kind, stoking his desire for her. He realized how much he relished her delight. He had bedded his share of women and believed he never left them unsatisfied, but this was different. Her ecstasy became his own; he had never experienced anything to match it.

After their exquisite joining, they lay silently in each other's arms as if neither wanted to break the enchantment of the moment, until one of the horses whickered softly, the noise bringing him back to the present. "As much as I hate to end this," he said, propping himself on his elbow beside her, "I suppose I shall have to take ye back."

"I suppose so," she agreed. "But feel free to waste your day with me anytime the notion strikes ye, Laird."

"Cheeky wench."

Chapter 12

After the extraordinary day they'd spent together, Niall sought her company much more often. Several days later he waited for her at breakfast again.

"More surprises?" she asked.

"I thought ye might like to see more of my land, perhaps meet some of the MacIan farmers."

"How much more land is there?"

"Ye can ride for several hours in any direction without leaving our holding. Most of the farmers live in small clusters scattered throughout our land. My men-at-arms serve sentry duty to ensure the safety of the whole clan, but I, too, make regular visits to make sure all is well with them."

"And here I thought you only built walls and trained warriors," she teased.

"Ah, my clever lass, ye do have a few things to learn. The warriors may be our clan's strength and protection, but the farmers are its sustenance, so they are every bit as important."

After breakfast, they rode out again with an escort, this time traveling northward. After they had ridden a while they neared a small field of oats. "You do have grain fields. I wondered because I haven't seen any until now. I'm sure you saw that Cotharach was surrounded by fields of wheat and barley."

"We do grow some grain and a few other subsistence crops, but the Highland environment is very harsh. Not to mention the fact that our land isn't well suited to growing much. We rely heavily on animal products, mostly wool, for income, with which we buy other things we need. A hail storm has little effect on our sturdy Highland beasts, but it can completely destroy a field of grain."

"I see. I guess that makes raiders an even bigger problem."

"Aye, it does. Even the loss of a few animals to raiders can devastate an already poor clan."

~ * ~

When they reached the first small cluster of crofts, the farmers and their families stopped their work to greet their laird. Niall introduced her, but the people seemed cautious around her. She tried to draw some of the women into conversation while Niall spoke with their husbands, but while they were not disrespectful, they were guarded. Not wishing to make them uncomfortable, Katherine let it go. Instead she watched Niall's interactions with his clansmen and saw a completely different side of him. After they remounted their horses and rode away, she commented, "You are different somehow when you talk with the farmers."

"Ye are different when ye gather herbs, but how am I different?"

"I'm not sure exactly. At Duncurra you are every inch the laird and military leader. You are firm and decisive. You tolerate nothing less than absolute respect and your clansmen willingly give it."

"Of course they do. I always consider the needs of the clan first. My clan knows my decisions reflect that, so I have earned their respect. Was it not so at Cotharach?"

"Do you really need to ask that question? My uncle thought of himself first in all things. My clan feared him, they didn't respect him. He gave no thought at all to the farmers unless they didn't produce enough to suit him. He told them what he wanted and punished them if they didn't deliver. He certainly didn't seek their opinions."

"No matter how I may wish to demand it, nothing I say will make the rain fall or the sun shine."

"Aye, that is true. However, it is more than that. Somehow here ye seem more open and receptive with them."

"As ye pointed out, I am a warrior, not a farmer. These men have knowledge acquired through years of working the land. More than that, they have the knowledge passed down from their fathers and grandfathers, just as my father and Malcolm's father trained me to be a warrior. I am still their laird."

"No doubt. Still, not every leader has learned that lesson."

"What lesson? How to talk to farmers? That's not so very hard," he jested.

She laughed, "Nay, when to seek information, and perhaps more importantly, listen to others."

He sobered a bit. "Your uncle was not a leader, Katherine, he was a tyrant. I am sorry ye suffered so at his hand."

"Thank you. It is true though that one can learn as much from a bad leader as a good one. Knowing what not to do has its value."

"Never fear, my sweet lass, I am certain there will be occasions to learn what not to do from me as well."

~ * ~

When they returned to the keep, Edna was full of questions about Katherine's visit to the crofters.

"Honestly, Edna, I don't think they liked me. I seemed to make them uncomfortable."

"My lady, Highlanders are not always the most welcoming folks. It has been a long time since we have had a laird's wife who paid any attention to the clan. Most of the farming families had precious little contact with Laird Alastair's second wife, but give them time and they will come around."

"How can ye be sure of that?"

"Lady Katherine, ye are kind and gracious and ye always manage to insinuate yourself into things. Frankly, ye are hard not to like."

Katherine laughed. "Insinuate myself? What does that mean?"

"Ye think no one notices how ye slip your way seamlessly into situations? One minute ye are chatting away with someone who is working, and the next ye are working right alongside them."

"I don't know what you are talking about."

"Don't ye? Didn't I see ye scrubbing pots in the kitchen yesterday?"

Katherine waved her hand, dismissing the notion, "That was nothing. Bridie needed a little extra help, that's all."

"Ye find a way to give a 'little extra help' to everyone ye encounter. Of course, the fact that the laird is so taken with ye will help too."

"Why would that matter?"

"Lady Katherine, ordinary people marry for love but noblemen and women don't have that luxury. We know neither of ye chose this union. The fact that there is affection between ye is practically miraculous. I think ye have won his heart, my lady, and that is something the clan can be thankful for."

Katherine didn't argue but she clearly remembered Niall saying, *my heart was never part of this bargain.* Nevertheless, she did as Edna suggested. She gave the clan time, and continued to be herself.

~ * ~

On another visit, she and Niall arrived at one of the small farming communities. An elderly farmer told them his wife, Maire, had been ill.

Excusing herself, Katherine went into his cottage, where she found his wizened wife trying to sweep the floor. "Hello, Maire, I'm Lady Katherine."

The elderly woman made a couple of swipes with the broom and sat down for a moment to catch her breath. "I don't believe I've ever met ye, lass," she said between breaths, then she stood and tried again to sweep.

"Nay, I'm sure we have never met," said Katherine. Taking the broom from Maire, she said, "How about if you sit and have a chat with me while I sweep."

"Now, lass, I couldn't let ye do that."

"Oh, please, I would enjoy a chat and I have been sitting all day."

"Well, I won't say your help isn't appreciated. I've had trouble catching my breath all day."

"Have you now?" asked Katherine as she made quick work of sweeping the small cottage. "Has your breathing been bothering you for a while, or is it just today?"

"Ah, lass, I'm getting old. I suppose it has been getting harder for me to do much for weeks, but now that ye ask, it has gotten worse these last few days."

After sweeping the dust into the hearth, Katherine put the broom away and said, "I know a bit about healing. Perhaps you wouldn't mind if I took a quick look. Maybe there is something I can do."

Maire chuckled and said, "Well, I don't think ye can turn back time. Now if there is a powder or a potion that will pep me up a bit, I'll give it a try."

Katherine knelt in front of her and found swelling that pitted to her touch in the old woman's ankles and lower legs. "Oh, my legs have been swelling up like that for a couple of weeks now," offered Maire.

Katherine put her ear to Maire's chest, hearing moist crackling sounds as she exhaled. "Well, Maire, I think there might be a few things we can do. First, I suspect you will be more comfortable if you take a bit of a rest with your legs up." With a little protest, she helped the woman into bed, elevating both her head and her feet with pillows. "I won't be a minute now—I just have to get something from outside." Popping out of the cottage, she found Turcuil standing in the yard, so she asked him for the dagger he wore on his belt. The confused giant of a man handed her his dagger without question and she proceeded to pry some dandelions from the ground nearby, getting as much of the root as possible.

Having done that, she carefully cut some nettles, gathering them with her plaid wrapped around her hand to protect her skin from the stinging hairs. Back in the cottage, the women chatted as Katherine prepared an infusion of the dandelion root, adding a little honey to sweeten it. She gave a mug to the old woman to drink. Then she put the nettles in a cauldron of water with onions and a bit of cold chicken she found. "It is rather late in the summer for nettles, so let them stew down well, otherwise they might be a bit tough."

"Now, lass, I thought ye had a potion or something for me. Were ye just making an excuse to cook my dinner?"

Katherine laughed. "Nay, Maire. You are holding on to a lot of water. You can see it there in your legs and that is what is making it hard for you to breathe. The dandelion root and the nettles will help you get rid of some of it. I am going to put the chamber pot here near your bed, so it is easy to reach."

Maire looked at her solemnly. "Och, lass, I've been on this earth long enough to know what's happening to me. I told ye, ye can't turn back time."

Katherine sat beside Maire, taking hold of her hand. "You are right. I can't turn time back, but these things will help make you more comfortable for a while. I've left some dandelion root there on the table, I'm sure your husband can find more as you need it. You can tell him how I made it."

"Ye are a good lass. What did ye say your name was?"

Katherine chuckled and answered simply, "Katherine."

"Just Katherine, is it? Are ye the laird's Katherine?"

"Aye, Maire, I am the laird's Katherine."

"Well, ye are a good lass, Katherine MacIan. That lad's done well."

Katherine smiled at her, but before she could respond, someone knocked on the door. She opened it to find Turcuil looking for her. Turning back, she said, "It has been lovely visiting with you, Maire, but I think my husband is ready to go. Now, remember what I told you and keep your feet up as much as you can."

As Katherine rode away, she felt the sadness she always did when there is little to do for someone who is ill except make them more comfortable. She knew eventually the fluid building up would overcome the dear old woman, but in the meantime she would be able to breathe a bit easier. After that day, Katherine always traveled with her bag of medicinal supplies.

~*~

Not surprisingly, knowledge of her skill as a healer spread very quickly at Duncurra. The clan had several midwives, but only Alan's wife, Effie, had healing skills extending beyond stitching wounds. With eight children, Effie found it difficult to tend all the hurts and ills at Duncurra. It didn't take long for the MacIan clan to turn to Katherine when they needed her skills. She was always willing to spend a few minutes chatting with them, celebrating their joys, or listening to their problems, and doing whatever she could to help. In this way Katherine learned a lot about the clan and the clan learned more about her. Soon her compassion won over even those who had been suspicious and mistrustful of a Lowlander.

Occasionally, when someone on an outlying farm needed a skilled healer, Niall took Katherine there. However, for the most part, the clansmen and women sought Katherine out at the keep. As their laird's wife, she suspected they weren't completely comfortable asking her to come to them.

Late one morning, she sat in the great hall reviewing the account books with Hendry. Caolin, one of the women who worked in the kitchen, rushed in and said, "My lady, I beg your pardon. Please, I need your help. I tried to find Effie, but she is delivering a bairn."

"What's wrong?"

"Tis my sister's child, she is terribly ill. She is coughing so much she can barely breathe. Kara lives in the village. Can ye come?"

"Of course I'll come. Give me a minute to get my things. Hendry, can we finish this later?"

"Aye, my lady. I've been itching to go down to the lake and fish for a spell, anyway," he said with a wink.

Katherine retrieved her bag of medicinal supplies before walking with Caolin to Kara's cottage.

"Kara's husband is one of the men-at-arms here and he is away on sentry duty," Caolin explained as they walked. "Their four-year-old daughter Ailis is terribly ill—she can barely breathe. Lady Katherine, they lost a baby last winter to a fever. Kara is beside herself with worry."

Caolin hadn't exaggerated. When they arrived they found Kara in a panic and Ailis struggling to breathe between coughing fits. Katherine stepped in, calmly taking control. The smoke from burning rosemary filled the house. Many people believed it would ward off infection, but Katherine had found the smoke seemed to make things worse, particularly for coughing illnesses. She had Kara remove the burning herbs from the cottage, then opened the windows and doors to help clear the smoke.

While Ailis' skin felt hot and her lips looked dry and cracked, Katherine didn't think the little girl had a dangerously high fever. The things Katherine had found to be most helpful in relieving a serious cough were steam and getting the patient to drink plenty of fluids. She bade Caolin heat a kettle of water. In the meantime, she held the child upright on her lap, speaking to her in a soft, calm voice while supporting her during the coughing spells.

Once the water boiled, Katherine poured some in a bowl placed on the table. Then she had Kara sit with Ailis on her lap. She put a linen towel over their heads, covering the bowl and trapping some of the steam. She replaced the water in the bowl as needed to keep it steaming. The child's breathing eased a bit, but she was still not out of the woods. Katherine knew she had to get some fluids into the wee lass, too, so she made a tisane of peppermint, chamomile, and lemon balm, sweetened slightly with honey. Even if it was just a spoonful at a time, she made sure Ailis drank as much as she could between coughing spasms. After several hours of spooning liquids into the lass, Ailis still hadn't used the chamber pot.

As afternoon faded into evening, Katherine saw Kara's exhaustion. Clearly another long night lay ahead for her, so Katherine insisted she rest. Caolin kept the water heating and Katherine continued to keep Ailis as calm as possible, encouraging her to breathe the steam and drink the tisane. As darkness fell, they heard a knock at the door. With her head under the towel with Ailis, Katherine couldn't see who had arrived, but she heard Caolin's gasp.

"Laird."

Katherine slipped her head out from under the towel to see her large, clearly angry husband filling the doorway.

"What's the matter?" Katherine asked, concerned.

"No one knew where ye were," he growled. His tone of voice caused Kara to awaken. Little Ailis began to tremble and Katherine felt warm moisture spread across her lap. At least that was a good sign.

"Mind your tone," shushed Katherine, "you're scaring the lass."

Niall arched an eyebrow and, if anything, his scowl darkened. Caolin and Kara both looked petrified.

"I don't understand why you are angry. Hendry knew I was coming here to care for the wee lass. She has been very ill."

"Did ye know Hendry was going fishing at the loch?" His voice sounded quiet and calm, but it covered barely controlled rage.

"Well, aye, I did know that," she admitted.

"So no one at the keep knew where ye were until he returned just now. Were ye trying to worry me?"

"Nay, of course not. Niall, I am sorry. I didn't leave the walls, so I didn't think it mattered."

"It does matter. Ye know there is always a guardsman in the castle. If ye leave for any reason I expect ye to tell him where ye are going."

"I didn't know that," she said meekly.

"What do ye mean, ye didn't know that? Is it not the same everywhere? Was it not that way at Cotharach?"

"There were guards, but no one cared where I went. We've been through this, Niall."

"Aye, we have and ye know I care where ye go, so I will make it clear for ye. When I am in the keep, ye don't leave without telling me, and when I'm not there, ye don't leave without telling a guardsman, even if you are just going to the village. If he thinks ye need an escort, he will arrange it. Do ye understand?"

"Aye, I understand. I don't understand why, but I understand what ye've asked."

"Ye truly don't understand why? By all the saints, Katherine, ye are my wife, that's why."

Katherine looked at the faces of the other women in the room. This obviously made sense to them, so she simply said, "Oh."

Niall shook his head in frustration. "Are ye still needed here?"

Katherine thought for a moment. Although Ailis still had coughing fits, they were less frequent and had eased a great deal. Also, the lass breathed much more easily between them now. Since she had obviously wet herself on Katherine's lap, the fluids seemed to be helping, too. Katherine knew she had done all she could do for now. "Nay, I think Kara and Caolin can handle it as long as they promise to send for me if something changes for the worse."

The women agreed. Katherine gave Ailis to her mother before leaving the cottage with Niall. They walked in silence for a few minutes. Finally Niall said, "Katherine, I am your husband and your laird. It is my duty to protect ye, but I can't do that if I don't even know where ye are. Do ye understand that?"

"Aye," she said quietly.

"Do ye really?"

"I understand you need to know where I am, so you will know I'm safe." She didn't fully understand why. After the whole 'don't leave the walls without an escort' incident she understood why he felt she needed protection outside the walls. Surely if she hadn't gone outside the walls, she could only be inside the walls and therefore safe. However, it was a simple enough request. "I truly didn't mean to worry you and I'll try not to disappear again."

"Try?" he questioned, lifting her chin to look into her eyes. "There is no 'try.' Don't," he commanded firmly. Looking at her as if seeing her for the first time, he said, "Ye are all wet."

"I said you scared the lass."

"That isn't ..."

"Aye, it is."

"I didn't mean to scare the wee thing," he said, feeling contrite.

"Och, don't fash yerself, laddie," she said in her best imitation of Bridie, "I'm sure she's not the first, nor will she be the last lass whose knees ye cause to quiver."

"Cheeky wench," he said with a grin. "I'd make your knees quiver here and now, but ye need a bath."

"That I do," agreed Katherine. She laughed heartily and turned to walk with him to the keep. Given the lateness of the hour, it would be much easier to bathe in the kitchen, but she suspected Niall would object unless she gave him a persuasive argument. "Niall, it's late, I think I'll just bathe in the kitchen."

"A bath can be brought up. Ye needn't do that."

"I was just thinking ye could get to the part of the evening where ye make my knees quiver much more quickly if I do."

"Och, yer a bold one, Katherine MacIan," he said with a salacious grin.

Katherine bathed in the kitchen that night.

Chapter 13

In August, the sentries reported another raid on the western border. Even though the clan's financial hardships had been resolved, Niall found the losses to theft insufferable. Frustrated and irritated, he discussed the problem in the great hall that evening with Diarmad, Alan, and Cairbre. Katherine worked on a tapestry, while Fingal played a game with Tomas near the hearth.

"How are we going to stop the greedy bastard? I would be insane to do more than retaliate with similar raids, but I can't sit back and let him rob me blind, either," Niall said.

"He seems to be targeting just us," said Cairbre. "There have been no reports of trouble with other bordering clans."

"He's not feuding with other clans," said Alan.

"He's not feuding with us, either," said Diarmad. "They've always been a prickly bunch, but that disagreement was resolved years ago.

"Apparently," said Alan, "no one told Tadhg."

"Malcolm thinks Matheson has a much bigger target than a few head of livestock," said Niall.

"What, Duncurra?" Fingal said.

"I have to agree with Malcolm. One way of ensuring the defeat of an opponent is to critically weaken him first," Niall explained.

"Well, that would be true if a few sheep would critically weaken ye, and it could have in the spring, but not now. Even if that was his intention, it no longer makes sense," Fingal rationalized.

"There's no chance Matheson doesn't know about the wedding?" asked Cairbre.

"I don't think there is a soul in the Highlands who doesn't know about the wedding," scoffed Diarmad.

"Is it possible the greedy bastard just enjoys pilfering our sheep?" Alan asked.

"I don't think so. These facts don't add up," said Fingal. "I know Tadhg Matheson better than any of ye do. He trained with Laird Chisholm when I was there. He is not stupid, and, to be frank, he never struck me as greedy, either."

"Men change, Fingal," scoffed Niall.

Fingal didn't argue with him, but the look on his face clearly told Niall he disagreed.

"Will we raid Matheson again to recover our loss?" asked Diarmad.

Niall considered things for a few moments and said, "I think not. Maybe if I don't retaliate he will stop. If he raids again, we will know he is after a bigger target, as Malcolm suggests."

~ * ~

Summer waned, and Duncurra brought in a bountiful harvest. The long days began to shorten, growing cold. In October, Matheson raided yet again. Niall rode out the next morning with Diarmad, Cairbre, and several other men to see the site of the raid. He had not returned by early afternoon. Fingal, too, was away from the keep, having left the previous day to lead a contingent of men to Inverness for supplies. It would be several days before he returned.

Katherine worked hard to prepare the household for the long frigid winter to come, when an unexpected chill arrived. Late on that frosty afternoon, the watch announced MacLennan riders approached. Katherine knew Niall would want Malcolm and his party to be welcomed, so she had rooms readied. She also informed Bridie there would be guests for dinner.

Malcolm arrived accompanied by an older woman with dark hair and dark eyes who was both a little taller and heavier than Katherine. She wore a dark green woolen mantle over a wine colored velvet gown and a gold kirtle that appeared to be made of silk.

Malcolm greeted Katherine heartily, taking both her hands in his and kissing her on the cheeks. "Katherine, ye are looking very well." Malcolm smiled. He gave her an appraising look and added, "Ye seem to be adapting nicely to the Highlands."

"Thank ye. It is very good to see ye again, Laird MacLennan," Katherine replied.

"Lady Eithne MacIan, I would like to introduce ye to Niall's wife, Katherine, Katherine, this is Lady Eithne MacIan, the late laird's wife," said Malcolm.

Katherine had learned little more about Eithne than Niall had told her that evening at Brathanead. Katherine was under the impression neither of her sons felt particularly close to her. Also, she had heard hints Eithne may have played some role in the MacIan's financial problems. No one seemed to think Eithne would ever leave Edinburgh, so Katherine certainly had not expected ever to greet her in Duncurra's great hall.

"It is a pleasure to meet you, Lady Eithne. Welcome. Please, come warm yourselves by the hearth and have some refreshment," Katherine said.

Eithne leveled a haughty stare at Katherine. "Katherine, dear, I have heard so much about you. I assumed, as you were a noblewoman from the Lowlands, you would have received proper training in decorum, but evidently not. You will address me as Lady MacIan, and it is unseemly for you to welcome me to my hall."

Eithne's insults momentarily stunned Katherine. Over the last few months it had not been necessary to hide her emotions, but she had not buried those skills very deeply. She immediately adopted her long-practiced, unemotional demeanor. "I beg your pardon, Lady MacIan."

Eithne sauntered into the hall and began giving orders. Eithne's stiff posture and clear dismissal told her her stepmother-in-law expected a stronger reaction, but

Katherine knew this game and played it well. When Edna looked to her lady for a signal as to whether she should do Eithne's bidding, Katherine gave her the slightest nod. As Alastair's widow and Niall's stepmother, by all rights Eithne held the title of "Lady MacIan." Therefore, unless Niall said otherwise, she could issue orders at Duncurra. Everyone spent the rest of the afternoon trying to meet Lady MacIan's demands.

Eithne responded to their efforts by criticizing, correcting, or otherwise throwing barbs, primarily at Katherine, who had spent years honing the skills needed to handle Eithne, but the younger woman worried her clanswomen would be hurt. She did her best to be polite, doing everything she could to please her husband's stepmother. Although he didn't rush to her defense, occasionally, Laird MacLennan offered a mild chastisement. "Now, now, Eithne, don't ye think ye are being rather harsh with Katherine?"

He did step in firmly when Eithne ordered the staff to remove Katherine and Niall's things from the laird's chamber so she could reside there for the duration of her stay. "I'm not sure that is wise, my lady," Malcolm murmured. "Niall is laird here."

"I suppose you are right," said Eithne, her eyes filling with tears. "My dear Alastair is gone and that chamber will be filled with too many memories. You can put my things in the room next to it. Malcolm, my old friend, it would give me such comfort to know you are near. You should occupy the other chamber on the second floor." As quickly as they had started, her tears stopped. "See to it, Katherine," she said imperiously, waving her away.

Tomas occupied the room next to theirs, but Katherine did not protest. She helped Fineen move his things into the laird's chamber for the moment, but she still worried. Everything in her screamed that Eithne was a feminine version of her Uncle Ambrose. Her instincts told her to keep Tomas away from her guest, at least until Niall came home.

"Fineen, I need you to do something. Please go find Tomas—I think he is in the stables playing with Nevan. See if he can stay with Effie or Shona for a while this evening. You can tell them I will send for him later."

Fineen nodded and left.

Katherine returned to the great hall and informed Lady MacIan and Laird MacLennan their rooms had been prepared.

"Well, I should hope so," said Eithne, "and my bath is ready?"

"Nay, my lady," Katherine said, "I was unaware you wanted one."

"Katherine, are you so simple minded that you must be instructed in common courtesy? Doesn't every weary traveler deserve a hot bath? It is a good thing I am here. I fear my home will become a Highland hovel under your tender care."

Eithne stood to leave and called to Edna, "Send up a bath. Now!" Turning back to Katherine she added, "We will have our evening meal when I return to the great hall. You will be dressed in proper attire and that rag will be removed from your head, or you will not dine at my table."

Eithne looked delighted when Katherine snapped, "My lady, I was under the impression you were a Chisholm and thus a Highlander, so you will understand why I will not remove my kertch."

Eithne slapped her so forcefully Katherine's head swung to the side and she tasted blood. She heard shocked gasps from everyone in the hall.

"How dare you address me in that manner?" screeched Eithne. "You will do as I say or you will not eat." She strutted from the room, heading to the tower looking happier than she had all afternoon.

Malcolm, too, rose to leave, chiding the younger woman. "Lass, Niall will be very disappointed to learn of the disrespect you have shown to his mother."

~ * ~

After Niall chose not to retaliate for the last raid, Matheson had sent a clear message by escalating this one. Not only did he steal sixteen head of sheep, but he torched several haystacks. They searched the area west of where the raid occurred, but the trail stopped shortly after they crossed onto Matheson land. "Fine," said Niall. "If Matheson wants this feud, by God, I will give it to him. We raid tonight and I want every one of those animals replaced."

Niall sent a rider back to Duncurra just before dark, instructing him to tell Alan the situation. "Will I deliver the same message to Lady Katherine?"

"Nay, she will worry. Just tell her we have decided to do some hunting and will return tomorrow." Well, it was true, really, he consoled himself. He was simply hunting another man's sheep.

~ * ~

Katherine glanced around the great hall: the servants appeared transfixed. After Laird MacLennan and Lady MacIan left, they rushed to Katherine, but she put up her hand and shook her head slightly. "Please attend to the tasks you have been given." Many of the MacLennan soldiers who rode escort were lounging in the hall. She worried they would interpret any sign of support for her from the Duncurra staff as disloyalty and report it to Lady MacIan.

At the moment she was most concerned about Tomas. Just as Uncle Ambrose had, she suspected Lady Eithne would instantly identify him as Katherine's most profound weakness. However, she was confident Niall would sort things out as soon as he returned. That thought had barely formed when she learned he would not be home that night. Very few things kept him away from the keep overnight, but it did occur occasionally. Still, of all nights, she wished it didn't have to be this one. She had hoped to finalize plans for the evening meal and send her regrets to Lady MacIan without defying her order, but now she had to explain Niall's absence as well.

Katherine had to get through this evening as best she could on her own. She needed to get Tomas back to the keep and tucked away as soon as possible. She found Edna to discuss her concerns. Edna agreed. "Don't worry, I will see to him. I'll send Maura for him and he can stay with us tonight." Maura, Edna's daughter, was a bright, responsible girl of four and ten, so Katherine nodded her assent.

"Edna, please let me know when he is safe."

~ * ~

The evening meal was nearly ready when Maura returned with Tomas. Katherine stepped into the west tower so the MacLennans wouldn't see her and kissed him good night, saying, "Tomas, I want you to stay with Edna tonight. Tomorrow, I want you to stay here in the west tower with Maura and Nevan until your da comes home. Do you understand?"

"Aye, Mama."

Feeling slightly relieved now, she went to the kitchen, where she found Bridie livid. "Lass, that witch cannae treat ye like this. She has no right to lay a hand on ye. The laird won't stand for it, I tell ye."

"Bridie, please, don't give her a reason to target you, I couldn't bear it. Let's just keep her ire focused on me until the laird returns tomorrow."

"Target me? Lass, what are ye talking about?"

"Bridie, Lady MacIan is like my uncle. I can protect myself, but if she thinks anyone here will stand up to her for me, she will retaliate against them to strike at me. Please ignore anything she says to me. I'm going to take some bread and cheese to my chamber and try to avoid her this evening."

Bridie continued to steam, but said no more.

When Katherine returned to the great hall, Lady Eithne and Laird MacLennan were already seated at the laird's table, with Eithne in Niall's place. Katherine approached and Eithne spat, "I told you to dress appropriately and to remove that rag from your head. Do you defy me? You may wear a proper veil if you feel the need, but you won't sit at my table looking like a common born Highlander."

"Eithne," Malcolm said in a disapproving tone.

Common? There was only one common born Highlander in this conversation and it wasn't Katherine. She knew better than to react. She knew not to take the bait. She had slipped earlier but she would not do it again. She took a deep breath and replied calmly, "I beg your pardon, Lady MacIan. It is not a question of defying you. I do not have more appropriate clothes than these. I only wish to inform you and Laird MacLennan that my husband has been detained and will not return to Duncurra until tomorrow. I do not wish to offend you any longer with my presence, so please excuse me."

"Well, dear," said Eithne, rising from the table, "if it is only a matter of you not having other clothes, I will be happy to loan you something. Come with me," Eithne commanded, reaching forward and snatching the kertch off Katherine's head, taking with it the last of Katherine's self-control.

Katherine grabbed the kertch out of her hand. "I am sorry, perhaps you misunderstood me. It isn't that I don't have other clothes. I consider these to be my most appropriate garments. Good night, my lady, Laird," she said, giving a nod to each of them before turning to leave.

"Stop!" commanded Eithne. "What is that you have in your hand?"

Katherine looked down to see the bread and cheese crushed in her left hand and turned back to her saying, "It is bread and cheese, my lady."

Eithne smirked, "I am sorry, perhaps you misunderstood me. When I said if you didn't dress properly you would not eat, I didn't mean just at this table."

"As you wish, my lady," Katherine said, shrugging. Resisting the urge to throw it at her, she put the food down on the nearest trestle table and, with supreme control, walked toward the east tower.

"Perhaps hunger will make you more agreeable in the morning," Eithne called.

"I doubt it, my lady," Katherine answered and ducked out the door.

~ * ~

Niall and his men had a successful raid. They stole a score of sheep. Niall decided to take a few extras rather than burning anything. When his men had secured the sheep well clear of the area, Niall pounded on the door of a farmer's cottage. The old farmer looked terrified by the furious warrior, but Niall did not intend to harm him. He said, "I am Laird MacIan and I want ye to give your laird a message from me."

"A—A—aye, Laird," the old man stammered.

"Tell him to stay the hell off my land!" Niall roared.

Chapter 14

"Stay off his land? What in the hell is he talking about?" Tadhg Matheson demanded furiously. He had barely finished breaking his fast when Hamish, one of his commanders, reported to him about the raid and MacIan's message. "Was anyone harmed?" he asked.

"He scared the wits out of old Angus, but nothing else, Laird."

"Hamish, I consider myself to be a reasonable man, wouldn't ye agree?"

Hamish chuckled. "As reasonable as they come, Laird."

"Last winter was a hard one, and ye know as well as I do Alastair MacIan had huge debts in Edinburgh, so when a few of my sheep walked away, did I grumble?"

"Now, Laird, would ye be asking me to lie?"

"Fine, I grumbled, but I didn't retaliate. I wasn't going to be the reason his clan starved."

"Exceedingly generous, Laird."

"Let's not go straight to 'generous,' at least not where the MacIans are concerned. I'll stick with 'reasonable'," Tadhg said dryly.

"Exceedingly reasonable, Laird." Hamish laughed.

"So, Alastair died, the MacIan debt was more profound than anyone imagined, and I ignored it when a few more head of sheep and cattle wandered across my border. Then Niall MacIan managed to marry one of the wealthiest heiresses in Scotland."

"As I hear tell, much to everyone's surprise, she is one of the bonniest as well."

"Rich and bonny, a lass after my own heart," sighed Tadhg. "So now MacIan has recovered financially and has a bonny wife to warm his bed. Why is he still raiding Matheson land and at the same time threatening me to stay off his? Hamish, I have grown tired of being reasonable. This time, we will retaliate."

"Tonight?" asked Hamish eagerly.

"Nay. Let's let Laird MacIan enjoy his success and feed my sheep for a couple of weeks before fetching them home."

~ * ~

Bone weary when he rode with his men to Duncurra late that morning, Niall wanted nothing more than his sweet wife and his warm bed. He knew something was wrong when Alan rode out to meet him. "What has happened? Is it Katherine? Tomas?"

"Laird, it's nothing like that. Malcolm MacLennan has arrived with Lady Eithne."

Niall gave a huge sigh of relief. "Is that all? Did ye think ye needed to meet me with that news? My mother, while unexpected, is only a minor irritation."

"I beg your pardon, Laird, but I'm thinking she may be more than a minor irritation. I understand your mother has claimed her right as Lady MacIan, taken over Duncurra, and sent your wife to bed last night without supper."

Niall swore and kicked his horse into a gallop, not stopping until he reached the keep. Giving his horse over to a stable hand, he strode into the keep in a black fury. Eithne sat chatting with Malcolm at his table in his chair, but he didn't see any sign of Katherine.

"Mother, this is a surprise," said Niall, trying to tamp down his rage.

"Well, darling, I don't see why it would be. You didn't give me nearly enough money to live on in Edinburgh, so there is nowhere else I can go. Malcolm was visiting the royal court and agreed to escort me home."

"Home?" Niall snorted in disgust. "Mother, I gave ye a larger stipend than ye deserved, considering how close ye came to ruining us. Ye had more than enough for a comfortable life. Where is my wife?"

Eithne pouted and tears welled up in her eyes, "You are being deliberately cruel. Your father would be so ashamed of the way you treat me."

"I see to the welfare of my father's clan, which is significantly more than ye did. Where is my wife?" he ground out through gritted teeth.

"As I warned you, son, that girl is totally unacceptable. She is unskilled, willful, and rude. You really must do something about her. She boldly defied me last night, in front of my clan. I told her perhaps going to bed hungry would sweeten her mood, and she stomped off. I have never been so embarrassed, so humiliated. Not that I care as long as I don't have to suffer her distasteful company, but I believe you will find her in your chamber."

Niall headed for the tower stairs, taking them two at a time. Reaching his chamber, Niall threw the door open and demanded, "What did ye do?"

~ * ~

Katherine, who sat by a cold hearth sewing, responded with disbelief, "What did I do?"

"Ye know what I mean," said Niall crossly. "What happened?"

Katherine told herself to stay calm. She shook her head slightly. "Niall, please don't be angry until you have heard the whole story."

"Katherine, my mother is a mean-spirited, bitter woman. I know this—everyone does. But by all that's holy, were ye unable to keep the peace for one day?"

Katherine's heart sank. Without knowing any of the facts, he was blaming her. In spite of assuring her he would make an effort not to assume the worst, he had done exactly that. She remembered the day in the glen when he said, I am a very flawed man, and set in my ways. *It may take a few tries before I get the knack of it.* Still, she believed once he heard the story he would understand.

"Damn it, Katherine, answer me!"

"Where shall I start?" asked Katherine, looking down.

"Start with why my mother says ye defied her in front of clansmen," Niall answered. "You remember the definition, don't you? Willful disobedience?"

Katherine remembered Malcolm's warning: Niall will be very disappointed to learn of the disrespect ye have shown to his mother.

Katherine sighed. "Your mother was retiring to her chamber for a bath. She said she wanted the evening meal ready when she returned and I should be dressed properly without—without my kertch on, or I would not dine at her table. I told her I understood she was a Chisholm and, as a Highlander herself, I hoped she would appreciate why I couldn't do that. Then she—she—"

"She became angry, ye were too hard-headed to give in, and decided to go to bed hungry instead. Why couldn't ye have just appeased her and changed your clothes? What were ye wearing, anyway?"

"I was wearing this," she said, pointing to the Highland clothes she wore.

"Is that when ye 'stomped off to bed?"

"Nay," she said miserably. "When she came downstairs and I hadn't changed, she asked me why I defied her. I said I did not intend to defy her, but I did not have more appropriate clothes."

"But ye do have other clothes. Ye have the Lowland gowns ye brought with ye."

"Niall, that's not the point. A gown is not more appropriate than what I am wearing. Anyway, that's essentially what I told your mother, and she told me to leave, so I did."

He shook his head and said, "Nay, Katherine, the point is, like it or not, and believe me I don't like it, when Eithne is in residence, she is Lady MacIan. Ye defied her in front of clansmen, which I will not tolerate. Are you going to try to convince me your behavior was not willful this time?"

"Nay, Niall, but—"

"No arguments. Put on a gown, come downstairs, and apologize, so we can restore some semblance of peace."

"Niall, I haven't told you everything," she tried to explain.

"I've heard enough. Ye were childish and disrespectful. Ye will make amends."

"But what about my kertch?"

"Leave it off."

"How can you ask me to do that? Shall I take off my wedding band, too? You're a Highlander; you know what it means."

"But ye aren't a Highlander!" Niall yelled at her.

That stung worse than Uncle Ambrose's whip ever had.

"Nay. I was just forced to marry one who always seems to believe the worst of me, to give him my wealth, to live in the Highlands with him, and to help care for his clan. You're right. I'm not a Highlander, how silly of me to think that," she snapped at him.

"Not. Another. Word." Niall looked furious. "I've had enough misery from that woman to last several lifetimes, and I will not have ye adding to it. Ye will placate her until she leaves. Change your clothes. Now!" Niall roared as he left the room.

Katherine felt crushed. She put her sewing away, removed her kertch, and changed her clothes. With rigid determination, she forced back her tears before descending to the great hall. She could tell by the looks of pity she received from the Duncurra staff that they had heard Niall shouting at her, telling her she wasn't a Highlander. They looked as shocked as she felt.

Niall stood with his back to the room, staring into the hearth. She approached the table where Eithne sat gloating. Adopting her mask of indifference, with her head bowed Katherine said, "My lady, I apologize for defying you in front of your clansmen last night. Please forgive me."

"Well, I was appalled and insulted by your behavior. See that it doesn't happen again."

"Yes, my lady. Please excuse me now, there is work I must do."

Eithne waved her away arrogantly. Katherine glanced at where Niall stood with his back still turned to her and, with her heart breaking, she escaped to the kitchen. There she found Bridie sobbing in Edna's arms.

Chapter 15

Niall introduced Tomas as their foster son that evening. Exactly as he expected, Eithne looked as if she had just smelled an exceedingly bad odor. Katherine had been right to shield Tomas until he returned. Malcolm's cool reaction surprised him a little, and Niall got the impression he disapproved as well. However, Tomas had been the child of a peasant, and Malcolm and Eithne had spent enough time at court to be overly class conscious. He knew it would be best to limit Tomas' contact with both of them.

Niall remembered vividly how Eithne had expressed her displeasure with him when he was little. Initially subtle, she would give him a hard pinch or a thump on the head. As he grew older, she slapped him or took a leather strap to his hands or legs. Niall believed if she felt perfectly comfortable treating her stepson and even her own son in that manner, she would have no compunction about doing the same to his foster son. One of his guardsmen would be assigned to stay with Tomas at all times.

~ * ~

Katherine chastised herself repeatedly. She knew how to protect herself from the likes of Eithne and was a master at controlling her anger and hiding her emotions. She had become complacent. Whatever gave her the idea she could have principles, much less stand on them? She became Katherine Ruthven once more, remaining quiet and calm, keeping her eyes downcast, and doing everything Eithne asked of her.

Having had no sleep the night before because of the raid, Niall looked exhausted by nightfall. After the evening meal, Katherine excused herself to put Tomas to bed. Niall, too, offered his apologies and followed Katherine and Tomas out of the hall. When they reached the second floor, Niall made to open the door to Tomas' room and Katherine stayed him. "Your mother is staying in that room. I've moved Tomas' things out for now."

"Why did ye do that? She could have stayed in the other one."

Katherine said pointedly, "Niall, Lady MacIan required this room for herself and the other one for Laird MacLennan. I put Tomas' things in our room for now."

"Fine," he said irritably, going to their chamber. He looked angry and Katherine suspected he wanted to be alone with her, but it couldn't be helped. She made a pallet for Tomas on the floor and slipped into bed wearing her shift.

"Are ye sleeping in that?" he asked angrily.

Katherine sighed. "What would ye have me do, with Tomas sleeping in the room?"

Niall growled, "Ye will find somewhere else for him tomorrow.

~ * ~

When Fingal returned the next day, and Keith filled him in on the events of the past few days, he became furious. "He did what?" Fingal roared. "He let that bitch get to him!"

He was not going to let this slide. Fingal put a lid on his temper and sought out his brother, who was overseeing some repairs to the defensive wall. "Niall, can we talk?"

"Leave it, Fingal," Niall warned.

With barely controlled anger, Fingal said, "Ye are my laird, and I would not show disrespect to ye, but ye are also my brother and that is who I want to talk to. Will ye talk with me privately?"

"Fingal, as your laird I am telling ye this is not a good day to talk to your brother."

Fingal tried one last time, speaking very low. "Niall, she is my mother and that is only by sad chance. She has never been a real mother to either of us. She doesn't have the capacity to love anyone but herself, and still ye give her free rein over your clan. Ye have a wife who has given ye her heart, and yet ye are letting the same woman who destroyed ye destroy her as well."

"Fingal, I warned ye. Ye are crossing the line. Ye will not tell me how to treat our mother, this clan, or my wife. I am your brother, and because of that I am not going to call ye out on this, but if ye raise the subject with me again, particularly if ye make any comment about my wife, ye will pay the price. Do I make myself clear?"

With gritted teeth, Fingal answered, "Aye, Laird. Ye have made yourself clear." He bowed and left, feeling frustrated and having nowhere to vent his anger.

~ * ~

For the next several days Niall had the peace he sought, but the strain nearly killed him. Eithne ruled Duncurra and he stayed away. Niall thought perhaps the tension was getting under Malcolm's skin as well because he returned home, but Lady MacIan begged him to come for Christmas and he agreed. Because of that, Eithne refused to allow Katherine to put Tomas in "Laird MacLennan's" room. Katherine put him in an empty chamber on the third floor, but Fingal woke most mornings to find his nephew on the floor of his room.

Each evening Katherine took Tomas to bed immediately after the meal. On the first two nights, Niall found her asleep beside the boy and he carried her to their chamber without waking her. The third night he wanted her so badly he ached. He laid her on the bed and undressed her, kissing and caressing her bare skin as he went. In her state of half-sleep, she responded to him instinctively. A little moan of pleasure escaped her lips as he continued the delicate assault. As she woke more fully, she returned his caresses and seemed to join with him willingly, but without the joyous abandon he found so erotic. Afterwards, Niall held her close, breathing in the clean scent of her, and feeling as if he had lost something.

~ * ~

She lay in his arms until she thought he had gone to sleep, then slipped out of bed. She put on a shift, wrapped an *airisaidh* around her shoulders, and sat on the floor near the hearth, resting her head on her knees as she stared into the fire.

"What are ye doing?" he asked.

"I thought you were asleep. I am cold."

"Katherine, come back to bed. I will keep ye warm."

"I just want to sit here close to the fire for a minute. I will come back to bed soon."

"Come now." He sounded irritated.

She hadn't shed a tear since Eithne arrived days earlier. She had held herself together with her forced calm and it had been grueling. She wanted to please Niall, but he allowed Eithne to run rough-shod over his clan. She didn't want these people, whom she had learned to care for, to suffer Eithne's malice, but she didn't know what to do about it. Right now, more than anything in the world, she just needed to cry.

"Niall, please, please let me be. Please, go to sleep. I will come back to bed soon. Please..." she was trembling.

"Enough, Katherine. Come to bed now," he demanded.

"Nay," she said. "Your quiet biddable wife will be back in the morning, I promise. I just—please...." She turned her head away from him as the first hot tears slid down her cheeks. She stayed as still as she could, knowing a sob would give her away. *Please just go to sleep.*

"Are ye crying?"

"By all that is holy, Niall," her voice cracked, "even Tomas knows I don't like to be seen crying. Can't you please, just this once, please let me be?"

He was out of bed instantly. When he scooped her into his arms, she could no longer hold back the sobs.

"Wheesht, lass. Why are ye crying?"

She sobbed. "B—be—because—y—you're an idiot."

"What did ye say?" he asked, astonished.

"I said—I'm crying—because you're an idiot."

"That's what I thought ye said." He said nothing more, but held her while she cried. When her tears finally subsided, he asked, "Do ye want to tell me why I'm an idiot now?"

"Niall, after you saw how badly Uncle Ambrose beat me, you made me promise never to hide anything from you. Then, that day in the glen, you said you would try not to assume the worst, but you have. The one time I needed you, I needed to talk to you and tell you something, you wouldn't listen. You ordered me to stop."

"Is this about the day my mother arrived?"

"Idiot," she said under her breath.

"Aye, that's been established," he said dryly, "and ye are right. Ye made me a promise and I made one to ye. I did warn ye it might take a few tries before I got the knack of it. Sweetling, I am sorry. I was tired and angry and I should have listened to you. Will ye tell me now?"

"Why bother?"

He tilted her chin up to look at her. "Because I asked you to."

Katherine shook her head in frustration, but launched into the whole story. She started with Eithne's chastisement for addressing her as "Lady Eithne." When she reached the point where Eithne scolded her for not having a bath prepared, Niall said reasonably, "But she hadn't asked for one."

"She called me simple-minded when I made that observation. That is when she told me to remove the rag from my head. I said I understood she was a Highlander and I knew she would appreciate why I didn't want to remove my kertch, and she slapped me. After that I was rude, and I should not have been, but—"

"She struck ye?" Niall's eyes grew dark.

"Aye but—"

"She struck my wife in the face? In front of clansmen?"

"That's what I wanted to tell you. That's why I hid Tomas. Niall, why wouldn't you listen? I swear I tried to keep the peace. I—" she couldn't hold back a sob.

"Wheesht," he said, carrying her back to bed. When the new wave of tears had quieted, he said, "Katherine, ye are right. I am an idiot."

The next morning when they rose, she started to put on a kirtle, but Niall shook his head, "Nay, Katherine, I was wrong." He handed her a *léine* and an *airisaidh*. "She was Lady MacIan, but I am laird now, and ye are my wife, the lady of this castle. He retrieved her kertch, and gave it to her. "In the future, I won't let anyone forget that."

"This isn't going to be pretty," Katherine said, tying her kertch on.

When they descended to the great hall, Eithne sat at the laird's table. "What's the meaning of this?" she spat when she saw Katherine's attire.

Niall answered, "Lady Eithne, there has been a mistake. Ye were my father's wife and ye are Lady MacIan." She smiled smugly. "However," Niall continued, "I am laird here now. Ye chose to leave this keep more than twelve years ago, and during that time ye managed to impoverish this clan."

Eithne opened her mouth to protest, but Niall put his hand up to silence her.

"Ye have given up the right to any authority at Duncurra. Ye are welcome to live here, or in Edinburgh, or anywhere else ye choose, on the allowance ye have been given, but Katherine is the lady of Duncurra. Ye will show her the respect she deserves as my wife, and which she has earned by caring for this clan."

Eithne appeared to burn with fury, but before she said anything, Niall added, "One more thing, Lady MacIan. If ye ever strike my wife again, I will banish ye."

Eithne stomped off to her chamber and did not emerge for the rest of the day.

Under Bridie's strenuous objections, Katherine did have the evening meal sent up.

Once again Duncurra ran smoothly, but with Eithne in residence, things were not always pleasant. Katherine continued to find herself in the role of protector as she had been at Cotharach. Although she had the authority to prevent some of Eithne's punitive behavior, she had no power to curb her acid tongue. Lady MacIan continued to be an irritant to everyone who lived or worked at Duncurra, and the comfortable rhythm existing before her arrival was shattered.

Chapter 16

As the days grew shorter in early November, the Highlands became unusually cold and the winds howled from the northwest, occasionally bringing snow. Katherine envied Niall, who could stay away from the keep for most of the daylight hours, limiting his exposure to the ever-present Eithne. When she could leave the keep to visit an ailing villager, Katherine relished her time away, but it came at a price. On her return she faced disgruntled staff and an even more caustic than usual mother-in-law.

As Niall had instructed, and to Tomas' delight, each day a different guardsman had the responsibility of keeping the boy well clear of Eithne. Each of them had different talents, interests, and stories, so Tomas always had fresh entertainment. To Katherine's amusement, so did the rest of Duncurra. This was especially true on "Turcuil days," as Tomas called them. Turcuil could strike terror into the hearts of lesser men with a simple scowl, but Tomas adored him. On "Turcuil days" he learned to wrestle and spar with a wooden sword. He also rode all over Duncurra on the shoulders of a bear, or a dragon, or whatever beast Tomas wanted Turcuil to be.

This alone provided rich entertainment for those witnessing it, but the real show came when the weather was bad or some other reason forced them to stay in the keep. Katherine finally saw why Fingal first described him as a changling, because on those days it was impossible for Turcuil to avoid Edna. Fingal and Niall hadn't exaggerated. When Edna entered a room, Turcuil watched her like a smitten puppy, becoming absolutely tongue-tied if forced to speak to her. When she spoke to him, he turned several shades of red and mumbled or grunted something unintelligible.

After several "Turcuil days," Katherine realized the rest of the castle staff actually enjoyed the sport of "Turcuil baiting" and created opportunities to engage in it. One morning Katherine heard Bridie say, "Edna, I'm just taking some sweet buns out of the ovens. Go tell Turcuil to bring Tomas to the kitchen." But then Bridie followed her to the door of the great hall with a grin on her face, to watch the show. Katherine mistakenly thought his fellow guardsmen might have more sympathy for him, but if anything, they relished "Turcuil baiting" more than the castle staff. Whenever possible, the men created errands forcing Turcuil to cross paths with Edna simply for the sport of it.

It was obvious that everyone watching found the whole comedy even more amusing because while Turcuil clearly adored Edna, she seemed sublimely unaware of his affection for her. Perhaps because of this, Edna treated him with the same terse efficiency she did everyone else, and the inexplicably shy giant could not push beyond her brusque demeanor.

Katherine supposed she really shouldn't interfere, but she liked both of them immensely. Not only did she hate to see Turcuil suffer, but she also believed Edna might welcome his affection if she knew about it. Edna had been a widow for a number of years, and even with two children and a castle full of people, Katherine frequently thought she seemed very lonely. Armed with this knowledge, the Lady decided to give the oblivious woman a little push if she had the chance to do so.

Such an occasion arose one day when Edna planned to visit the cooper. Seeing the opportunity, Katherine decided not to pass it up, so she went along, ostensibly for some fresh air and a walk. As they strode down the path, Katherine asked, "Edna, how long do ye plan to torture Turcuil?" knowing full well Edna did not recognize the effect she had on the guardsman. Still, Katherine had learned the element of surprise had value in any battle.

"Turcuil? What—what are ye talking about?"

"Turcuil. Ye know, the great bear of a guardsman."

"I know who Turcuil is, my lady," she said in exasperation. "Why do you think I am torturing him?"

"I don't know why ye are torturing him, that's why I asked ye."

"Nay, that's not what I meant and ye know it. I am not torturing Turcuil, as if anybody could. What makes ye think I am?"

Katherine stopped and looked her in the eye. "Ye needn't be coy with me. Ye can't have missed it. Anyone with eyes can see that man is mad about ye. I am just wondering how long ye plan to lead him along like a bull with a ring in his nose."

"My lady," gasped Edna. "I have never—surely you don't think that I—why would—he what?"

"He is mad about ye. He absolutely adores ye. He can't take his eyes off ye. If ye so much as twitched your little finger in his direction, he would fall at your feet."

"My lady, ye are mistaken," Edna said, blushing profusely. "The oaf rarely even speaks to me except for the occasional grunt."

"He can barely form thoughts in your presence, much less words."

"Well," said Edna indignantly, "that hardly bodes well for getting to know him better, does it?"

Katherine laughed heartily. "And why should the course of true love run any smoother for ye than for the rest of us? A strong man who adores ye can learn to talk to ye with a little encouragement."

"But—my lady, are ye certain? Turcuil?"

Katherine smiled and said confidently, "I am more certain of Turcuil's affection for ye than I am of the sun rising on the morrow. Mind ye, I certainly would understand if ye aren't interested in the man. He has his faults, and trying to get through to him would be a challenge."

Suddenly indignant, Edna said, "Now what on earth would make ye say that? Turcuil is a fine man whom any woman would be lucky to have." She stopped her tirade when she registered the small sly smile on Lady Katherine's face. She blushed again, laughed, and said, "Ye are a wicked lass."

"I'm nothing of the sort," replied Katherine, even as her mouth split into a very wicked grin and she continued walking toward the village.

"Well, my lady, since ye are so very certain of his affections, how do ye propose I—uh—encourage him?"

Now Katherine blushed. "Are ye honestly asking me that question? I'm hardly the expert at capturing a man's heart. Have ye forgotten the king had to force a man to marry me? Nay, I'm just showing you where the road is. Ye'll have to find the way on your own."

"It seems to me, having captured the heart of a hard-headed man who was, as ye say, forced to marry ye, ye might be able to share some wisdom, my lady."

Katherine smiled sadly. "Edna, I believe the laird has grown fond of me, as I have of him, but he said himself his heart was never part of the bargain. It is different for ye and Turcuil, because Turcuil is prepared to offer ye his heart."

"Fond, my lady? Ye and the laird have grown fond of each other? What was it ye said to me, 'Anyone with eyes can see?' Well, anyone with eyes can see there is more than fondness between the two of ye."

Katherine wished it were true and couldn't keep the sadness out of her voice. "I think ye are mistaken."

They had reached the cooper's workshop and Edna said, "With all due respect, my lady, I think *ye* are mistaken. Ye have captured the laird's heart as securely as he has captured yours."

Katherine looked doubtfully at her and Edna added, "I am surer of that than I am of the sun rising on the morrow."

Katherine laughed as she realized how happy Edna's words made her. If Edna could tell Katherine loved Niall, perhaps Niall was growing to love her as well.

~ * ~

That evening, after her chat with Edna, the older woman appeared to pay closer attention to Turcuil. When he entered the great hall for the evening meal, Edna wished him a good evening and asked if he would go with her to fetch a keg of ale from a storeroom. He became even more flustered than ever and blushed crimson, but as he followed her to the storeroom, Katherine noticed the small knowing smile on Edna's face.

Later, when she and Niall had retired to their bedchamber, Niall said with a sly grin, "I think Edna has finally taken notice of Turcuil. I didn't think that would ever happen."

Katherine stopped combing her hair. She turned to look at him. "I have to confess, I, too, was convinced it wouldn't happen, so I gave Edna a little push."

"Katherine, what did ye do?" Niall asked, the grin on his face belying his severe tone of voice.

"Nothing that shouldn't have been done ages ago. Although it was plainly obvious to everyone else, Edna herself was completely oblivious to Turcuil's affections. I just pointed that out to her."

"Wife, I am not sure ye should be interfering in the love lives of my men."

"Well, that isn't what I did, is it? Not unless you have recently made Edna a guardsman? I simply shed some light on the situation for her. What she chose to do with that newly found knowledge was completely up to her."

Niall snorted. "Turcuil has no chance now."

Katherine glared at him. "How long would ye like to continue this little offended act, Laird? Ye are sadly mistaken if ye think I don't know ye yourself have been—what was the word you used? Interfering? Yes that was it—ye yourself have been 'interfering' in Turcuil's love life for weeks now."

At the look of shocked indignation on Niall's face, Katherine arched an eyebrow. "Tell me ye have not assigned Turcuil to Tomas twice as often as any other guardsman."

Niall still tried to feign innocence. "Have I? I was unaware."

"Unaware, were ye? And I suppose ye were also 'unaware' Turcuil is the only guardsman assigned to Tomas when the weather is bad?"

Niall had the good grace to smile and look guilty.

"I thought so," said Katherine smugly. "Well, sir, ye should realize even if ye toss the right ingredients into a pot and stir, it doesn't become soup without adding some heat."

Niall grinned, pulling her into his embrace, "I'll give ye some heat, my impudent little matchmaker."

Chapter 17

By the end of November, winter's icy grip firmly held Duncurra. Unusually cold, even for the Highlands, Katherine found fewer valid reasons for escaping the keep, thus having to tolerate Eithne's company for longer periods of time. Even though Niall had clearly assigned all authority to Katherine, she still tried her best to be gracious and to show Eithne a reasonable amount of respect. Some days she found the effort required to do this simply exhausting.

On one snowy afternoon after attending to all other tasks that could possibly keep her out of the great hall, Katherine finally had to tackle some needlework she had been avoiding. As she sat sewing by the hearth, she listened to Eithne criticize and complain for what seemed like hours. Katherine hadn't been well for a couple of days. She felt more tired and less patient than usual. She could barely tolerate the forced confinement with her mother-in-law. As Eithne railed on at her, Katherine thought time spent with the unpleasant woman must surely rival purgatory. God must have given her this penance for some reason, but she couldn't imagine what horrible sin she had committed to deserve it. Finally she stood up saying, "Pardon me, Eithne, I have to…go out."

"In this storm? Why, of all the idiotic things to do."

But Katherine had already left the great hall before Eithne could say more. Not taking time to fetch a heavy mantle, she pulled her *airisaidh* over her head, stepping outside the front doors of the keep. The snow fell heavily, blown by the biting wind, which easily penetrated her woolen garments. In her haste to leave, she forgot to inform a guardsman of her destination. She had no real idea where she was going anyway.

She stood on the steps for a moment, looking around, and her eyes landed on the chapel just across the courtyard. Perhaps she would find the peace she sought in the stillness there. She crossed the courtyard and slipped inside the little building, shutting the door behind her. With no fire to warm it, Katherine could see her breath in the frigid air, but without the biting wind she could tolerate the cold.

Sitting on one of the benches in the sparsely furnished chapel, she took a deep breath, inhaling the faint aroma of beeswax and incense that seemed to linger in every church. The tension she couldn't seem to escape in Eithne's presence slipped away, leaving her feeling calmer than she had in days. She missed this. She prayed quietly for a while. When she reached the end of her litany, she simply sat in the stillness, savoring the tranquility. She felt a holiness in simply being still that she couldn't quite explain, but of all days, today she needed the sacred silence. She wasn't sure how long she sat there, but a commotion outside drew her from her contemplation and she went to see what was amiss.

"There she is," she heard Turcuil call, and then she saw her husband striding towards her.

"I thought ye were lost. Why didn't ye tell anyone where ye were going? Eithne said ye went out into the storm hours ago." Niall was cross but his voice held a note of fear.

"Well, that is a gross exaggeration," Katherine said, "and I didn't tell anybody because when I left the keep I didn't know where I was going. I just needed to escape and find a few moments of peace, but I am sorry I worried you."

"Ye are freezing," he said and, scooping her up, carried her across the snowy courtyard, into the keep, straight upstairs to their chamber. He stoked the fire in the hearth and asked, "If ye needed quiet, why didn't ye just come up here where it was warm?" He still sounded cross with her.

"There is a difference between quiet and peace. I have been tired and irritable lately. I used to go to Mass every day and I thought maybe a few minutes in the peaceful stillness of the chapel would help. That is the only thing I have ever missed about Cotharach."

He considered her a moment. "Would ye like to have a priest here, Katherine?"

"You mean a resident priest like Father James, not just an itinerant? Is that possible?"

"It can be arranged. Since ye are the reason we have adequate resources, the least I can do is give ye a priest if that is what ye want."

"If it really isn't a problem, I would like that very much." She wrapped her arms around him and kissed him.

~ * ~

The storm blew out during the night and the day dawned clear and bright. Niall sent a messenger with an appropriate offering to the Dominican abbey several hours ride away. It thrilled Katherine when the messenger returned the next day, accompanied by Father Colm. As big and strong as any warrior, only his priest's robes revealed his true calling. His crystal blue eyes sparkled with vitality, but his white hair and beard suggested he had at least three score years behind him.

Katherine had a room prepared for him in the east tower and he immediately became an important fixture at Duncurra. Although clearly a very spiritual man, he was warm and friendly, always more than willing to help with whatever work he could. This endeared him to the clan instantly, and it was common to see him lifting stones to mend a wall, or helping to repair a roof. If anyone hesitated to accept his help, he informed them he considered the work a "corporal act of mercy," and in failing to allow him to help them, they would deny him the opportunity to perfect his soul. Coming from a priest, this argument sounded reasonable, and upon hearing it, the villagers nearly always accepted his help. Katherine suspected the old priest just liked to stay busy.

In the evenings Father Colm usually joined those gathered at the hearth, often telling stories that had everyone enthralled. On one of these evenings shortly after he arrived, Katherine finally learned why this gentle priest looked like a warrior. He was a warrior, or at least had been one before becoming a priest. In fact, he had been a mercenary, an extremely talented swordsman.

The youngest of five brothers, he had been an ambitious young man. He had sought wealth and glory with his sword arm. He hired himself out to whatever lord or baron would pay him the most. Travelling throughout England and France, soon he cared little about the nature of the duties assigned to him, as long as the purse that came with them was heavy enough. Because of his skill and reputation for ruthlessness, the purses became heavier and heavier.

"One day I found myself in the midst of a fierce and bloody battle. I had either forgotten the reason for the fight or never knew what it was in the first place. I was simply there to kill. I showed no mercy. In truth, my soul was empty—I had no mercy to show. I was covered in blood and gore, but none of it was my own. Opposing warriors lay dead all around me. I'm sure the stench of death permeated the air, but I didn't notice. My broad sword was raised over my head, prepared to cleave yet another warrior in two, when for some reason I hesitated. I truly believe God stayed my hand, for in that moment of hesitation, I realized it was not a warrior standing before me."

"Who was it?" asked Tomas, enthralled.

"It was just a scared lad, Tomas, a squire of no more than four and ten. His lord had fallen, he wore no armor, nor did he wield a weapon. In the moment I hesitated, he ran. I was horrified by what I had almost done. After that battle, I wondered how many faceless men, perhaps even boys, I had slaughtered for no other reason than to fill my own purse. Make no mistake, there are just wars. Certainly there is nobility in defending one's home or fighting an injustice, but there was nothing noble in what I was doing. That realization shattered me. I asked to be released and I came home to the Highlands.

"Once home, I realized simply walking away was not enough to soothe my conscience. My sins haunted me for years, but I found solace in faith. That is why I eventually became a priest. I used the riches I had acquired to help those in need."

"Can ye still wield a sword?" asked Tomas, rapt.

"Aye, lad, I can, but while I would if I had to in defense, I shall never do so again for personal gain."

~ * ~

While she continued to feel ill and more tired than usual, Katherine loved being able to attend daily Mass once again. And she wasn't the only one. She learned Highlanders in general tended to be very devout, so the chapel was often full.

Edna, too, attended daily Mass, often with the giant Turcuil at her side. As conversation wasn't his strong suit, Katherine suspected Turcuil felt less self-conscious with Edna when in an environment where the only words he had to speak were the responses of the ancient liturgy.

As they neared the end of Advent, a time of prayer and fasting, Katherine threw herself into preparing for the feasts and celebrations of Christmas and the Epiphany. She ensured the entire keep was cleaned and decorated with holly, ivy, and bay. As he had promised, Laird MacLennan returned to Duncurra with a small retinue for the Christmas celebrations.

Katherine had mixed feelings about Laird MacLennan. Clearly both Niall and Fingal respected him, considering him part of the family. Yet when he had first arrived with Eithne, Katherine would have welcomed more support from him. However, when he arrived days before Christmas, charming and affable, she thought perhaps she had overreacted. Malcolm's presence brought one unexpected but welcome benefit—Eithne focused her full attention on entertaining him. This gave Katherine a much needed respite from her sniping. Soon she wondered why she had ever dreaded his arrival.

After the flurry of activity leading up to it, Christmas came reverently. Duncurra celebrated the three traditional Christmas Masses, the Angel's Mass at midnight, the Shepherd's Mass at dawn, and the Mass of the Divine Word later in the morning. Then, in the afternoon, the clan celebrated with a huge feast. It had been several years since the MacIans had sufficient resources to allow for a celebration like this, so they threw themselves into it whole-heartedly. After the feast, those assembled removed the trestle tables so the music and dancing could begin.

Katherine found the dancing captivating. As a member of the Scottish Lowland nobility, in her younger years she had learned formal courtly dances similar to those performed in England and France. However, the dances performed on this Christmas night were unique to the Highlands. She had never seen anything like them and she watched the beautiful, joyful dances with longing.

Shortly after the music started, Niall, perhaps noticing her wistful expression, took her hand. "Dance with me."

She felt acutely ashamed and without meeting his eyes, began to stammer. "Niall—I—I can't—I would love to—but I—I don't know how."

"Then ye shall learn," he said, ignoring her embarrassment and pulling her into the center of the room. She was terrified, knowing she would humiliate them both, but he only grinned at her. "Katherine, relax, it isn't that hard."

As he guided her through the opening steps of the dance, she desperately tried to follow him. Astonished by how well her warrior husband could dance, Katherine felt even worse about her own lack of skill. When the pattern repeated, she found she had less trouble, until by the end of the dance, although not proficient, she felt more comfortable and was enjoying herself. When the dance was over, Niall pulled her into an embrace, kissing her, much to the delight of the other revelers. She stumbled through several more dances with him before begging him to have mercy on her. Breathing heavily, she retreated to her seat at the table.

With the courage coming from a few tankards of ale as well as the urging of his comrades, she watched Turcuil pluck up his nerve and ask Edna to dance with him. Until that moment, Katherine let herself believe her dance skills weren't terrible for her first time, but she became acutely embarrassed again when she watched the giant of a man dance the sometimes intricate country dances with ease. Noticing her discomfit, Malcolm asked, "Lass, what has ye so distressed?"

Flushing even more deeply, Katherine answered, "It is a little embarrassing that every warrior in this room seems to be able to dance, while I stumble like a drunkard."

Malcolm laughed and patted her arm warmly. "Katherine, of course they can dance; they are Highlanders. Highland warriors practice intricate dances to help build their agility, and then they celebrate victory by dancing them. Ye have nothing to be embarrassed about. Even though these country dances are not simple, ye did very well for your first attempt."

He leaned a little closer and, lowering his voice conspiratorially, he said "Ye know very well if there had been much room to criticize, Lady MacIan would not have missed the opportunity, but ye will notice she doesn't dance at all."

Katherine had to laugh at the notion that it was possible to consider silence from Eithne as praise. It did give her the confidence to try again when both Fingal and Father Colm asked her to dance later in the evening.

The merry-making continued well into the wee hours of the morning. Katherine sat by Niall watching the festivities. So exhausted she could barely sit upright, but not ready to leave the celebration, she decided she would just rest her eyes for a moment.

Father Colm sat on Niall's other side with Diarmad, Fingal, and Malcolm, telling more stories from his young warrior days that had the other men roaring with laughter. Katherine was startled by one particularly explosive burst of laughter and raised her head, looking at the priest in confusion. Father Colm nudged Niall, inclined his head toward Katherine and said with a grin "I think it's time ye took that one to bed."

~ * ~

The yuletide festivities continued for twelve days. The day after Christmas was the feast of St. Stephan the Martyr. After the extended festivities of the evening before, Katherine was surprised to see so much activity in the keep the next morning. There were baskets filled with hay, salt, and oats in the great hall. Upon seeing this she whispered to Niall, "What is all of this for?"

"Did ye not seek St. Stephan's blessing in the Lowlands?"

"When I was little my papa gave coins to the poor on St. Stephan's day, but Uncle Ambrose certainly didn't."

"Here we ask St. Stephan's blessing on horses and livestock. Father will bless the hay, salt, and oats during Mass and it will be distributed amongst the farmers. Then the blessed items will be given to sick or injured animals during the year. Father will also bless the horses in my stable after Mass."

Katherine had never heard of this custom. "Why? St. Stephan was a martyr who was stoned to death because of his faith in Christ. What is his connection to livestock?"

Niall's eyes twinkled as he said, "There are several answers to that question, lass. The first is, according to legend, St. Stephan had a horse that he loved, but the horse became very ill. Christ cured St. Stephan's beloved horse and that is why Stephan's faith was so strong."

"It sounds as if ye don't believe that legend."

"Well, sweetling, I have had some fine horses in my life and I surely would thank God if he intervened to save one of them. However, I'm not sure I would face a stoning for the love of a horse."

"But it wasn't for the love of a horse, it was—oh never mind," she said when she realized he was teasing her. "What are the other reasons for blessing livestock?"

"Some say because little work is done between Christmas and Epiphany, it is a holiday for the livestock as well, particularly for beasts of burden like horses and oxen. Since St. Stephan's day falls on the first day after Christmas, it is a good a time as any to bless them."

"I guess that is reasonable, but I can tell by your grin there is more."

"Now, ye see, lass, in ancient times, before we all became God-fearing Christians and heathens roamed the land, it is said horses were sacrificed at the winter solstice. When Christians put a stop to animal sacrifices, the horses in the Highlands, being good Christians themselves, were exceedingly grateful and thanked the first saint whose feast day fell soon after the solstice. St. Stephan would have been an ungrateful sot if he had refused to be their patron, so it was really a case of the Highland horses picking the saint as opposed to the other way round."

Katherine laughed and Niall found himself thanking all the saints for giving him this beautiful lass, whose laughter must surely be sweeter than the songs of angels.

~ * ~

The celebration continued the next day on the Feast of St. John the Evangelist. Father Colm blessed kegs of wine called "The Love of St. John" in the morning to be served later at the feast. This was a tradition Katherine was familiar with, however the Clan celebrated in another way, as well. Because St. John lived to be a very old man, the eldest members of the clan were honored at this feast and sat with Niall and Katherine at the laird's table. Niall watched her with pride as she listened to their stories, laughing merrily with them. Once more he realized how fortunate he was she had accepted his clan as her own and treated these elders with the kindness and respect they were due. His mother, Lady MacIan in name only, didn't even attend this feast.

When the music started he claimed Katherine for dance after dance until she begged him to stop.

"Aren't ye tired of me stepping on your feet yet?" she laughed.

"Was it ye who was stepping on my feet? I thought sure it must be Turcuil," he said with a wink and laughed at her mock outrage. "Truthfully, Katherine, I would rather dance with ye all night and suffer bruised toes than dance with any other partner, regardless of how skilled she might be."

Katherine laughed. "That is the Love of St. John talking."

Niall laughed, too. He suspected love had something to do with it, but perhaps not the blessed wine. Taking her in his arms, he said, "Have I thanked ye yet?"

"Thanked me for what?"

He motioned to the celebration around them. "For this."

"Planning a feast is no great ordeal."

"Not for planning it, pet. The MacIans haven't had much to celebrate, and nothing to celebrate with, for the last few years. It is only because of ye the clan is safe and whole."

"Nay, Niall, ye sought the king's help, saving me and Tomas in the process. I have a home and family again." The warmth and love Niall saw in her eyes took his breath away.

Fingal, who stood nearby, said, "Perhaps ye would honor a member of your new family with a dance, then?"

Katherine laughed. "If your toes can stand it, I suppose I can."

~ * ~

The third day after Christmas was Childermas, honoring the young boys in Bethlehem who were killed by King Herod. In the same way that elders were honored on the

Feast of John the Evangelist, sometimes children were given special treats on Childermas.

At the midday meal, Eithne asked, "Has young Tomas had his beating yet today?" Tomas' eyes grew wide with fear and Father Colm looked up from his conversation with Cairbre.

"We don't observe that tradition at Duncurra," Katherine said coolly. Tomas had had more than enough beatings in his life. He didn't need another one to fully understand the cruelty of men.

"I am glad to hear that, my lady," said Father Colm. "It is a ridiculous custom and one that I don't hold with, either."

"Come now, Father, Katherine," Malcolm said, "some people think a child is destined to have bad luck if he doesn't receive a few whacks in memory of the Holy Innocents." Malcolm called to Niall, who was deep in conversation with Diarmad, "Niall, what's this I hear about not beating children on Childermas?" Wide eyed with fear, Tomas slid off his chair, maneuvering very close to Katherine.

Katherine found Laird MacLennan's satisfied smile, as well as the pleasure he appeared to derive from Tomas' discomfort, very disturbing.

Before Niall could respond, Katherine said, clearly very irritated, "Laird MacLennan, please cease this discussion now. No one will be beaten here, today or ever."

"Katherine, dear, please calm down" said Niall. "I think Malcolm was just teasing."

She didn't think Malcolm was teasing and she knew Eithne wasn't. She answered, "I apologize if I misunderstood you, Laird. Please understand, I don't see the humor in beating a child or anyone else." Katherine excused herself from the table, leaving the great hall with Tomas, who still looked terrified. She wanted to reassure him, so she took him to her room and sat with him by the fire.

"Why does Laird MacLennan want to beat me?"

She tried to explain Childermas and the reason for the custom, although it had always seemed absurd to her. "Tomas, it must have been a terrifying day when Herod murdered all the little boys in Bethlehem. Think how scared they must have been. There are people who think if children feel just a little of that fear and pain, they will remember the sacrifice of the Holy Innocents."

"But ye don't think so?"

"Nay. In fact, I think it may be easier to think about the Holy Innocents if we aren't worried about ourselves, don't ye?"

"Aye," he agreed solemnly.

"Sweetheart, ye know I won't let anyone hurt ye?"

"Aye, but what if someday ye aren't near? I don't like him. I don't like Da's mother, either."

"I know, pet, some people are very hard to like," Katherine agreed. "Sometimes it is just best to stay away from them."

~ * ~

"Well, that was rude," snapped Eithne, when Katherine left the hall.

Niall glared at Eithne and said to Malcolm, "I'm sure ye can understand, Malcolm, my wife is sensitive about the subject of beating."

"Niall, I am so very sorry, how thoughtless of me. How could I possibly have forgotten? I should go and apologize to her."

"That won't be necessary, I'm sure she understood." Niall assured him. "I promised Tomas we would go out for a ride this afternoon. I will tell Katherine again that you intended no harm."

Fingal watched the entire exchange, dumbfounded. Katherine had nearly died in Malcolm's keep. He understood his mother's callousness, but Malcolm's surprised him. Fingal found Niall's calm acceptance of the situation extremely irritating as well. When was he going to wake up?

Chapter 18

After the small upset on Childermas, the festivities continued until the Epiphany, which celebrated the visitation of the Magi. On this day, people exchanged gifts in commemoration of the Magi's gifts to the Christ child. When Katherine and Niall woke that morning, before leaving their chambers, he gave her his gift. Katherine fingered the delicate silver filigree brooch, inlaid with small precious stones, reverently. "It is beautiful, Niall, thank you." She attached her *airisaidh* around her shoulders with it. "I have a gift for ye, too." She smiled. "But I can't give it to ye today."

"Why not?" He feigned disappointment.

"Because it isn't ready yet."

"When will it be ready?"

"Early August, I think." Katherine grinned.

Niall looked at her in confusion until the meaning of what she had said sank in. "Katherine, are ye with child?" he asked.

"I think so. I have all the signs. I am tired, cranky, and I feel sick half the time. When I missed my monthly courses in November, I thought maybe it was just from the upset over Eithne, but I have passed the time they are due in December now, too."

Thrilled, Niall pulled her into his arms and kissed her. He couldn't have been happier; the woman he loved was going to give him a child. *The woman he loved.* In spite of everything preventing him from admitting it, he did love her, deeply and passionately. How could he ever have tried not to? Finally, he asked, "How long have ye known?"

"I have suspected it for a couple of weeks, but I spoke with Effie yesterday and she confirmed it. I wanted ye to know as soon as I did. But it's still so early in my pregnancy,

I was thinking perhaps we should not announce this news just yet. Maybe we could wait a little longer."

"We will wait as long as ye wish, Katherine."

~ * ~

After they attended Mass and broke their fast, Niall said to Tomas, "Are ye ready to see your gift now?" Tomas nodded eagerly. "Well, we will have to go outside to see it."

Katherine laughed as Tomas grabbed her hand and dragged her to the door with them. Pulling their plaids over their heads to block the cold, Niall and Katherine led Tomas to the stable where he found his present, a sturdy Highland pony.

The boy could barely contain himself. "Does he have a name?"

"Nay," answered Katherine, "but your pony is not a 'he'. Ye will need to pick a lass's name."

He thought for a moment, looking very serious, "Then I want to call her Mab," he finally said.

"Why Mab?" asked Niall.

"I think it's a pretty name and Maura told me a story once about a fairy queen named Mab."

"Then Mab it is," said Katherine.

Niall helped Tomas saddle the little pony, letting him ride in the courtyard. The tolerant pony seemed undaunted by the boy's youthful exuberance. Niall stayed close, giving Tomas instructions on how to hold the reins to control where the pony went. Niall had selected this animal carefully and, watching them together, Katherine knew he had made a good choice. Gentle enough to be safe, Mab also had enough pluck to be a worthy mount for an energetic lad.

As Katherine watched them, she remembered the pure joy she had felt when her father had given her Stormy. Giving Tomas the pony had been Niall's idea, but she wholeheartedly agreed. In this moment, she felt truly and completely happy. She did not want to break the spell, but she had responsibilities she could not ignore, and the wind also grew fierce and cold. "I am going to freeze solid if I stay out here any longer. Besides there is still much to do."

"Please, can I ride longer, Mama?" Tomas asked.

Niall answered, "We will let your mama go inside before she freezes, but ye can ride a few more minutes before we see Mab tucked in."

Katherine walked over to give them each a kiss before she went inside. She whispered softly in Niall's ear, "I think it would be a good idea for Tomas to have a rest this afternoon before the feast."

Niall grinned and said, "That could be a challenge. I seem to remember unsuccessfully ordering his mother to 'rest' once."

Katherine laughed. "Do what ye can."

"Speaking of his mother resting, I know I cannot order ye to sleep, but I want ye to lie down in bed and close your eyes for a while this afternoon. The evening will be long for ye, too. Was that specific enough?"

"Aye, Laird," she said, grinning at him. She turned to reenter the keep, thinking "a while" still left a lot of room for interpretation.

~ * ~

Much too excited to sleep, Tomas laid down on the bed that afternoon as his da had told him to do. *Only babies took naps.* He frowned and stared at the bed's canopy, thinking about his new pony. Finally, he decided if he could just check on Mab one more time and make sure she didn't need him, he could try to sleep then. He got out of bed and peeked out the chamber door into the hall, looking for anyone who might object. Seeing no one, he slipped very quietly into the corridor and down the stairs. He made it all the way past the second floor without meeting a soul, but before getting to the armory, he heard voices whispering at the bottom of the stairs. He crouched down so whoever was there wouldn't see him, listening impatiently for them to leave. At first he couldn't understand what they were saying, but as he listened more closely, he heard something that terrified him.

"Everything has been arranged as ye required. It can only end in Niall's death this time, and Duncurra will finally be yours."

"I am ready to be done with this mockery. I have pretended to be jovial and devoted for too long. I am just sorry I won't be the one to kill him. Part of me wants him to know it was me."

As quietly as he could, Tomas slipped back up the stairs. He wanted to stop at his mother's room, but afraid whoever was at the bottom of the stairs would hear him, he went to his own room and shut the door. He didn't know what to do. They had been talking about killing his da. He needed to tell someone, but was so afraid of running into the bad people he couldn't leave his room. He sat crouched by the fire for what seemed like hours when Fineen finally tapped on his door and entered. "Tomas, your mother sent me to bring ye down to the feast."

"I need to talk to Mama," he said.

"Well, come on then, she's downstairs." Tomas worried about the people in the stairwell, but if he was with Fineen he would be safe until he could talk to Da or Mama.

His parents sat at the head table, but Lady Eithne, who was sitting near Mama, scared him. He didn't like Laird MacLennan either, but he was sitting near Da. Tomas would have to wait until he could talk to one of them alone.

He went to the table and his mama gave him a kiss. "For someone who wasn't tired, that was quite a nap."

Tomas just nodded, moving as close to her as possible.

She cocked her head to one side, "Tomas, is everything all right?"

He nodded again but didn't speak.

"Do ye want to go sit with Uncle Fingal and have something to eat?"

Ceci Giltenan

"Katherine, you do not give children options. They should be told what to do and taught to obey," Eithne scolded.

"Thank you, Eithne, we will have to disagree on that. Life is full of duties and obligations. I see no benefit in creating more where it isn't necessary," his mother said mildly, but he did not want to stay near Lady Eithne anyway. He backed away and ran to where Uncle Fingal sat.

Tomas had never experienced feasts and celebrations like the ones at Duncurra. He loved the little pies filled with shredded meat and spices. He had never had one before, but they had been served every evening since Christmas. Nevan had told him it was good luck to eat one on each of the twelve days, but Tomas wasn't very hungry tonight.

On all of the other nights he didn't want the fun to end, but now he was anxious for the celebration to be over. He needed to talk to Mama, but every time he tried, there were too many people around. He remembered thinking he would just put his head on the table for a minute. He awoke the next morning snuggly tucked into his own bed.

Dressing quickly, he hurried downstairs, stopping to tap softly at his mother's door, but no one answered. He listened cautiously from the top of the stairs to the first floor to make sure the stairwell was empty before hurrying down to the great hall. Neither his parents nor Uncle Fingal were there, but thankfully, Lady MacIan and Laird MacLennan were absent as well. Father Colm sat at the table chatting with Diarmad, so Tomas went to them.

"Have ye seen my mama?" Tomas asked, climbing into a chair beside Diarmad.

"Not yet, Tomas," answered Father Colm.

Diarmad added, "I saw your da before he went out hunting and he said ye might want me to take ye to ride your pony this morning." He motioned for a serving maid to bring a bowl of porridge to Tomas.

"I don't know," said Tomas feeling very worried. "I need to talk to my mama." He ate his porridge with his brow still furrowed.

"Ye don't know if ye want to go riding?" asked Diarmad. "Your da had to pry ye off that pony yesterday."

"I want to ride Mab, but I really need to talk to Mama."

"Is something bothering ye, lad?" asked Father Colm, looking concerned.

Tomas liked both Father Colm and Diarmad. He really needed to tell someone about what he had heard, but the people he overheard had whispered. Not being able to recognize their voices, Tomas didn't know whom to trust. He didn't think it could have been Diarmad or Father Colm, but he would feel much better talking to Mama. "Well, I—," Tomas saw Lady MacIan and Laird MacLennan enter the great hall. Looking at Diarmad, he said, "I would like to ride my pony. Can we go now?"

~ * ~

That morning, Katherine slept much longer than she usually did. Between the late night and her pregnancy, she knew she probably needed the rest, but she felt guilty anyway. She hurried down to the great hall to find the castle servants well about the business of the day. Lady MacIan commented, "Katherine, dear, it is a wonder anything at all gets done around here with the lady of the castle sleeping half the day away."

Father Colm laughed, saying, "Now, Lady MacIan, I would hardly say half the day is gone. Why, ye yourself have only just arisen."

Lady MacIan glared, but she said no more.

Grateful for the support, Katherine flashed the priest a quick smile. For once Eithne's sharp tongue had actually given Katherine a valid reason to escape for a while instead of only the impotent desire to do so. "As I am getting a later start than usual today, I'm sure you will excuse me if I don't join you for your morning meal. I have duties to attend to."

Katherine walked toward the kitchens, followed by Father Colm, who asked, "Lady Katherine, do ye mind if I walk with ye? There is something I would like to discuss."

"Not at all," she answered.

Father Colm inclined his head toward Eithne and Malcolm and said, "Please excuse me." After they left the great hall he said, "Lady Katherine, your son seemed anxious about something this morning. He wanted to talk to ye. Diarmad and I tried to find out what was bothering him, but as soon as Laird MacLennan and Lady Eithne arrived, Tomas said no more. He has gone to the stables with Diarmad."

"That doesn't surprise me. I'm sure you have noticed Niall assigns one of his guards to keep an eye on Tomas every day."

Father Colm chuckled, "I had noticed Tomas always seemed to have a guard with him. The days when Turcuil becomes a fierce dragon who needs taming are humorous indeed. I did not know the reason."

Katherine laughed, too, and went on, "Well, the primary reason is to keep Tomas away from Lady MacIan."

"That seems like a wise choice. It also explains a few things. Clearly the lad is cautious of both Lady MacIan and Laird MacLennan. I have found children and dogs to be uncanny judges of character. I will keep an eye on Tomas as well."

"Thank ye, Father. I will find Tomas as soon as I have spoken with Bridie."

"It is probably nothing, but I'm sure he will feel better once he tells ye what it is," Father said with a reassuring smile. "Let me know if I can be of any help. I have some things to take care of in the chapel this morning."

It took much longer for her to seek Tomas out than she had anticipated. Before Katherine finished with Bridie, a servant came rushing into the kitchen looking for her.

"My lady, there has been an accident on the training field. Fingal is hurt. They're bringing him up to the castle now."

"Please go to my chamber quickly and bring me my bag of supplies." Katherine sent other servants to prepare Fingal's chamber and to bring other supplies she would need. Then she rushed to meet the men carrying him.

From a distance she saw blood drenched his left side, but he was still alert. When she reached him, she assessed his wound quickly. It looked more severe than it actually was. Relief flooded her and she thanked God and his angels for their protection. "This isn't nearly as bad as I feared. Why, it is a scratch, really," she teased.

Fingal groaned. "Just a scratch, is it? It hurts a tad more than any scratch I've ever had."

"Well, perhaps it is wee bit deeper than most scratches. I will clean and stitch it, but ye'll be fine. The bleeding has already slowed. How did this happen?"

Rab explained, "One of the young soldiers in training made a wild swing and lost his balance. As he fell, he slammed into Fingal's back. Fingal was forced forward onto Bruce's blade, with whom he was sparring. Bruce saw it happening and tried to avoid Fingal, but still managed to give him that wee scratch."

When they arrived in Fingal's chamber, Edna awaited them with all the supplies Katherine required. Katherine asked Turcuil to stay, fearing that he might need to hold Fingal still while she worked. "Drink this,," she said, giving her patient a potion.

He swallowed it, shuddering when the cup was empty. "God's bones, what kind of poison is this?"

"I'm sorry, I know it's bitter, but it will help with the pain. Here is some ale to get rid of the taste."

"Couldn't we have started with the ale and skipped the other?"

"This is likely to hurt quite a bit. I'm sure ye'll be thankful for both."

"I believe ye; thousands wouldn't."

She gave the potion a few minutes to begin working before she started stitching. She had hoped between the potion and the pain, he would lose consciousness, but he didn't. With his jaw set and fists clenched, he remained silent as Katherine worked. By the time she tied off the last stitch, he looked pale and exhausted from the ordeal.

"Try to rest now. The potion I gave ye should make ye sleepy. Turcuil, please stay with him and let me know if anything changes."

"I don't need a big, ugly nursemaid. Now, if perhaps the fair Fineen wanted to tend to my needs, I wouldn't turn her away."

"Ye are a rogue, Fingal MacIan. I think it would be best for ye to keep your mind and your hands off the 'fair Fineen' until your side is healed. I don't want to have to sew ye up again. Edna will bring ye some broth shortly and I want ye to drink it all." Katherine laughed when Fingal pouted, looking very much like Tomas did when disgruntled. It reminded her that she needed to find Tomas. "If he won't let ye stay, Turcuil, would ye please look in on him frequently for me? I need to find Tomas, he was looking for me earlier."

"Aye, my lady. I'll try to forget he called me a maid."

"He called ye big and ugly, too," observed Edna.

"Aye, love, I won't argue about being big and ugly, but I am no maid."

"Well, if Fingal doesn't want me to put bitter herbs in his broth, he'd better not call ye ugly, either."

Fingal rolled his eyes, causing Katherine to laugh as she left them to look for Tomas.

~ * ~

She found him tending Mab in the stable. "Father Colm said ye were looking for me earlier."

"Aye, I was. I have to tell ye something, but we need to be alone."

"We could go to my room. Will that do?" He nodded and they walked to the keep, going straight to the east tower. Katherine had barely shut the door to her chamber when

Tomas' arms were around her, holding tight as if he were afraid of something. "Tomas, what is it, sweetheart?"

"Da told me to rest yesterday and I went to my room but I just couldn't sleep. I kept thinking Mab might need me. Mama, I only wanted to go out to the stable for a few minutes to check on her, and I was going to go back to my room and rest like Da said to."

"So ye snuck out to the stables when ye were supposed to be resting? Is that what has ye so upset?" He seemed awfully distressed over something so small.

"Nay, I didn't get to the stables. When I walked down the stairs, I heard two people talking in the stairwell. They were whispering and I couldn't understand most of it, but one of them said Da was going to die."

"What? Maybe ye misunderstood."

"One person said something was going to end in Da's death and Duncurra would finally be the other person's. Mama, I don't want Da to die." Tomas was near tears.

"Tomas, don't worry, Da isn't going to die. Sweetheart, did ye hear them say anything else?"

Tomas nodded, tears slipping down his cheeks, "The other person said something about pretending to be something for too long, and being sorry he wouldn't be the one to kill Da, because he wanted Da to know it was him."

"Then the people ye heard talking were men? Did ye see them?" Katherine asked.

"I think they were men. I don't know, they were whispering. I didn't see them. Mama, I was scared and I went back to my room. I was afraid to come out. When Fineen brought me downstairs I wanted to tell ye, but I didn't want—anyone to hear. Then I tried to find ye this morning, but I couldn't."

"It will be all right, Tomas. Stop crying, sweetheart. As soon as your da comes home, we'll tell him. He will know what to do." Katherine tried to reassure him, but her own mind spun as she tried to process what the boy had told her.

She didn't understand what, and perhaps more importantly, who Tomas had overheard.

"I don't want to go down to the great hall. I want to stay here with ye."

"Ye can stay here, Tomas. I will just let Edna know ye are not feeling well, so I will be here with ye here for a while. That way she can find me in case anyone needs me." She decided not to worry him more by telling him Fingal was injured. "I will be right back."

He nodded, looking forlorn.

Katherine went downstairs, found Edna, and explained that Tomas wasn't feeling well and she was going to sit with him for a bit. She asked Edna to send up some soup and bread, then returned to Tomas. Diarmad was on his way downstairs after having checked on Fingal, and met Katherine on her way up. "Diarmad, Tomas isn't feeling well, if ye see Niall, will ye ask him to come up?"

"Certainly, my lady, but the laird went out with a hunting party and I don't expect him back until late this afternoon. Tomas seemed upset earlier, is there anything I can do?"

"Nay, thank ye, Diarmad, it is probably just a combination of rich food and late nights," she assured him. Because Tomas had no idea who he had overheard, she did not intend to tell anyone the real problem until she had talked to Niall.

Chapter 19

Finally, very late in the afternoon, Niall returned from hunting. He learned of Fingal's accident immediately and left his horse with the stable master. He intended to go straight upstairs to check on his brother, but Malcolm called to him when he entered the great hall. "Niall, lad, come join me," he said, motioning to a servant to bring another tankard of ale.

"I'll be down in a few minutes, I just want to see how my clumsy brother is faring."

"There is no need to rush to Fingal's side," teased Malcolm. "It was merely a flesh wound and your wife has tended him well. She has been absent from us all afternoon. I'm sure if there were any problem with Fingal we would know about it. Come, sit and warm yourself."

Niall scowled. "If it was only a flesh wound, why was it necessary for Katherine to spend the afternoon tending him?"

"Well, ye know women—they all love the attention of handsome young men. A captive audience is irresistible." He winked.

Niall fumed as he headed for the east tower. He went straight to Fingal's chamber and entered without knocking, only to find Fingal alone and asleep. As he left the room, Niall met Diarmad in the corridor.

"How fares your brother this evening?" asked Diarmad.

"He is asleep."

"He has been most of the afternoon. Katherine gave him a potion when she stitched him up."

"Katherine didn't stay with him?"

"I don't know, I don't think so. Turcuil and Edna have kept an eye on him and were to notify Katherine if anything changed. Although with love blossoming, I am not sure they would notice. I believe she is in your chambers with Tomas now. He apparently is not feeling well. She wanted to see ye as soon as ye returned from hunting."

"Tomas is ill, too?" Niall headed to the stairs without waiting for an answer. When he reached their chamber, he found Katherine sitting with Tomas on her lap telling him a story.

She looked up and her face flooded with relief, "Oh Niall, I am so glad you're home." She stood Tomas on the floor and crossed the room to hug him.

He returned her hug, and put his hand on Tomas' face, saying, "Diarmad said Tomas is ill." Although the boy appeared to be upset, he didn't feel feverish.

"He isn't ill," Katherine explained. "Something very upsetting happened yesterday and I wanted to talk to ye about it. I thought it better to keep him away from—everyone, until I did. Tomas, tell your da what ye told me."

Tomas told the same story about slipping downstairs unnoticed and overhearing the whispered conversation. "Da, I don't want ye to die," he said as he burst into tears again.

Niall felt the anger rising in him but he tried not to let it show. "Stop crying, Tomas, I am not going to die, but I need ye to tell me as much as ye can about what ye overheard. Were they men? Did ye recognize either voice?"

"They were whispering and I couldn't hear them well. I think they were men, but I don't know for sure."

"What exactly did they say?" pressed Niall.

Tomas looked scared and Katherine said, "Tomas, Da isn't angry with ye, he just wants ye to try to remember everything ye can."

"One person said everything was arranged and it would end in your death, Da, and he said Duncurra would belong to the other person then. The other person said he pretended to be something for too long. He was the one who said he was sorry. He wasn't the one who would kill ye, because he wanted ye to know it was him. That's all I remember."

Seething, but not wanting to scare Tomas more than he already was, Niall said, "It will be all right, don't worry." Then the laird sent for Rab and instructed him to take the boy to his chamber and to let no one other than himself or Katherine into the room. When they were finally alone, he turned to Katherine and said with barely contained wrath, "It must be Fingal."

"Fingal?" Katherine said, aghast. "Niall, it certainly is not Fingal. He is loyal to ye—he loves ye."

"Nay, Katherine, he loves ye," Niall spat. "It can only be him. He thinks he would be Duncurra's heir if I died. My dear little brother may have waited too long. He doesn't realize there is another heir on the way."

"Niall, I think ye are jumping to conclusions. Talk to Fingal about this rationally."

"I will talk to Fingal, but I can't right now because he is sleeping off the potion ye gave him," Niall snapped. The stunned look on Katherine's face did not cool his anger, even though part of him knew he was being irrational.

Katherine stammered, "I-I just gave him something to help with the pain."

"Well, we certainly wouldn't want Fingal to be uncomfortable, would we?"

She remained silent for a moment, then said softly, "What are we going to do about Tomas?"

"*We* aren't going to do anything. Tomorrow, after Fingal wakes, I will get to the bottom of this. If ye aren't too busy tending my brother, I will take ye down now for the evening meal. Don't speak of this to anyone."

Katherine said no more. During the meal Niall knew by his people's reactions his unusually short-temper was clearly apparent. Katherine remained subdued and quieter than normal. *Fine, everyone will assume we are arguing and there will be nothing to explain.* As soon as dinner was over, Niall offered his apologies to Malcolm and Eithne, retiring with Katherine. On their way up the stairs, Katherine said, "I would like to check on—"

"Fingal?" Niall said sharply. "Don't ye think ye have offered him enough comfort for one day?"

Katherine folded her hands in front of her and took a deep breath before saying with a controlled, calm voice, "Niall, I would like to check on *our son* before we retire. It is not necessary for me to check on Fingal. His wound is not serious. I'm not sure what I've done to anger ye, but I have not seen Fingal since I stitched him up this afternoon. As soon as I bandaged his wound, I gave instructions to Turcuil and Edna to look after him. I have not been back since then. If anything goes awry, they will let me know."

Niall wondered why she would say this when Malcolm had clearly told him she was with Fingal, but he didn't call her on the lie. "I will go check on Tomas. Ye go to bed."

"Niall, he is afraid. I want to see him and kiss him goodnight."

"Do not argue with me tonight," he growled, opening the door of their chamber for her. She walked silently past him and he shut the door before she could say anything else.

When Niall returned, he found Katherine combing her hair, getting ready for bed. She looked so very beautiful, and even though he was angry, he ached with need for her. Why had she spent the afternoon with Fingal and lied to him about it? He pulled her roughly into his arms. With one arm he held her to his chest, knotting his other hand in her hair so she could not turn away. His lips slanted across hers and his tongue plundered her mouth relentlessly. She responded to him by wrapping her arms around his neck and returning his kiss ardently.

He broke the kiss. "Why did ye lie to me?" He searched her face for a clue to what she was thinking but saw only confusion.

"Niall, I don't know what ye are talking about. I have never lied to ye and I never will. I love ye."

He gave her another searing kiss, wanting to believe her. He remembered the unbearable pain of betrayal at the hands of a woman whom he thought he loved, and didn't think he could live through that again. When he drew away from her, he said fiercely, "Ye are mine, Katherine. Ye are mine. I will not share ye!"

"Aye, Niall, I am only yours, completely and forever. I love ye."

He wondered if he was mad for believing those words, but he wanted them to be true. He carried her to the bed and made love to her urgently and passionately. She responded to his every touch with abandon. He wanted her, needed her, as he had never wanted or needed another person. How could she possibly understand that, and how could she possibly feel the same way about him? He poured his searing need into their joining, as if by the sheer intensity of his love-making he could convey all of this to her.

~ * ~

Afterwards, when they both lay spent, his slow, regular breathing signaled that he slept. She lay with her head over his heart, gently stroking his chest and shoulder. She wondered if he would ever release the pain and doubt plaguing him, which made him so uncertain of her devotion. Eventually her mind turned to the events of the day.

Who had Tomas overheard? Katherine didn't want to believe, couldn't believe, Fingal was one of the men involved, nor could she understand why Niall believed it with such assurance. She decided surely Niall would realize this when his anger cooled. Perhaps in the morning he would see things more rationally.

In the wee hours of the morning they awoke to the sound of Diarmad pounding on their chamber door. "Laird, wake up! There has been a raid to the southwest. The fires have been spotted by the watch."

Niall jumped out of bed, dressing in an instant. He strapped on his sword before turning to Katherine, who had arisen and was dressing as well. "Ye stay here in this room.

Don't leave for any reason until I come back," he ordered sternly. "I mean it, Katherine," he added even more forcefully, and strode out of the room, slamming the door.

Katherine stared after him in wide-eyed shock. She wasn't sure if he had confined her to their chambers for her own safety or for some other reason, but she would not provoke his ire further by defying him. She did not leave the chamber.

~ * ~

By the time Niall and a contingent of his men reached the site of the raid, the small cluster of farmers' cottages and barns had burned to the ground. The raiders had completely destroyed everything in the dead of the night. Unlike the other raids, in which they stole animals or burned hay, this time they had senselessly slaughtered the animals and set fire to the whole lot. The only thing for which Niall could be thankful was that the raiders had pulled his people from their homes before they torched the buildings. Even so, they killed three men, who had apparently tried to interfere. Surveying the ruins, he knew Matheson intended to send a message by leaving this devastation.

Diarmad approached him. "Do ye want to send men to follow the raider's trail?"

Niall shook his head. "There is no need. We know the trail will lead to Matheson and we have little hope of catching them now. We must get these people back to Duncurra. When they are safe, I will decide what needs to be done."

Diarmad nodded. "Apparently, Matheson has returned your message. Old Una just told me the leader said to tell ye, 'Duncurra is next.'"

~ * ~

Niall brooded silently as they rode back to Duncurra, arriving after daybreak. He and Diarmad went to the great hall, and he asked Cairbre and Alan to join them. He trusted these three men above all others. Once they arrived, he dismissed the servants and told his men about the conversation Tomas had overheard.

Diarmad said, "Do ye think the pair he heard were somehow involved in this raid?"

Niall shook his head in frustration. "I don't know. He heard them say 'everything was arranged,' but he also seemed to think whatever they were talking about would end in my death."

"Maybe they were lying in wait, assuming ye would follow the raiders," Diarmad suggested.

"Ye didn't track the raiders?" asked Alan.

"It seemed pointless. They had already wrought the destruction and I decided it was more important to get my people safely back to Duncurra. Now I wish I had followed the spineless curs."

"Well," said Cairbre, "if they were lying in wait, ye can bet ye would have been significantly outnumbered. Cowards are more likely to rely on numbers than skill. They lose more of their own, but achieve the outcome they desire. If it was their plan to ambush ye, your compassion for your clan has thwarted their attempt."

"Perhaps," said Niall, "but regardless of whether this attack was what the conspirators were discussing or not, I have a much bigger problem. Someone here at Duncurra is plotting my death, and the evidence points in one direction—Fingal."

The men stared at him in astonishment. Cairbre was the first to respond. "Laird, that isn't possible. Fingal has worshipped ye from the moment he could toddle. There is no one more loyal to ye than your brother."

Niall turned on him darkly. "Really?" he asked with derision. "Whoever it was admitted to pretending to be something he wasn't. Fingal's devotion could all be pretense. Tell me, who else would inherit Duncurra?"

"Laird, I know it looks damning, but I, too, can't believe Fingal is behind this," Diarmad insisted.

"What is Fingal behind?" asked Malcolm casually as he walked into the great hall.

"Well, ye may as well know, too," said Niall, before quickly running through the events of the last few days.

Malcolm looked shocked and concerned. "I have trouble believing your brother could be involved in a plot against ye, Niall. Perhaps young Tomas misheard or imagined the whole thing. Maybe he just made it up for the attention."

Niall shook his head. "Nay, I have questioned him at length. His story doesn't vary, and he's terrified. I believe the boy heard what he said he did. My brother thinks he is the one who would inherit Duncurra."

"Isn't he?" asked Malcolm.

"Nay. Katherine wanted to wait to make the announcement, but she is with child. If something were to happen to me, the bairn stands to inherit, not Fingal."

Niall's men congratulated him, their happiness dampened somewhat by the serious circumstances in which they found themselves.

Niall said, "Perhaps Fingal worried about something like this. The attacks increased after I married. Maybe he was hoping to seize control before there was an heir."

Alan said, "Niall, I can't explain what Tomas overheard, but like Cairbre and Diarmad, I cannot believe Fingal is behind it."

"If ye are sure the lad is telling the truth, now, as I think more about it, I'm not so sure it isn't Fingal," Malcolm said. "He certainly would expect to inherit Duncurra. He also knows, and by all accounts, was friendly with Tadhg Matheson while they were in training. If Matheson was aiding him, it would explain why the conspirator bemoaned his loss in not being the one to kill ye. He expected Matheson or one of his men would. Maybe Fingal staged his own accident to ensure no one suspected him."

"I think it is time we had a chat with my brother," said Niall, his expression dark and cold. "Diarmad, please go and invite him to join us."

"Laird, he is injured. Perhaps we should go to him."

"My wife assures me Fingal's injury is not serious. I am certain he can make it down the stairs with your assistance," Niall said with barely controlled rage.

"Aye, Laird." Diarmad bowed his head slightly and went to fetch Fingal.

Malcolm furrowed his brow. "I hear your wife is an extremely skilled healer. I'm sure Fingal is doing very well today after her tender ministrations."

Niall scowled.

"Ye don't suppose," continued Malcolm, "Fingal knew Katherine was expecting?"

"That makes no sense," said Niall crossly. "If he knew, there would be no reason for him to seek my death. He wouldn't inherit Duncurra anyway."

"Unless," said Malcolm, so quietly only Niall could hear him, "he planned to eliminate Katherine as well."

Niall's heart stopped. If he thought that was a possibility, he would kill Fingal with his bare hands. He wouldn't let anything happen to Katherine and the baby.

"Or perhaps the bairn isn't yours."

Niall's expression suddenly turned murderous.

Malcolm rushed on. "Nay, think about it, Niall. Ye said Katherine didn't want to announce the pregnancy yet. Perhaps they both know the bairn could be Fingal's. If he were to eliminate ye before Katherine's pregnancy was announced, he could marry the grieving widow and no one would be the wiser. Ye wouldn't be the first man to have someone else's bastard hidden under your protection."

Niall seethed; Malcolm could be right. He had foolishly let his guard down. "Cairbre," barked Niall, "fetch my wife here as well."

"Aye, Laird." Niall didn't miss the worried look Cairbre gave Alan.

Ceci Giltenan

The laird sat in stony silence, considering what Malcolm had said. How could it be anyone except Fingal? But was Katherine involved, too? Fingal was young, much closer to Katherine's age, and charming. Most women found him attractive. How many times had he heard Katherine's musical laughter over something his brother said? When he suggested Fingal was at the bottom of this yesterday, she had jumped to his defense. By all that's holy, she had spent the afternoon tending an injury that she herself said was not serious. Then she lied to him about it. How could he have let this happen again? What possessed him to open his heart to a woman, giving her the opportunity to destroy him?

Diarmad arrived in the great hall with a pale and drawn looking Fingal, just moments before Cairbre arrived with Katherine, who looked confused but guarded.

Chapter 20

One glance at Niall told Katherine he was dangerously angry, and for the first time since she'd married him, she was truly afraid.

"Good morning, brother." Niall nodded to Fingal. "Wife." He nodded to Katherine. "I am so pleased ye could both join us this morning. I think it is high time we discuss what has been going on around here."

Looking completely confused, Fingal said, "I'm sorry, Niall, it was only an accident. I should have kept the men farther apart on the training field. It won't happen again."

"I'm not referring to your accident. I am more concerned about the little conversation Tomas overheard before the feast on Epiphany."

"I'm not sure I understand. Tomas didn't mention a conversation to me."

"Nay, I'm sure he didn't," Niall said smoothly, "because he overheard two people plotting to kill me, and one of the two thought Duncurra would become his upon my death. Now, who could that have been?"

Fingal looked stunned, "Ye aren't suggesting I—"

"Silence," barked Niall. "Don't dig your grave deeper with your denials. What I want to know now is how Katherine is involved? Are ye lovers? Is the babe she carries yours?"

Katherine, who had been staring in utter astonishment at Niall, snapped, "Niall, how could ye think that, much less even speak it? Before anything else, I am your wife. I am devoted to ye, and I love ye with all my heart. Why do ye refuse to believe that?"

Niall sneered. "Ye give every indication of loving Fingal, too. I understand ye spent a cozy afternoon with him just yesterday."

"Ye blind idiot!" Katherine shouted as a rage every bit as hot as his own overtook her. "I have no idea why ye think I spent a 'cozy afternoon' with Fingal. I stitched and bandaged his wound; Turcuil and Edna were there the whole time. When I finished, I spent the afternoon with our son, who was terrified by what he had heard. I told ye that. Why would ye believe something else?"

Too angry to speak, Niall just stared as Katherine continued, "And as to loving Fingal, of course I do. I love Fingal as a brother, as your brother, because I love ye. What's more, Fingal loves ye, and even if I were inclined to be unfaithful, he would never betray ye. Why is it so hard for ye to fathom that? Am I betraying ye by loving Tomas? How about Father James and Father Colm? I love them, too, but Niall, ye are the heart of my heart, my soul mate. How can ye not see that?"

"He can't see it because he doesn't believe it's possible," spat Fingal. "He couldn't manage to earn my mother's love, but who could, Niall? Do ye think she loves me anymore than she does ye? The only person she truly loves is herself, and yet ye will never give up trying."

Turning back to Katherine, Fingal continued, "Perhaps you didn't know this, but several years ago my brother fell for the wiles of a faithless, grasping bitch who betrayed him with another. She was never worthy of your love, Niall, but ye have been so tainted by her deceit, ye can't recognize genuine devotion when ye see it."

Then, sounding defeated, he said, "I don't know whom Tomas overheard, or why they would believe Duncurra would become theirs, but it wasn't me. The only thing I have ever wanted was your respect. When ye appointed me to your guard, I thought I had finally earned it, but that must have been an illusion as well. If my presence here causes ye such distress, as soon as I can travel, with your permission, I will leave Duncurra and return to Laird Chisholm."

Niall stared at both of them, speechless. Katherine trembled, forcing back her tears. She felt as if he had mortally wounded her. Fingal, ashen and obviously in pain, looked...lost. Niall shook his head and said in a calm voice, "Ye're not going anywhere except back to bed, Fingal. Katherine, give him something for pain. I will join ye in our chamber shortly."

Katherine ran out of the great hall and up to their chamber. Safely behind the closed door she broke down and sobbed. She had been afraid when she saw Niall's raw anger. She felt the same heart- stopping fear she had when she knew Uncle Ambrose was going to beat her. This man she loved so desperately had hurt her more deeply than anything Uncle Ambrose could have done. *You have learned the surest way to open yourself to hurt is to love, and yet you love anyway.*

How could he have accused her of something so awful? How could he doubt her so profoundly? After a few minutes, she pulled herself together, washed her face, and prepared the potion to give to Fingal—the same one Niall had seemed angry about yesterday. She shook her head at the irony.

Diarmad was helping Fingal into bed when Katherine arrived. He looked miserable.

"Here, drink this," she said, handing him the potion. "It will help with the pain."

"Is it the same bitter swill ye made me drink yesterday? Thanks, I think I'd rather be in pain."

Diarmad frowned at him and Fingal took the potion from her. "Still, I wouldn't want to be accused of not following orders," he said wryly. He swallowed it, grimacing at the taste.

"I'll send Edna up later to change your bandage," Katherine said flatly and turned to leave.

"Katherine, wait," called Fingal. She stopped but didn't turn around as he went on. "I don't know where that came from, but I am sorry. I know he loves ye; he didn't mean to hurt ye like that."

"Still, Fingal?" Katherine asked, turning slowly to look at him, "After he verbally scourged both of us for some imagined wrong, ye would still defend him and apologize for him? I think your attempts at winning your brother's love and approval are as vain as my own." She turned and left the room, returning to her chamber quickly lest she cry again.

~ * ~

Niall remained in the great hall brooding. Alan and Cairbre didn't interrupt. Niall knew they would simply wait until he either dismissed them or drew them back into the discussion. Malcolm did not show the same deference, finally asking, "Ye don't believe them, do ye?"

"Aye, Malcolm, I do," said Niall irritably.

"Niall, I am afraid ye are becoming just like your father. He was too willing to trust people. That was his greatest fault. I hope it doesn't destroy ye." Niall didn't respond and Malcolm continued, "Well, I had planned to return to Brathanead today, but if ye would like for me to stay until things are sorted out, I would be happy to."

"My thanks, Malcolm, I don't think that will be necessary. I don't know whom Tomas overheard or what it means, and I really can't see any solution to this issue with Matheson at the moment. Laying siege to Cnocreidh would be a colossal waste of resources. I will increase security along my western border and raid again to try and recover some of our losses, but I will not allow revenge to drive me to wreak the kind of destruction he did. If there is any way ye can help, I will send ye a message. Have a safe journey."

"I'm sure you know best," Malcolm said before he left the hall.

Diarmad returned as Malcolm was leaving. He approached Niall and said, "Fingal is in bed and your wife awaits ye in your chambers, Laird."

Niall nodded but said nothing.

Diarmad shook his head. "Laird, I know it isn't my place to tell ye this, but even at the risk of worsening your foul temper, I find myself agreeing with your lady wife."

"Diarmad, I think we all agree with her," said Cairbre dryly.

"Agree with what?" Niall snapped.

"Begging your pardon, that ye're a blind idiot, Laird," answered Alan.

Niall simply rubbed his temples and said, "Oh that, aye, that has been fairly well established."

~ * ~

When Niall entered their chamber, he found Katherine sitting on the hearth hugging her knees to her chest with her head on them and he knew she had been crying. She had pulled her kertch off and it lay on the floor beside her. He went to her and gently pulled her up off the floor, putting his arms around her. "Katherine, I'm sorry."

"I can't do this anymore," Katherine said so softly he could barely hear her.

"Can't do what anymore?"

"I can't love ye. Father James was wrong. This hurts too much and I can't do it anymore."

"Katherine, please don't say that."

"Why, Niall? At dinner on the day we arrived here, ye told Cairbre your heart was never part of this bargain, but I had already given ye mine. Nothing I do or say seems to convince ye of that. Ye seem determined to punish me for the other women who have hurt ye. I thought I could stand anything, but the pain ye inflict is more than I can bear."

Niall knew he deserved that. "Katherine, I'm sorry, I was wrong."

"Aye, ye were," she agreed, her voice catching, "but this pattern doesn't change. Ye are always willing to believe the worst about the people who love ye the most. Fingal can leave. I can't. I have to protect myself. I don't want to love ye anymore." Her voice broke with a harsh sob.

Those words cut him deeply. "Katherine, please, ye don't mean that. Sweetling, I do love ye. I love ye with all my heart. Ye are right, I didn't want to because I didn't want to risk getting hurt as I had in the past. I know I have hurt ye and I am sorry. Please, Katherine, forgive me. Tell me I haven't lost ye," he said desperately. He tipped her chin up, looking directly into her tear-filled eyes. The pain he saw rent his heart. "Katherine, I need ye. Please don't stop loving me."

She sobbed again, "I don't think I could stop if I tried, but don't do this to me again. It will kill me." She was unable to force back her tears any longer.

He pulled her close again and buried his head in her hair. "Wheesht, lass."

Chapter 21

January had been unusually cold and stormy but not within his keep, thought Niall. It had been three weeks since he had admitted to himself he was hopelessly in love with his bonny wife, and she with him. He basked in the heat of that love. Several nights ago, under the crystal clear sky that follows a storm, he had led a successful raid against Matheson, replacing most of the livestock that had been slaughtered. However, he had spent the other nights with Katherine. Her passion continued to thrill him. He thought the sight of his delicate wife lying in his arms, cloaked only in her soft honey-colored curls, looking drowsy and replete after their love-making, was the most beautiful sight on earth. The thought made him grin as he stared into the fire in the great hall.

"Ye haven't been listening, have ye?" asked Diarmad.

"Nay, I'm sorry, I was distracted," Niall said, his grin widening. "What were ye saying?"

"I was saying," Diarmad repeated indulgently, "things have been quiet since we increased the number and frequency of patrols on the border. Maybe the show of strength is all it will take."

"Let's hope so," said Niall, but he didn't believe the trouble with Matheson was over.

Moments later he received a message from the watch. A small group of men approached Duncurra under the MacLennan banner.

"Malcolm is returning so soon? That's odd," he said.

Diarmad chuckled. "Perhaps not. When he was here, he spent most of his time in Lady Eithne's company. Maybe he will rid ye of that thorn in your side by marrying her."

"One can only hope," answered Niall.

~ * ~

When Malcolm arrived, it was not to visit Eithne, and he did not bring good news. "Niall, I came as soon as I heard. The daughter of one of my clansmen, who is married to a Matheson, tells me they are planning something at Candlemas or there about. Matheson may be planning a siege on Duncurra."

"A siege?" Niall was incredulous, "in the dead of winter?"

"He believes ye to be weakened and unable to withstand a siege for long."

"Why would he think that?" asked Cairbre. "Duncurra is more secure and has better resources than it has had for several years."

Malcolm shrugged. "Who knows why rash young men do the things they do? The fact is ye can expect him on your doorstep soon."

"Well, we can certainly withstand a siege during winter within Duncurra better than he will be able to survive outside the walls," Niall declared.

His commander and captains nodded in agreement.

"I'm sure that is true," agreed Malcolm, "but will ye risk the lives and health of your wife and mother by keeping them here? I thought perhaps it would be best if I escorted them to Brathanead to keep them safely out of harm's way. Once they are secure, I will send a contingent of my men to support ye."

"That is a very kind offer, and certainly if Lady Eithne wishes to, she can return to Brathanead with ye, but Katherine will stay here. A siege on Duncurra would be folly on Matheson's part. I don't believe he will follow through with it."

"Niall, don't make this decision hastily, or based on what ye think another man's rational choices should be. Matheson has already demonstrated his brutality. What do ye think he will do to Katherine if his siege is successful?"

Niall paled. He remembered the threat conveyed after the last raid: *Duncurra next*. The thought of his wife, his pregnant wife, at the hands of Matheson made his blood run cold.

Malcolm assured him, "She will be safe with me, regardless of what happens."

"Don't speak of this to anyone for now," Niall warned. "There are things to discuss and I need to consider all options."

~ * ~

The Laird was preoccupied during dinner, but he didn't share the most recent news with Katherine. After dinner he suggested she retire early, telling her he needed to discuss a few things with his commander and captains. They discussed strategy late into the night. None of them liked the idea of sending Katherine to Brathanead. Furthermore, Niall knew he would have a battle on his hands convincing her to go, but as they discussed it, he became even more certain it was the right choice. He and his guard would escort them with the MacLennan soldiers. When she was safely ensconced at Brathanead, he would return to Duncurra to prepare for a siege.

The next morning, he told Malcolm the plan. "I can understand your desire to see her safely to Brathanead, but do ye think it wise to leave Duncurra with a siege eminent? What will your people do if ye and your elite guard are gone when Matheson attacks?"

"Surely I can take the two days needed to escort Katherine safely to your keep and return."

"Are ye sure enough to risk everything on it? The only information I have is that Matheson has planned something at Candlemas, which is in two days, but we can't be sure he won't attack before then."

Niall realized Malcolm was right. Time was precious and even taking one day to ride with them was folly. He agreed Katherine and Eithne would travel to Brathanead at dawn, under Malcolm's care. He considered sending Tomas, but he wouldn't be able to send a guard with them and he didn't trust Eithne. Furthermore, he reasoned if Matheson was successful, a boy would be less a target than his wife. Tomas would stay at Duncurra.

Niall waited as long as he could to tell Katherine the plans for her safety.

~ * ~

After the noon meal was finished, Niall asked Edna to take Tomas out of the great hall.

Assuming he intended to talk with his men, Katherine said, "I'll take him. He wants to show me what a skilled horseman he is."

"Nay, Katherine. There is something I wish to discuss with ye."

"Tomas, shall we go find Maura and Nevan?" asked Edna as she ushered the lad outside. Diarmad, Malcolm, Eithne, and Fingal remained at the table, making Katherine instantly wary. Her gaze flitted around the group, but Fingal's was the only face registering the same uneasiness she felt.

When Tomas was out of earshot, Niall took Katherine's hands in his. "Sweetling, we have received word Matheson is planning to lay siege to Duncurra any day now."

"What? Why would he do that?"

"It doesn't matter why. The point is we will be under attack very soon, and I do not want ye here when it starts. I need to protect ye."

"What are ye saying, Niall? Are ye sending me away?"

"My love, I am keeping ye safe. Ye will go with Eithne and Malcolm to Brathanead until the siege is over."

"What about Tomas?"

"Tomas will be safe here."

"Niall, this doesn't make sense. If Tomas will be safe here, I will be safe here. Ye don't even know why Matheson is attacking. Why are ye so sure he will?"

"Katherine," said Niall, frustrated, "apparently, he believes we are vulnerable and he can take Duncurra. I believe we can withstand a siege, but I don't want to risk your safety or that of our bairn."

Katherine felt panic rising. There was something desperately wrong here. This didn't make sense. Even if it were true, she certainly would not leave her home when she should be helping prepare for its defense. She glanced around the table again, looking for support, but she found none. Even Fingal's mouth was set in a grim line. She did not want to argue with Niall in front of an audience, so she leaned toward him and said very softly, "Please, Niall, can we discuss this privately?"

Niall shook his head. "There is nothing to discuss."

Katherine glanced around the table again and caught Diarmad's eye. He looked at her and, shaking his head, said, "My lady, ye should not be here during a siege."

Malcolm said, "Ye will be safe at Brathanead, my dear, and that will give your husband peace of mind. He does not need to be distracted at a time like this. Once ye are safe, I will send men to help defend Duncurra. It will be over soon and ye can return."

Katherine tried one more time. "Niall, please, can we talk alone?"

"There is nothing to talk about. I have made my decision," Niall said sternly.

"Katherine, it is obvious Niall loves you," said Eithne. "He only wishes to keep you safe. Your behavior is very unseemly."

Katherine ignored her. "Nay, Niall, please don't make me do this. Don't send me away. If there is a siege the clan will need me."

Niall would not relent. "I protect what is mine, Katherine."

"Then protect me here. This is where I belong."

Niall had obviously reached his limit. He stood up and said harshly, "I am not arguing with ye about this any longer. I will not risk losing ye and ye will be out of harm's way at Brathanead. Ye will leave with Malcolm in the morning. Do ye understand me?"

She looked him in the eye and gave the slightest nod of her head, but she felt shattered.

He pulled her into his arms. "Please, Katherine, try to understand. I will come for ye when I have dealt with Matheson and it is safe for ye to return."

~ * ~

Niall had not informed Fingal of his plans for Katherine in advance and wasn't surprised when his brother sought him out privately.

"Niall, can I talk to my brother?"

Even after everything that had happened, Niall found it difficult to believe Fingal was not involved in this somehow. "Ye can unless ye are going to tell me that I should not send my wife to safety."

"I'm not going to say that," said Fingal with a grin. "I do have trouble believing Matheson intends to lay siege to Duncurra." Niall arched an eyebrow at him as he continued, "But I agree she should not be here if there is any chance of it at all."

"So, if ye agree with me, what is your concern?"

"I don't think ye should send her to Brathanead with Malcolm."

"Tell me, Fingal, what, in your vast experience, leads ye to draw this conclusion?" Niall asked mockingly.

"Niall, please listen to me. There is something wrong with all of this, and somehow I think Malcolm is involved. He has been subtly agitating from the day we arrived at Brathanead after the wedding. He was the one who suggested to ye that Katherine and I were somehow in league together against ye. His closeness to Mother has me worried."

"Ye are worried about your mother?" asked Niall, aghast.

"Nay, not about her. I worry that she has sucked Malcolm into something. Niall, I don't trust him anymore and I am worried about ye sending Katherine away with him."

"Where would I send her, then?" asked Niall patronizingly.

"Ye could send her to Chisholm. Fearghas Chisholm would keep her safe. I trust him, and Da trusted him."

Niall sighed. "Little brother, I know ye mean well, but I trust Malcolm, and Da trusted Malcolm, too. Katherine will be safe there and he's ready to take her in the morning. It would take a day or perhaps two to get a message to Fearghas and have him return with a large enough force to protect her. Matheson could already have begun the siege by then. Furthermore, Fearghas Chisholm is a close ally of Matheson's too. If it came to it, I am not sure whose side he would take. Nay, Fingal, it is safest if my wife goes with Malcolm."

Chapter 22

The next morning as they prepared to leave, Malcolm pulled Niall aside. "Stop worrying. Ye have made the right decision and she must accept it. I will protect her well at Brathanead. Even your mother, who rarely agrees with ye on anything, sees this is the best course."

"I know ye are right. I just hate to send her away so unhappy."

"Niall, ye know women wield pouting and sulking the way ye and I do a broadsword. Don't let her manipulate ye into making a decision that could put her in danger. Now bid your lady farewell, or we will not make Brathanead before nightfall."

As Katherine waited for a stable hand to lead Eachann from the stable, Niall went to her and pulled her into his arms. She returned his embrace and he lifted her chin to look into her eyes. "Katherine, I love ye with all my heart. Ye know that."

"I love ye, too, and I don't want to leave."

"I know, sweetling, but this is the best way to protect ye. I will come for ye when it is safe, I promise." Looking miserable, she gave another little nod but didn't speak. Niall kissed her before lifting her onto Eachann's back. When she had settled herself in the saddle, Malcolm gave the signal for them to leave.

~ * ~

As they rode farther from Duncurra, Katherine adopted the emotionless mask that had served her so well in the past, while Eithne chattered away about inane topics. Katherine tried to be polite without joining the mindless conversation. The snow on the ground forced them to travel at a slow pace, and the sun was well past its zenith when they stopped on MacLennan land to water the horses. They had brought a light meal of bread, cheese, and cold mutton from Duncurra, but Katherine ate very little.

Malcolm encouraged her to eat more. "Lass, that is not enough to keep a bird alive. Ye must have something else. I promised your husband I would take good care of ye. What will he think if ye waste away to nothing under my watch?"

"Aye, Laird, thank you," she answered, accepting the piece of brown bread and cheese he offered, but she didn't actually eat any of it.

When they set out again, Eithne rode near the front of the group beside Malcolm. Katherine heard her talking endlessly, but she was too far back to understand the words. She was just happy for a respite from the spiteful woman. After a while, she noticed Malcolm and Eithne had ridden out well in front with many of Malcolm's men. In fact, they were completely out of sight occasionally. The party rode through a wide mountain pass on a trek skirting close to the mountain on their left.

Katherine knew the Highlands held many similar passes. When she had first travelled this way as they journeyed to Duncurra, Niall explained such spots were a favorite place for thieves to lay in wait. When riding through these areas, Niall remained alert, moving quickly and quietly, with his men riding close around them. They were on MacLennan land and with six MacLennan soldiers encircling her, she should feel completely safe, but she worried. Maybe it was just Niall's caution making her nervous, but something felt wrong. She tried to push the pace a little in an effort to rejoin those in front.

"We seem to be falling behind. Can we speed up a bit to catch up with Laird MacLennan?" she asked her escort.

One of the MacLennan soldiers said, "There is no need, my lady. Laird MacLennan doesn't wish for you to risk hurting yourself. Besides, they aren't that far ahead. It's just hard to see them because the path bends to the right and the forest is heavy. Ye'll see, they're just around the corner and we'll catch them up soon."

"I will not break if we pick up our pace a bit. I'm sorry, but I don't think they are 'just around the corner' because I can't hear them anymore. Please, I want to catch up to them."

"My lady," the soldier said, his voice thick with irritation, "ye can't hear them because the snow deadens the noise, and I will not risk my laird's ire to indulge your whim."

In spite of her concerns, they continued to hold the same plodding pace. A moment later she did hear horses, only it wasn't Malcolm's party.

Armed men surrounded them and in an instant they were under attack. Although the attackers did not outnumber the MacLennan soldiers, they had far superior skills. Still, she expected to see Malcolm and the rest of the men come riding back to help, but they never did. Before she knew it, the MacLennans capitulated, laying down their weapons.

There was only one thing Katherine could do; she turned Eachann and bolted.

Leaning low over the horse's neck, she rode to the north as fast as she could manage. She heard a horse thundering behind her, but didn't look back. It was barely a moment before the huge black warhorse drew alongside Eachann on her right and someone lifted her off her saddle. The other rider's vise-like arm closed around her, pulling her onto his horse as he slowed the beast.

She screamed, kicked her legs, arched her back, and pushed against him, trying to twist out of his grip, but it was no use.

"Wheesht, lass, I won't hurt ye, but ye'll hurt yourself if ye keep fighting."

She stopped struggling for a moment. "Please let me go. I don't have anything valuable, and the MacLennans have surrendered. Please just let me go."

"Now, lass, my conscience wouldn't allow me to let as sweet a thing as ye ride out unprotected. Ye might be set upon by brigands," he said with a chuckle. "Beside which, I'm not interested in the MacLennans. Ye are the prize I seek." At this pronouncement, Katherine renewed her struggle to twist free. He held her with both arms, and with his left leg, trapped her legs against the horse. He spoke in a more serious tone. "Wheesht. I don't want to bind ye, but I will if I have to. I will not risk ye hurting yourself," he grunted as she managed to dig an elbow into his stomach, "or me." He tightened his grip, "Which is it to be?"

Katherine stilled. She was terrified. Finally she asked, "Who are you and what do you want with me?"

He released her legs, but he still kept one arm firmly clamped around her waist. He nudged the black into a trot towards Eachann. "My lady, I am Tadhg Matheson, laird of Clan Matheson. Am I right in assuming ye are Niall MacIan's wife?" She gave a little nod. "Then, my lady, what I want is for ye to be my guest at Cnocreidh." By this time he had ridden close enough to the brown gelding to take hold of the reins. Then he turned both horses back in the direction from which they had just ridden.

Katherine turned her head so she could look him in the face. "My husband will kill you," she said, with more bravado than she felt.

He smiled at her and said mockingly, "And just where is he, lass? If ye were my wife I wouldn't trust a group of cowardly MacLennans to see to your safety."

Tears threatened and she looked away. "He thought he was keeping me safe," she said defensively, adding, "Laird MacLennan is one of his oldest friends, and Niall trusts him."

"Well, as it appears Laird MacIan's trust was misplaced. His oldest friend has abandoned ye."

She knew he was right. If Malcolm and his other men were 'just around the corner' as her escort had said, they should have heard the attack and ridden back.

She bowed her head, feeling completely defeated. "Why do ye want me?"

"Lass, have ye never seen your reflection? There are many reasons a man would want ye."

She snapped her head around in fear and he quit teasing.

"Ye are in no danger, I swear. I am going to take ye to my home and keep ye safely there until I can get your hard-headed husband to stop raiding my holding."

By this time they were back at the scene of the ambush. Her MacLennan escort had been relieved of their weapons and sat on the ground bound at the wrists and ankles. The Matheson warriors sat on their mounts, waiting for their laird to return. One of them asked, "What do ye want us to do with them, Laird?"

"Take the horses. We'll leave the cowards trussed. I expect MacLennan will send someone for them, but one never knows what a cur will do. Just in case, leave a dagger. Maybe they will manage to free themselves before Laird MacIan can kill them. Oh, and lads, one last thing," he said, addressing the MacLennan soldiers. "Please make sure Niall MacIan gets this message. His lovely wife will be my honored guest at Cnocreidh until he is willing to discuss a truce." Then he signaled his men to leave and the Matheson warriors rode fast and hard to the northwest with seven new horses and Katherine MacIan.

He might consider her "his guest," but she knew that was a farce. After her initial fight he had loosened his grip on her. She suspected that he believed she had resigned herself to the situation. He was mistaken. If he thought she would make this easy for him, he had another think coming.

She might not be able to escape easily, but she could make him miserable, so she launched a more insidious attack. She fidgeted and twisted on his lap, forcing him to constantly readjust in order to maintain balance. Occasionally she bumped his chin with her head, knocking his head backwards, or dug her sharp elbows into his ribs. Each time she issued a polite, sweet apology. Katherine was prepared to make him suffer the whole journey, but before long he must have realized these were not accidents. "Enough! Ye will sit still," he commanded, clamping an arm around her waist and once again pulling her firmly against his chest.

Having effectively curtailed her attack, she was left with nothing to do but endure the ride and think. She tried to fit all the pieces together. She could not find an explanation for Malcolm's abandonment or the fact that her MacLennan escorts had barely raised a sword. Laird Matheson had said something about getting Niall to stop raiding, but it was Matheson who kept harassing the MacIans. Nothing made sense. She needed Niall. She was afraid and she needed to escape, but as long as Laird Matheson held her on horseback, she couldn't. She would have to find an excuse to get down and get away.

~ * ~

Tadhg had hoped if they pushed, they would reach Cnocreidh before sunset, but when darkness fell, they were still about an hour's ride away. However, the temperature dropped and a bitter cold wind whipped up. He had no intention of sleeping on the frozen ground with this particular hostage. The moon was bright and they rode over familiar terrain well within Matheson territory, so he pushed on at a slower pace.

After hours of silence from her, his hostage turned her head and, looking up at him, said, "Laird Matheson—"

"Please call me Tadhg." He looked at her for a moment. Even in the low light, the fear he saw in her eyes concerned him.

"I would rather not," she said.

He chuckled. "Well, lass, if ye want me to answer, ye will have to."

Ignoring him, she asked, "Will it be much longer?"

"Perhaps an hour," he answered.

"Well, I...um...I need some privacy," she said shyly, bowing her head and looking away.

He had expected this and signaled for his men to halt. He lifted her chin and gently turned her head so he could look her squarely in the eyes. "I will allow ye to have some privacy, but first answer me this. Do ye have any idea where ye are?"

She looked back at him, apparently confused, and by way of clarification he asked bluntly, "In which direction would ye go to get back to Duncurra?"

As realization dawned on her, he saw tears fill her eyes. She tried to blink them back and said, "I don't know."

"I didn't think so. I know ye are scared, and I know ye want to go home, but running away from me would put ye in danger and I can't allow that."

"And I'm not in danger with you?" she challenged.

"Nay, ye are not," he said firmly. "But I warn ye, if ye try to escape, I will find ye. This is my land and tracking ye through snow will not be difficult. Furthermore, if I have to traipse through these frigid, snowy woods tonight searching, when I do find ye, I will bind ye until we reach Cnocreidh. I will not let ye put yourself at risk. Do I make myself clear?"

Still fighting tears, she nodded before looking away. He hated threatening her but knew it was necessary. He added more gently, "Ye will get through this and I will get ye back to your husband unharmed." He dismounted and lifted her to the ground, motioning for her to go into the woods. As she walked away he added, "One more thing, lass." She looked back at him and he said with a wink, "He won't kill me."

~ * ~

They did arrive at Cnocreidh within the hour, and Katherine felt utter despair set in. The massive fortress appeared to be as impenetrable as Duncurra. It stood on the top of a hill with a huge swath around it cleared of trees, making it impossible to approach or leave without being seen. Not only that, but two thick, fortified walls surrounded it, an inner curtain wall enclosing the keep, and a second wall encircling the village around it. They entered through a manned barbican set in the outer wall; the heavy portcullis opened as they approached. The inner curtain wall appeared to be higher and thicker than the outer wall and she could see sentries on the top. They crossed through another manned barbican and portcullis to reach the enormous keep. It looked as if all of Duncurra would have fit within the central section of Cnocreidh, between its four massive towers. Katherine thought dismally that finding her way out of the keep alone would be a challenge. Escaping the walls appeared to be nearly impossible.

"Welcome to Cnocreidh," Tadhg said as they entered the courtyard. He dismounted, lifted her to the ground, and handed his horse to a stablehand. Taking Katherine's elbow, he led her to his keep and through the doors into the great hall. Fires roared in two hearths and the flurry of activity suggested the evening meal was nearly ready. As they walked in, he called to an older woman, saying, "Elspet, our visitor, Lady Katherine MacIan, has arrived. Turning to Katherine, he said, "Elspet manages the staff here."

He spoke quietly to Elspet for a moment. Although Katherine had ridden in his lap for hours, she hadn't actually gotten a good look at him until now. He had dark hair and green eyes, and while he stood as tall as Niall, she thought he was perhaps less broad through the shoulders. However, he had crushed her against him long enough for her to know he had the same powerful muscles. He hadn't been unkind to her, and he swore to her she was in no danger, but her heart ached for home.

~ * ~

When he finished speaking with Elspet, Tadhg turned back to Katherine. "I will show ye to your chamber. I have arranged for ye to have a hot bath, and dinner will be brought up. I suspect ye could use some rest."

She nodded, following him up the stairs to a well-appointed fourth floor chamber. A fire crackled in the hearth and the room was warm and inviting. She walked in, standing there for a moment with her back to him. Tadhg thought she looked very small and fragile compared to the virago he had pulled off her horse earlier. Even though he had warned her about the danger of escaping, he suspected she had still hoped to try until they rode into view of Cnocreidh. At that moment he had felt her shoulders droop. Now she looked very alone and afraid. Even though he was the cause of her current consternation, he wanted to comfort her.

"Lady Katherine, I know none of this is your doing. The difficulties between the Mathesons and MacIans go back many years, and I'm sorry ye have become a pawn. I want ye to be comfortable here. I would rather not lock ye in this room." She turned sharply to look at him and the fear he saw in her eyes disturbed him. "If ye will agree not to take one step out of this keep unless I give ye leave and someone accompanies ye, I will let ye have your freedom within it. Will ye promise?"

She looked down. It was clear she didn't want him to lock her in. He watched as she seemed to wage an internal battle. Finally, barely above a whisper, she said, "Nay. I will not promise to stay. If an opportunity arises to escape, I will take it."

"Damnation, there is no way for ye to escape Cnocreidh, surely ye realize that? Even if ye did manage to escape to the woods without someone seeing you, it is winter and ye have no idea how to get back to Duncurra. Ye would be in terrible danger alone. This will be over soon, don't make me treat ye like a prisoner."

She looked him squarely in the eye, and once again he saw the spirit and determination he had originally encountered. She said, "I am a prisoner and I won't make that promise. If I have the chance, I will return to my husband."

Elspet arrived, followed by servants carrying a tub and buckets of hot water.

Tadhg shook his head in frustration. "As ye wish, my lady." Before leaving he turned to Elspet, saying coldly,

"Lock her in. She is not to leave this room without my permission and an escort." He left.

~ * ~

Katherine's bag of belongings had been tied to her saddle, and Elspet brought it to her while she bathed. "The laird thought it would be better if ye didn't have a weapon," the woman said. "He asked me to tell ye he will return it to ye when ye leave."

"Of course he did," replied Katherine in frustration, remembering she had packed her father's jeweled dagger. She rose from the tub and wrapped herself in the soft linen towel Elspet held for her. She dried, changed into a clean *léine*, and sat by the fire combing her wet hair.

Servants removed the tub while Elspet tidied up before laying the meal on a small table. Katherine thanked her, but didn't make any attempt to eat it. "My lady, please eat something," Elspet said gently.

"I will," replied Katherine, "in a bit."

"Is there anything else ye need?" Elspet asked.

Katherine looked around, really taking in the room for the first time. It was small, but comfortably furnished. She shook her head and said, "Nay, thank you."

Elspet opened the chamber door to leave and said, "I'm sorry, my lady, I have to lock the door."

"I understand," said Katherine sadly. "Would you answer a question before you go?"

"If I can."

"When we entered the hall this evening, Laird Matheson said to you, 'our visitor has arrived.' When he left today, how did he know he would be coming back with me?"

"I'm sorry, my lady, that is something ye will have to ask the laird. Is there anything else?"

"Nay, thank ye."

Elspet left, locking the door behind her. Katherine made a half-hearted attempt at eating the food set out for her, but she was exhausted, her head ached, and she felt ill. She finally blew out the candles before curling up in bed. It was warm and comfortable, but she would rather be sleeping on the cold ground in Niall's arms than without him anywhere else. As she lay there, unable to sleep in spite of her fatigue, she once again tried to put the pieces together.

She became more and more certain Malcolm had abandoned her. Laird Matheson had said, "Our visitor has arrived." *He knew I would be traveling to Brathanead and intended to capture me.* That's where things fell apart for her. Malcolm had only arrived at Duncurra two nights ago. Niall had made the decision to send her to Brathanead yesterday afternoon. How could Matheson have known?

Based on the conversation Tomas overheard, there had been at least two people at Duncurra who were conspiring against Niall, one of whom expected to gain Duncurra for himself. Niall was right, that would appear to point to Fingal. He was among the first to know she would be traveling to Brathanead, but she would not believe he had betrayed Niall in this manner.

This puzzle had too many missing pieces. Her head ached worse the longer she thought about it, but she was more firmly convinced than ever Laird Matheson could fill in some of the blanks. She resolved to try to speak with him in the morning, then finally gave in to her exhaustion.

~ * ~

When Elspet knocked gently on the chamber door, Katherine was dressed and sitting in a chair by the hearth. Elspet bustled happily into the chamber saying, "Good morning, my lady, are ye well? It is good to see ye are already up and dressed."

"Good morning, Elspet. I am quite well, thank you," answered Katherine automatically.

"I've brought ye a nice hearty breakfast, my lady." Her beaming smile dimmed when she saw the uneaten dinner from last night still on the table. "What was he thinking?" she grumbled under her breath.

Choosing to ignore the comment, Katherine said, "Elspet, I need to speak to Laird Matheson as soon as possible. Please, can you ask if he will see me?"

She looked at Katherine and observed bluntly, "My lady, ye don't look 'quite well.' Ye didn't eat a thing and I'm guessing ye haven't eaten since sometime yesterday afternoon. What's more, ye look even more pallid and drawn than ye did last night."

"Please, I need to speak with your laird."

"Laird Matheson will be livid if he sees ye looking as ye do, and finds out ye haven't eaten. I think it would be a very good idea for ye to break your fast before I tell him ye wish to see him."

Katherine sighed and shook her head with an air of defeat. "You are right, I don't feel well and I cannot eat right now. I will eat something later, I promise. However, I must speak with Laird Matheson. Please, will you ask if he'll see me?"

Elspet stared at her for a moment. Shaking her head in frustration, she responded, "I will give your message to my laird, but please, lass, ye need to eat something. I'll check back in on ye soon. Is there anything else ye need before I go?"

"Nay, thank you, Elspet."

The woman left, taking Katherine's uneaten dinner, and once again locked her in.

Chapter 23

After Katherine left Niall spent the day preparing for the siege. He sent messages to outlying farms so as many people and as much livestock as possible could be moved to Duncurra for safety. He did everything possible to fortify his stronghold, driving himself well into the night, until Diarmad finally convinced him to rest briefly. When he lay down, he fell into an exhausted sleep, but the image of Katherine's face as she begged him to let her stay haunted his dreams. When he woke after only a few hours, he rose and continued preparing for the imminent siege. Even though he believed sending Katherine to Brathanead was the right thing to do, after his few restless hours of sleep, he couldn't shake the feeling he had failed her.

That evening one of his men-at-arms approached, saying "Laird, the watch reports there is a MacLennan messenger riding hard toward Duncurra."

This could not be good news. Perhaps Malcolm had learned additional information about Matheson's movements. He called for Diarmad, Alan, and Cairbre to join him in the great hall, where preparations were well underway for the evening meal. When the messenger arrived, Niall received him immediately. The messenger's news stunned everyone.

"My wife was kidnapped by Matheson?" Niall roared. "Tell me now the men guarding her were killed, because I swear they will die at my hand if they weren't."

"Laird MacLennan said Matheson attacked with an overwhelming force. Most of the MacLennan soldiers fell under the sword or were gravely injured. Laird MacLennan himself was seriously injured. He begs your forgiveness and swears he will help ye seek vengeance. MacLennan soldiers will be arriving to support ye tomorrow."

"Did Matheson also take Lady Eithne?" Diarmad asked.

"My laird said Laird Matheson only took Lady Katherine. Apparently she was bound, gagged, and thrown across Matheson's lap." The messenger began to look very uncomfortable.

"Does he intend to ransom her?" Niall asked, his panic over Katherine rising.

"The laird said Matheson didn't mention a ransom, but—"

"But what? What else is there?"

"I'm sorry, Laird. Apparently, Laird Matheson said to tell ye—if ye still wanted your wife when he was done with her—ye could come to Cnocreidh and beg for her."

The message had its desired effect. Niall exploded in rage. "I will raze Cnocreidh!" he roared. "We leave at first light." Turning back to the messenger, he said, "Matheson has never attacked the MacLennans; he must have known Katherine was with them."

"Aye, he did. He told Laird MacLennan he had 'received an invitation' from Duncurra."

This statement confirmed Niall's suspicions. Consumed with fury, in a deadly calm voice he said to Cairbre, "Bring Fingal to me now."

"Aye, Laird," answered Cairbre, but before he left, he said, "Laird, I cannot believe Fingal would betray ye."

"I don't care what ye believe. It can only be him. He would not only need to see me dead, he would need to eliminate Katherine and the bairn as well to inherit Duncurra. Get him now!"

Cairbre nodded and left.

Niall had never felt this kind of rage. He saw the concerned glances passed between Alan and Diarmad. "What?" he demanded.

Just as Cairbre had, Alan tried to reason with him, pleading for caution, "Laird, he is your brother, at least hear him."

"Have no fear, Alan, I will hear his confession before I kill him."

"Laird, I'm sending Caolin to fetch Father Colm," said Diarmad, motioning the women out of the hall.

Niall snorted in disgust. "If ye think anyone will stop me from seeking justice, ye are wrong, Diarmad."

Father Colm arrived at the great hall just as Cairbre returned with Fingal. Fingal stopped short, looking wary and cautious. "What has happened?" he asked.

"I think ye know," answered Niall, barely able to contain his wrath.

"Niall, I don't understand. Please tell me what's wrong."

"Ye will address me as laird, for ye don't have the right to call me brother anymore," snarled Niall. "Who did ye send to Matheson?"

"Laird, I sent no one to Matheson, I've had no contact with him."

"Stop lying! Ye're the only one who could have told him Katherine was on her way to Brathanead—the only one with a motive for wanting both of us dead!"

Clearly alarmed, Fingal took a step back. "I am not lying to ye, Laird. For the love of God, tell me what's happened."

Through clenched teeth, Niall said, "Matheson attacked with an overwhelming force as Malcolm was escorting Katherine to Brathanead."

Fingal blanched at his words. "Is she all right?"

Niall continued as if he hadn't heard Fingal. "Most of Malcolm's men were killed or injured. Even Malcolm himself was seriously injured. Matheson kidnapped Katherine and apparently does not intend to ransom her." Niall grabbed Fingal by the shoulders and bellowed, "Tell me what ye know, now, or I will tear ye limb from limb!"

"I swear to ye, on our father's soul, I had nothing to do with this. I would never harm either of ye, Niall, I swear it."

Niall threw him to the floor. Fingal was back on his feet in an instant, but Father Colm stepped between them. "Get out of my way, Father," demanded Niall.

Without flinching, Father Colm looked Niall squarely in the eye and said, "Laird, I will not let ye do something in anger ye will regret. Ye do not have proof your brother betrayed ye, and ye know as well as I do ye are angrier with yourself for not escorting her than ye are with anyone else. Ye need to focus on getting Lady Katherine back. Vengeance will wait."

Father Colm looked every inch a warrior in that moment, so Niall had no doubt he would have to battle the old priest before laying a hand on Fingal. Furthermore, what the priest said was true. "Ye are right, Father," Niall said, glaring at Fingal. "I have no proof, and nothing can interfere with getting Katherine back. However, I will find proof of your perfidy, brother, then I *will* kill ye."

Addressing Diarmad and his two captains, the laird said, "We will leave only a few men here to secure Duncurra. Everyone else should prepare to ride to Cnocreidh at first light." To the MacLennan messenger, Niall said, "Eat, rest, and return to your laird. Tell him I will gladly accept the support he offers, and I will have vengeance on Matheson." Finally, turning back to Fingal, Niall said with rancor, "Ye will stay here. I don't trust ye to protect your inheritance, so ye are relieved of all duties and confined to the keep." With that, he strode out of the hall, followed by Diarmad, Alan, and Cairbre.

~ * ~

Fingal felt angry and hurt, but more than anything else, he was confused. How could this have happened? He agreed with Niall, Matheson had to have known Katherine travelled with Malcolm in order to have ambushed him, defeating him so soundly. He looked at Father Colm and said sincerely, "Father, nothing that's happened makes sense. If something happens to Katherine, I am the only person who stands to inherit Duncurra, but I swear, I did not betray my brother." Dejectedly he sat in a chair by the hearth.

Father Colm considered him for a moment before joining him. "I believe ye. Unfortunately, it is difficult to identify anyone else with a strong motive. If it isn't ye, the only thing that makes sense is that whoever is behind this expects to conquer Duncurra, not inherit it."

"That is the only answer I can see, as well," said Fingal, "but the conspirator was here on the Epiphany and Matheson certainly was not. I didn't want to, but I can't help but think Malcolm is involved. I worried about Niall's decision to send Katherine with him, but Malcolm was our father's dearest friend. He has truly always been like an uncle to us. My distrust has more to do with my mother's involvement with Malcolm than anything else."

"Ye seem to have very little affection for your mother," observed Father Colm.

"Truthfully, Father, she wasn't really a mother to either of us. She went to court for the first time when I was five. Eventually she chose to live there permanently."

"Without your father?"

"Our father loved the Highlands, but my mother didn't, and after I was born, she was never able to carry another bairn to term. I think the fact that she lost so many other pregnancies trying to give him more children made him want to do whatever it took to make her happy, so he let her stay there." Fingal shook his head at the memories. "He turned a blind eye to everything she did, and while she was there, she practically destroyed this clan single-handedly."

"How did she manage that?" asked Father Colm.

"She acquired a massive debt, the true magnitude of which was only discovered after my father's death. The clan was on the brink of ruin. Niall was forced to seek help from King David, who provided a solution, in the form of marriage to a Lowland heiress."

"The Lady Katherine?"

"Aye."

The old priest smiled and said, "I would hardly call that a sacrifice."

Fingal smiled too. "There would be many who would agree with ye, Father, but for Niall, at the time, it was. Years ago the woman he intended to marry betrayed him. The entire clan witnessed her deception and his heartache. He vowed never to marry. However, for the sake of the clan, he did marry Katherine, paid off all the debts, and is trying to help the clan not only survive, but to prosper."

"That sounds an awful lot like admiration from someone who is supposedly seeking his brother's downfall."

Fingal smiled, but he felt profoundly sad. He had just lost the only thing that ever mattered to him. They both sat silently in contemplation for several minutes. Then Father Colm said, "Based on what Tomas overheard, the conspirator expects he will gain Duncurra for himself, but someone else will kill Niall. Could Laird Matheson be an accomplice?"

"I admit it has been a number of years since I have had any close association with him, but this is completely out of character. He is one of the wealthiest lairds in the Highlands and has never been covetous of others," said Fingal.

"Men do change," offered Father Colm.

"Perhaps, but I can't see what Tadhg could hope to gain by helping someone bring Niall down."

"Then, other than ye, who would have a reason to destroy Laird MacIan? Does he have any enemies?"

"Father, Niall has a temper, but with one notable exception," Fingal said dryly, motioning to himself, "he usually does not release his anger without serious cause. He is a force to be reckoned with, but he is also generally considered to be fair—much more so than our father was."

"Perhaps someone from Katherine's past? A family member or a disappointed suitor?"

Fingal snorted. "Her only family was a merciless uncle who damn near beat her to death, and he made sure she had no suitors."

Father Colm looked askance.

"Tis true. Nay, her uncle benefitted by her marriage to Niall. He was happy enough. Frankly, Katherine lost the most, but there was no one to champion her."

Father Colm nodded, saying, "Fingal, lad, I can understand why the laird thinks ye are behind this. Ye have argued against it being anyone else but ye."

Fingal answered wryly, "Aye, Father, even I am beginning to suspect me. The fact is my brother is a good man, and well respected. The only person I know who neither likes nor respects Niall is my mother."

"If there is so little fondness between them, why did she leave court and return to Duncurra?"

"After Niall resolved all the debt she accrued, he made it clear she was no longer to be extended credit. He gave her an annual stipend on which to live, but she arrived here after spending the lot in a few months."

"Could she be the one behind this?"

"Not alone. She has become very close to Malcolm, and in recent months he has not only stirred discord between us, he has done the same between Niall and Katherine."

"He was here at the Epiphany. It could have been Malcolm who Tomas overheard."

Fingal thought for a moment before saying, "Tomas said one of the people he overheard said something about 'pretending to be something for too long' and he was 'sorry he wouldn't be the one to kill Niall.' That could certainly be Malcolm, if the loving uncle role was just an act. Malcolm could have been behind the raids and the kidnapping. It was his idea to take Katherine to Brathanead in the first place. Instigating a war with Matheson would weaken us sufficiently to allow Malcolm to successfully lay siege to Duncurra, and could certainly get Niall killed."

Fingal rose to his feet, saying, "Holy Mother of God, Niall told the MacLennan messenger he would 'gladly accept the support' Malcolm will send. Niall is only leaving a handful of men here. Malcolm could ride in with an army and be welcomed. I have to find Niall and tell him."

"Wait," cautioned Father Colm, putting a hand on Fingal's shoulder. "Your brother is furious with ye and is not likely to graciously hear accusations against an old and trusted friend."

"Father, I can't let Niall ride off and leave Duncurra vulnerable to a siege."

"Lad, if ye go to him now with these suspicions, he is likely to separate your head from your shoulders before ye can tell him anything. Can ye close Duncurra after he leaves, and defend a siege until he returns?"

"Duncurra can be defended for a short time with a small number of men. Now that Niall doesn't trust me, it is unlikely the men left behind will follow my orders, particularly if they think the arriving army is Niall's ally."

"Is there someone else who ye trust from whom ye can seek help?"

"Laird Chisholm. I could reach his keep in a few hours, but if Niall finds out I've left, he will believe the worst."

"If ye don't, ye risk losing everything ye hold dear."

Fingal knew the old priest was right. In the bustle of activity surrounding the preparations to leave the next morning, as well as the continued effort to bring as many of the clan as possible behind the walls at Duncurra, Fingal slipped out without notice. He rode as fast as was safe in the dark and reached Currancreag, the Chisholm stronghold, shortly after midnight.

Chapter 24

Laird Matheson returned from the hunt in the early evening. They had been successful and he was in a particularly good mood. Looking extremely anxious, Elspet approached him as he entered the courtyard.

"How is our stubborn visitor today?" he asked.

"Laird, I think ye have an unexpected problem on your hands. I tried to find ye so I could tell ye early this morning, but ye had already left."

Tadhg raised an eyebrow at her. "Care to enlighten me now?"

"Why don't men ever stop to think about the consequences of their actions? She is scared and has eaten almost nothing. This kind of upset could be disastrous," she said, wringing her hands.

"Elspet, what are ye talking about?"

"Laird, I suspect your visitor is with child."

Laird Matheson swore loudly and, rubbing his forehead, asked, "What makes ye think that?"

"I helped her bathe last night, and although she is very slender, her belly is rounding. I thought it possible, but this morning she seemed ill and unable to eat, which isn't unusual if she is expecting."

"Damnation. MacIan might kill me. Hell, I'd kill me, if I were him."

"Laird, an upset the likes of this one could cause a lass to miscarry."

"God's mercy, Elspet, I know that."

"Good. I'm glad to see ye are sufficiently worried, because I've done something ye may not like."

"What have ye done?" he asked warily.

"Laird, I know ye ordered me to keep her locked in her chamber unless ye gave permission for her to leave, and I have never defied an order, but I reasoned that when ye gave that order, ye didn't know about her condition. Laird, I was worried about her, and no matter how good your intentions were, if something happens to that lass or her bairn, well, there is no telling what Laird MacIan would do."

"Ye didn't keep her locked up?" Tadhg asked, but the relief was evident in his voice.

"Nay, Laird, I didn't," said Elspet, trying to appear contrite. "But I followed half the order. I told Hamish ye ordered that Lady MacIan should have an escort ere she left her chamber, and he has been by her side all day, as ye required."

"Where is she now?" he asked wearily.

"I thought it best to keep her distracted. She had needlework packed in her bag. I gave her a few things she needed, so she spent most of the day in the great hall working on it. She is clearly uneasy still, but much less so than last night. Laird, she asked to speak with ye as soon as ye returned."

"I will see her now," he said, walking past Elspet to enter the keep. Then stopped and turned back to her. "Elspet, does Hamish know Lady Katherine did not have my permission to leave her chamber?"

"Nay, Laird, I didn't mention that bit. I—ah—only told him ye wished her to be escorted."

Tadhg chuckled, "And so I did."

He continued walking towards the keep but Elspet stopped him again. "There is one more thing ye should know." At his expectant look, she went on, "It's a terrible thing, really. I feel sorry for the wee lass, but while she was bathing last night, I noticed Lady Katherine's back is covered with scars from a whip."

"He beats her?" Tadhg asked, sickened by the thought.

"I couldn't say, Laird. While I don't think anyone has beaten her recently, some of her scars aren't terribly old. I just thought ye should know."

He nodded and continued on into the great hall in search of Lady Katherine. He found her as Elspet had said, sitting by the hearth, her needlework in her hands.

~ * ~

As Laird Matheson approached, Katherine clearly saw the concern in his expression. "My lady, I understand ye wished to speak with me, but I need ask ye something first. Elspet tells me ye have scars on your back. Does MacIan beat ye?"

"Oh, by all the saints, of course not. Niall would never hurt me. My Uncle Ambrose gave me those scars."

"Ambrose Ruthven?"

"Aye."

"If I ever see him again, I may have to kill him."

"Kill him over whipping his niece, who you kidnapped? I think if your house is made of glass, you'd best not throw stones."

Tadhg threw his head back and laughed. "Ye are a feisty bit of goods, my lady."

When he had stopped laughing, Katherine said, "Laird Matheson, I need to talk to you about, this—this whole situation."

"Which situation, specifically?" he asked, sobering. "Your husband's raids on my land, my taking ye as a hostage, or the fact that ye let me lock an expectant mother up like a prisoner?"

Shocked, Katherine snapped her head up at his last comment.

"Elspet is very observant," Tadhg said by way of explanation.

"Well, I am a prisoner, so I don't see how your last point is relevant, and I haven't exactly been locked up, but it is the first two that concern me. Laird Matheson—"

Exasperated he said, "Please, call me Tadhg."

Katherine ignored him and continued, "There is something very wrong. My husband did not instigate the raids on your land. He was only retaliating for raids against us."

"Lass, I know ye would like to believe—"

"Nay, hear me out. He did *not* start the raids. This last one was in response to a brutal attack on our border. The animals weren't stolen, they were slaughtered, dwellings were burned, and three clansmen were killed the day after Epiphany."

"And he thinks I did that?"

"Every indication was that ye did."

"That is ludicrous," he said, his ire rising. "That kind of destruction serves no purpose. He has raided me numerous times over the last year. I didn't retaliate last winter or spring because I had heard of the MacIan's financial troubles. I wasn't going to steal food from their mouths. The fact is, I have only led one raid on MacIan lands and it was this past fall, well after their financial issues had been solved." Tadhg gave her a pointed look and continued, "and they were still raiding my land."

"If ye weren't behind the raids, who was and why?"

"I can only guess someone wanted to provoke your husband into attacking me."

"What would be gained by that?"

"I'm not sure. I can certainly withstand such an attack. The only thing it would really do is weaken the MacIans."

"But Niall knew that. He wasn't considering attacking ye. We received word ye were planning to lay siege to Duncurra."

"That is, without a doubt, the most ridiculous thing I have ever heard. I have no intention of laying siege to Duncurra," Tadhg said vehemently. "I have no interest in Duncurra at all. Who told ye this?"

"Two days ago, Laird MacLennan arrived at Duncurra and told Niall an attack from ye was imminent. He said ye were planning to lay siege close to Candlemas, and convinced Niall I would be safer at Brathanead."

"He said Candlemas? Are ye sure?

"Aye."

"And when did Niall make the decision for ye to travel to Brathanead?"

"Two days ago, when Malcolm came with news of the siege."

"Katherine, I found out more than a week ago ye would be traveling to Brathanead yesterday."

"That is not possible. As I said, Niall only decided after Malcolm came, two days ago. I left with Laird MacLennan yesterday morning. How could ye have known for a week?"

"The wife of one of my clansmen is a MacLennan. She returned from visiting her sister with news that Laird MacLennan was having a huge feast for Candlemas and ye would be accompanying Lady MacIan."

"What? I would not go to Brathanead for a celebration without Niall. In fact, I would never have willingly accompanied Eithne anywhere alone. I didn't want to this time, but Niall insisted because he was afraid for my safety. Malcolm convinced him not to escort me by telling him your attack could come at any time, so he shouldn't risk being away from Duncurra even for a day."

"Well, that was a wise move on Laird MacLennan's part if he wanted me to kidnap ye. I never would have attempted it if Niall and his guard were escorting ye. I have no doubt he would die protecting ye. But, my lady, the MacLennans practically presented ye as a gift."

Katherine frowned at him. "If Niall led an attack on ye, it would leave Duncurra less well protected, wouldn't it?"

"Aye, probably dangerously so."

"Allowing someone else to successfully lay siege?"

"Aye."

"Then it has to be Malcolm at the root of this. He has been behind the raids against us, but he made it look as if it were ye. He has tried over and over to goad Niall into attacking ye, and Niall wouldn't. He knew it would critically weaken him. So Malcolm did the one thing that was sure to cause my husband to attack. He made it easy for ye to capture me. If he could get Niall to attack ye, he can take Duncurra. That explains what Tomas overheard."

"Tomas?"

"Our foster son," said Katherine. She told Tadhg about the whispered conversation in the stairwell. "Niall suspected Fingal. It sounded as if the person talking intended to inherit Duncurra."

"Unless things have changed drastically, Fingal would never have plotted against Niall. Fingal all but worshipped him. Besides, ye are expecting, are ye not?"

"Aye, but at that time we hadn't told anyone yet— Fingal didn't know. It had to be Malcolm, and he meant to seize Duncurra, not inherit it."

As Tadhg processed this information, he realized its full implication. "If Malcolm MacLennan is behind this, the message Niall will receive today is not likely to be the one I sent, asking to discuss a truce. He will ride on Cnocreidh to rescue ye, leaving Duncurra vulnerable."

Katherine went ashen. "Niall is expecting Laird MacLennan to send men to Duncurra. They won't be seen as a threat until it's too late."

Tadhg leapt into action. He called to Hamish, who was in the hall a discreet distance away. He explained the situation and gave orders to prepare a large contingent of men to leave at first light. "Lady Katherine, I have to ride on Duncurra before your husband has the chance to leave."

"But he will think ye are attacking. The battle will be underway before ye can get to him. Even if ye ride under the white flag, I doubt he will believe ye."

"I have to try. I refuse to let MacLennan get away with this," Tadhg said angrily.

"Niall will believe ye if I ride with ye. He will not attack if I am there," Katherine said.

"Absolutely not," Tadhg said, and stalked away to prepare.

God save me from over-protective men. Oh, and while ye are at it, please, God, save them from each other.

Chapter 25

Fingal knew Fearghas Chisholm and his wife Ena had been asleep for hours, but he told the guard this couldn't wait. "Damnation, Andrew, ye know I wouldn't insist on waking Laird Chisholm if it wasn't extremely urgent."

"Fingal, ye are generally level-headed, and the laird and lady are fond of ye, but by all that's holy man, they won't be happy if they find out this could have waited until morning."

"I promise ye, Andrew, it can't wait. I have to talk to the laird right now."

"All right, wait there by the hearth and I will get him."

In just a few minutes, both Fearghas and Ena greeted Fingal in the hall.

"My lady, I am so sorry, ye needn't have come down," Fingal said as she embraced him.

"I tried to tell her morning would be soon enough to greet ye, Fingal, but that battle was lost the moment she heard it was ye."

"If either of ye think I could go back to sleep, worried about what has brought Fingal here in the middle of a bitter winter night, ye are daft."

Fingal smiled at her warmly; she was the closest thing to a real mother he had ever had. "Ye look like the devil has been riding on your heels, lad, what's happened?"

The older couple listened as Fingal laid out the whole story for them. Fearghas agreed it was very unlike Tadhg Matheson to raid without provocation. "Now, I wouldn't put kidnapping a bonny lass past him," Fearghas added with a chuckle.

"I'm not even sure he has Katherine," said Fingal. "If Malcolm is behind this, the abduction could be a ruse as well, simply meant to draw Niall out of Duncurra."

"Ye could be right about it all, lad. Malcolm MacLennan has always been an ambitious man, but not one to take risks. If he had his eyes on Duncurra, he would want to make sure the conquest would be easy."

"Fingal *could* be right? Do you doubt him at all? Malcolm MacLennan has never been trustworthy, and neither has Eithne" said Ena indignantly.

"Ena," Fearghas said, "Don't start that, she is the lad's mother, after all."

"He may as well know, Fearghas." Fearghas shook his head in resignation as Ena continued, "Ye know Eithne was married to one of Fearghas' younger brothers and she lived here after her husband died in battle."

"Aye, I remember, ye told me that when I was a lad."

"Well, she was the most unpleasant, demanding, and embarrassingly indiscreet woman I had ever had to deal with. She threw herself at any man who would have her, regardless of whether he was married or not. She even flirted shamelessly with Fearghas. It doesn't surprise me she has her eyes on Malcolm MacLennan now. She cozied up to him any chance she could, even back then. He was married, but I wouldn't have put it past him to take what she offered. I think the only thing she really wanted was to be a laird's wife. As soon as she heard Beitris had died, she hounded Fearghas mercilessly to arrange a marriage with your da. Alastair was distraught, he wanted a mother for Niall, and he agreed to it. I have to admit I was glad to be rid of her."

"Ena, that is water under the bridge."

"Nay, it isn't, Fearghas. She's a scheming hag, and if she has her claws in Malcolm again, there is no telling what she's up to." At Fearghas' skeptical expression, Ena added, "Surely ye don't think Fingal is behind this?"

"Nay, my love," said Fearghas, "I know Fingal would never do this. Fingal, ye say the raids began before your father died?"

"Aye, they did."

"But ye were still living here, son. Ye didn't return to Duncurra until after his death. Surely Niall must realize it can't have been ye."

"Actually, Laird, I think that is precisely why he thinks I'm behind it. He knows Tadhg and I were friends, and suspects I cooked up the whole scheme with him." Fingal looked at his hands, unable to look Fearghas in the eye when he said, "It pains me to admit this, but I think that is why he requested I come home and join his guard. I suspect it had more to do with his wanting to keep an eye on me than any skill he thought I had."

Ena looked distraught. "Oh Fingal, ye mustn't believe that. Ye trained harder than any lad ever fostered here. Ye were smart and skilled, but ye were never arrogant. Until ye, I had never seen a lad who could best someone while sparring and still leave his pride intact. I always suspected ye remained humble because ye continually compared yourself to Niall and felt ye came up short. But ye are a fine man and a skilled warrior, never doubt that. Niall may be too hard-headed to see another explanation now, but when ye hold Duncurra for him with Chisholm warriors, he will see his little brother is a man to be reckoned with."

Fingal smiled at her, but Fearghas looked annoyed.

"Ye can remove that indignant look from your face right now, Fearghas Chisholm, ye know full well ye're planning to send him back with an army," she said, daring him with her eyes to challenge her. When he just smiled and raised his hands in surrender, she said to Fingal, "Try to get some sleep lad, I suspect ye will be leaving at first light." She rose and left the hall.

Fearghas chuckled after she was out of earshot and said, "Of course ye will return to Duncurra tomorrow at first light with Chisholm soldiers, but I suspect if I hadn't offered, my little Ena would be leading the troops."

Chapter 26

Try as she might, Katherine had not been able to convince Laird Matheson to let her ride with his army towards Duncurra.

"Laird Matheson—"

"Tadhg."

"Ye must let me ride with ye."

"I've told ye, it's too dangerous. I'm hoping we can reach Duncurra before Niall leaves it defenseless."

"Ye know that isn't going to happen. If Niall received word yesterday that I was kidnapped, and I am sure he did, it is likely he is already on his way to Cnocreidh."

"We will be riding under a white flag."

"Laird, I don't think that will matter. He will be furious."

"All the more reason for ye to stay safely here."

"But ye don't understand—"

"I understand perfectly. Now go rest, or I will lock ye up again."

Frustrated, Katherine went to her chamber as ordered, but she could not sleep. Just before dawn, she made one last attempt. She found Laird Matheson in the stable with Hamish and several of his other men, saddling their mounts. He arched a brow at her and said, "I am fairly certain I told ye to stay in the keep. Ye are as hard-headed as your husband."

"Aye, I am," she agreed, "that's why I'm here. Ye must take me with you."

"We've been through this. I told ye, we will be riding under a white flag."

"But what if he doesn't see it, or he's so angry he ignores it?"

"I have considered that. I sent scouts ahead to confirm Niall's movements. If they learn that he rides on Cnocreidh as expected, my men and I will take up a position on a stretch of moorland he will need to cross. The open ground will give him plenty of opportunity to see the white flag."

"Surely ye realize, believing what he does, Niall will not wait to hear ye out. Nothing short of seeing me well and unharmed will soothe his ire long enough to get him to listen. Even then he won't believe ye, unless I tell him what happened. He trusts Malcolm. Please listen to me. It would be tragic, if after all this, Malcolm wins because ye are forced to destroy the MacIan army." Katherine didn't completely believe Tadhg would be the victor, but she knew regardless of who won the day, a battle would leave MacIan men dead and weaken the clan.

"Lass, what ye describe could happen even if ye are there, and ye could be injured or killed in the melee."

Then Katherine did something she had avoided ever since her father died. She burst into tears in front of him and all the other men in the stable.

"Och, lass, don't cry." Tadhg resisted the urge to pull her into his arms, but he took her hands in his and said, "Please, don't work yourself up over this. Everything will be all right."

"Nay, it won't," Katherine sobbed. "Why can't ye be reasonable? Ye are likely to kill my husband today, and I can't bear the thought of it."

"Wheesht, calm yourself, lass. It isn't good for ye to get so upset with a bairn on the way."

"Tadhg," she implored, using his Christian name for the first time, "please take me with ye. Let me try to prevent a battle."

Tadhg looked completely at a loss. Evidently, he had no idea how to deal with a weeping woman. Katherine saw him catch Hamish's eye, silently imploring him for help. Hamish grinned and shook his head, "Laird, I hate to disappoint ye, but I think Lady Katherine may be right. The sight of her may be the only thing will hold Laird MacIan's temper in check long enough to listen to reason."

"But look at her. She is exhausted, she won't eat, and she is expecting his child. The sight of her could be enough to incite murder."

"That may be, Laird, but she'll look no better if you don't stop her tears."

Tadhg's shoulders sagged and she knew she had won.

"Wheesht, lass, I'll let ye go with us." Katherine struggled to regain control, and when her tears had quieted, he said, "Ye can go, but ye will do what ye're told. If things get out of hand, I need to know ye'll be safe." She nodded. "Go, get your things, then."

~ * ~

After she left the stable he looked at Hamish and said, "That was a useless warning, wasn't it."

"Aye, Laird, I fear it was."

"God save me if anything happens to her."

When they were ready to leave, he assigned eight men to guard her, knowing that, unlike the MacLennans, his men would guard her with their lives. As the first light of dawn pinked the horizon, the Matheson army rode east with their laird and Katherine MacIan in the lead.

~ * ~

As dawn broke, Fingal MacIan and Fearghas Chisholm led the Chisholm army west towards Duncurra. Fingal hoped to reach Duncurra and secure it before Malcolm arrived. He would prefer to take up a defensive position within Duncurra, rather than battle MacLennan in the open, but he feared he might not be welcomed or believed.

~ * ~

Niall and the bulk of his army left Duncurra at dawn heading west towards Cnocreidh. His fury was boundless but Father Colm had been right, he was angriest at himself. How could he have let her ride away from Duncurra without his protection? He would rescue her, he would kill Tadhg Matheson, and he would send as many Matheson clansmen to hell today as was humanly possible.

~ * ~

As morning dawned, confident of an easy victory, Malcolm MacLennan positioned his army at the MacIan border. They were prepared to ride as soon as he was sure Niall had departed for Cnocreidh. Malcolm fully believed his army would not do battle today. Convinced he would be welcomed at Duncurra, he believed he would secure it as his own before clan MacIan became fully aware of what had happened. The news that Niall suspected Fingal to be the traitor absolutely thrilled him. Fingal's presence at Duncurra would not be a problem at all. The entire plan unfolded almost more smoothly than he expected. However, he left nothing to chance. He would not allow victory to slip from him because of an unforeseen circumstance.

Chapter 27

Cairbre remained at Duncurra with a handful of men to secure it. Midmorning, he received word from the watch that an army under the MacLennan banner approached from the south. He expected reinforcements from the MacLennan's, but he was a bit surprised at the early hour. Malcolm must have sent them at least part of the way yesterday. It relieved Cairbre to know Duncurra's additional protection would arrive soon.

That relief didn't last long because moments later, the watch informed him an army also approached from the east riding hard under the Chisholm banner. Could he have been so wrong about Fingal? He hadn't seen the laird's brother all morning, and assumed Fingal was in his chamber. Cairbre sent for him, determined to discover what treachery was behind this. When the servant returned, it was Father Colm rather than Fingal who accompanied him.

"Father, ye cannot protect him this time. Niall was right, Fingal has to be responsible for this. With the bulk of our army riding on Cnocreidh, Duncurra is vulnerable and the Chisholm army approaches from the east. I will kill him where he stands before I let him wrest control of clan MacIan and Duncurra from Niall's hands."

"Cairbre, ye are wrong about Fingal."

"Are ye telling me the Chisholm army riding full out towards us is a figment of my imagination? Or perhaps Chisholm just happens to be paying a friendly visit with his full garrison?"

"I'm not telling ye either of those things. In fact, I suspect Fingal is at the head of the Chisholm army, as that is where he was going last night. However, he is not preparing to seize Duncurra, but rather to defend it."

"Are ye daft, old man? Defend it against whom?"

"The MacLennan army, whom I believe also approaches."

Father Colm proceeded to tell Cairbre what he and Fingal had discussed last night. "Cairbre, ye know in your heart Fingal is not a traitor; he is devoted to his brother. Ye have defended him time and time again to Laird MacIan. Laird MacLennan, on the other hand, seizes every opportunity to create discord. Think back to Childermas, man. He and Lady MacIan gained obscene pleasure in upsetting Lady Katherine and scaring young Tomas. Most scoundrels have no difficulty dissembling with their peers, but it's harder to conceal their true nature when they deal with those over whom they have power. The urge to feel that power is too great."

Cairbre knew Father Colm's insight into human nature was accurate, and he wanted to believe Fingal was loyal, but what would the cost be if he was wrong? "Father, if ye are wrong, and I open Duncurra to Chisholm, Fingal will seize it."

"Cairbre, if ye are wrong and ye open Duncurra to MacLennan, Malcolm will seize it. Who do ye trust more?"

"I trust Fingal, but my laird, to whom I have sworn fealty, does not."

"Then open Duncurra to neither, and the truth will out. If neither of them intends to conquer Duncurra, there will be no battle."

Cairbre saw the wisdom in this and told the few men-at-arms left not to open the gates to anyone. Both armies continued to approach, but the Chisholm army reached Duncurra first. From the wall, Cairbre called to Fingal, "I won't open Duncurra to ye, Fingal."

"I didn't think ye would. I'm not here to lay siege to my home, Cairbre, but I believe that is Laird MacLennan's intent."

"I won't be opening Duncurra to him, either. Father Colm told me of your suspicions. I don't know whom to believe, so I will take no chances."

"Then that will be enough for getting on with. Laird Chisholm and I will not allow Malcolm to approach, but neither will we attack. I only mean to defend Duncurra until Niall returns."

Fearghas directed his men to create a defensive line from the bottom of the crag on which Duncurra stood, extending westward.

~ * ~

So confident he would be able to ride into Duncurra unopposed, Malcolm allowed Eithne to ride at his side. Baffled by the appearance of an army between him and his prize, he took a few appropriate precautions before drawing too close. His messenger assured him Niall had ridden on Cnocreidh at first light, so this could not be his army. It didn't take long for him to recognize Chisholm's banner and he halted his men.

"What is the meaning of this?" demanded Eithne. "Who dares prevent me from entering my home?"

Malcolm cast a baleful glance at her and said, "There is no audience for your act here, Eithne. Ye have never considered Duncurra your home. Ye have spent more of your time at court or in my bed than ye ever did here. Your designs on it have only ever been driven by spite."

"And yours are driven by greed, my love, but spite and greed make excellent bedfellows."

Malcolm chuckled, "Ye are ruthless, my dear. Niall's only crime against ye was being born first."

"Until he left me destitute in Edinburgh."

"That's a bit of an exaggeration, wouldn't ye say? Twas nearly the other way round. Ye tucked Alastair's money away for years, creating crushing debt instead."

"I had to build my own wealth. Otherwise Alastair could have forced me to return to the Highlands whenever he wished, just to save a few coins. You wouldn't have had me in your bed then. Not to mention the fact that you needed to weaken them in order to successfully lay siege."

"Aye, that I did. It almost worked, but who would have thought King David capable of finding Niall a copper? I should have married that rich bit of goods myself."

"What of me, then?"

"Don't pout, it doesn't become ye. Besides, marriage has never been an obstacle to either of us. No matter, it will be resolved soon. His bonny heiress has become a greater weakness than any I could have hoped for."

"Aye, with Niall chasing after the bitch, we should have been able to ride into Duncurra unhindered. What will you do now?"

"Never fear, my devious little vixen. All may not be lost. Do ye see who is riding with Fearghas?"

"Why, it is my own dear son, Fingal. What makes you think he will be of any help? He has had his head up Niall's arse from the time he could toddle."

"Aye, but darling, just as I planned, Niall believes all his recent ills can be laid squarely at Fingal's feet. My messenger said Niall was ready to kill him last night. Hopefully, he injured Fingal's pride enough to finally dim his radiance in Fingal's eyes. Perhaps the lad can be tempted now. I think it is time we had a chat with him."

A sly smile spread slowly across Eithne's face. "You could be right, my love. He stands ultimately to gain both Duncurra and Brathanead by joining us. How could he not choose that over being second to a brother who hates him?"

~ * ~

Fingal and Fearghas watched Malcolm's army halt well to the south, on the western shore of Loch Craos. "It looks like we have spoiled Malcolm's plans. I suspect the cur is too cowardly to actually fight for something he wants," observed Fearghas.

When the MacLennan army made no further moves, Fearghas chuckled. "I wonder how long he will sit there until he turns tail and runs."

Then they saw two riders break away from the stationary army and ride towards them. "Who is riding with Malcolm?" asked Fearghas.

"Damnation," swore Fingal. "I suspect it is my mother."

Fingal rode out to meet them in the open area between the two armies.

Eithne said sweetly, "Fingal, dear, what are you doing? Niall asked Malcolm to come to his aid. Surely you know that. Have Laird Chisholm's army stand down and we can discuss this in Duncurra."

"Duncurra is closed to all of us, Mother." Fingal turned to Malcolm, "Ye are looking well, Malcolm. Ye seem to have recovered quickly from the grave injury ye received at Matheson's hand." Fingal shook his head in disgust. "Niall trusted ye above anyone else. How could ye betray him?"

"I did it for ye and your mother, Fingal."

"For me and my mother? You're not serious." Turning to his mother, he said, "What were ye thinking, Mother? Did ye believe if ye got Niall out of the way, ye could manipulate me more easily than ye did him or Father?"

"Fingal, you wound me. I only want the best for you, and it is time you knew the truth. Alastair was not your father, Malcolm is."

"The hell he is!"

"Darling, it is true. Malcolm and I met before I married Alastair. He and his wife were guests at Currancreag. He felt trapped in a loveless marriage, and I missed my husband so desperately. We didn't intend for it to happen, but in a moment of indiscretion, we turned to each other for comfort."

Fingal snorted. "Comfort? Is that what ye call it? I guess one woman's comfort is another woman's adultery."

Ignoring his comment, Eithne went on, "In just two weeks I suspected I was carrying. Malcolm and I loved each other, but he was already married. I talked Fearghas into arranging a marriage to Alastair. Neither of them knew."

"Stop your lies, Mother."

"These are not lies, Fingal. You need only peer into a looking glass to see how like Malcolm you are. He knew the first time he saw you as a boy. I feared others would notice it as you grew, but no one at Duncurra ever guessed Alastair wasn't your father."

"That is because he was my father," Fingal ground out angrily.

"Alastair may have raised ye, Fingal, but I am your father. That is one reason why I spent so much time at Duncurra. I knew I couldn't claim ye, but I wanted to know my son. When it came time for ye to begin training, I asked Alastair to send ye to me, but Niall had trained under my father and Alastair said he wanted to send ye to Laird Chisholm. Your mother, after all, was a Chisholm. Now Alastair is gone, I can claim ye and name ye as my heir. Not only can all of my holdings be yours, but Duncurra and all of the MacIan's new wealth as well."

Fingal just stared at Malcolm, marshaling his emotions. He knew this was not a ruse. Why had he never noticed the similarities he bore to Malcolm? They seemed plainly evident now. He asked, "Does anyone else know ye fathered me?"

Fingal noticed how pleased Malcolm looked. *Does he think I'm tempted by this offer?*

"A few of my clansmen know, and many more suspect it. Son, we can do this together. Ye can explain to Fearghas ye made a mistake and send his army back. Ye and I can walk into Duncurra, unchallenged. It will be yours with neither of us having to shed a drop of blood. Matheson has Niall outmanned, but even if Niall isn't killed, when he returns, he will not prevail against my army with the remnant he'll have left. He will have to lay siege to the fortress he so diligently prepared."

Fingal remained very calm as he heard Malcolm's plan. "Ye have been working toward this for a long time, have ye not? Ye were responsible for the raids last spring?" Fingal asked blandly.

"Aye, I had hoped to heat up the old feud between the Mathesons and the MacIans. Unfortunately Tadhg Matheson is not as fractious as his father was. He picked an inconvenient time to become a bloody black friar, so I had to keep raiding. Nothing seemed to draw Niall out, not even the destruction my men wrought after Epiphany."

"So it was ye Tomas heard." Fingal thought carefully about his next move for a moment. "It was rather clever of ye to arrange for Matheson to kidnap Katherine."

"I realized she was Niall's weakness. It is funny, really; he always scoffed at men who professed to love their wives. He said it made them weak, it was one reason he shunned marriage. Well, it might not make them weak, but it certainly does give an enemy a target. I realized nothing short of fear for his little heiress was going to draw Niall into battle, and I needed him to leave Duncurra with the most of his men."

"I can understand how ye managed to pull off the raids. That wouldn't have been too difficult. I don't understand how ye managed to get Matheson's help with the abduction. I didn't know ye were particularly close with him."

"Fingal, my son, Matheson was completely unaware of his role in this." Malcolm chuckled maliciously.

"So he didn't kidnap Katherine? Ye still have her?"

"Nay, for once Matheson took the bait, but his intention was only to use her as leverage to negotiate a treaty. Good men are predictable and they're so easy to manipulate, especially when they think the cause is noble. Of course, I would have faked the kidnapping if it had been necessary. However, once under attack, it might not have taken Matheson long to convince Niall he didn't have her. I really need Matheson to inflict serious damage on Niall's army, and Niall himself, if that is possible."

"I see, so Matheson still has her. Do ye know if she is safe?"

Malcolm grinned slyly. "Fingal, are ye concerned for the lass? She is a pretty thing. Do ye want her, son? We can arrange that. She is carrying Niall's brat, but your mother knows ways to scathe the baby away."

The statement sickened Fingal as many things suddenly became clear, but he needed one more piece of information. "Niall thinks I'm behind all this. Ye would not have had an heir if he had killed me yesterday as he wanted to."

"I did want Niall to believe it was ye, but I knew he would never kill ye. He thinks ye are his brother. As I said, good men are predictable, but I also knew he would not take a traitor into battle with him. I wanted ye to be safe at Duncurra when I arrived." Malcolm chuckled. "Although I didn't think ye would have raised an army against me."

"Ye didn't?" asked Fingal mildly. "I was the one Niall blamed, but I knew I had done nothing. As you predicted, Niall confined me to the keep, so I had plenty of time to think through all that was happening. Did ye think I wasn't smart enough to figure this out, or did ye think I wouldn't have the initiative to do anything about it?"

Malcolm looked slightly puzzled.

"Oh, I see, ye thought I was as faithless as the woman who spawned me, and would willingly betray loved ones." Fingal finally let the rage he felt show. "Ye were wrong, Laird MacLennan. In this case, the apple has fallen far from the tree—both trees it would seem."

"Fingal, my son, ye misunderstand—"

"No, Laird, ye misunderstand! Tis my misfortune your seed resulted in my birth, but my father was Alastair MacIan and my brother is Laird Niall MacIan and it is to him I have sworn my fealty. I want no part of ye or your craven scheme."

He started to turn his mount away, but stopped and warned, "If your army continues to approach Duncurra, ye will be driven back and I will pierce your black heart myself if need be." Then Fingal turned and galloped back to the Chisholm army, leaving Malcolm and Eithne astonished and staring.

Chapter 28

When Niall's army neared Matheson land, they found the Matheson army had assumed a stationary position on the western edge of a stretch of the moorland that straddled their border. The MacIan army rode hard across the heath, prepared for battle, when Niall saw Katherine, surrounded by Matheson guards at the forefront. He signaled for his men to halt. "What in the hell is he doing?" Niall roared, "Is he trying to get her killed?"

As they reined their horses in, some distance away from the Matheson's position, Diarmad saw the white flag. "Laird, they appear to be surrendering, do ye see the flag?"

"It has to be a trick. This is the bastard who slaughtered animals and burned buildings. He is capable of hiding behind a white flag, or even a woman, it seems."

"I don't think this is a trap, Laird. Matheson's warriors surround Lady Katherine, but Tadhg Matheson is in the open, well away from his men. Ye could kill him before they ever reached ye. Perhaps ye should move closer and see what he wants."

Although terrified for Katherine's safety, he knew Diarmad was right. He also knew Matheson could have Katherine killed before his eyes, and he would be too far away to reach her. There was nothing else to do; he had to ride forward and talk to the bastard. "Diarmad, ye are in command until I return. If I give the signal, show no mercy."

Niall rode forward and stopped his mount about twenty paces from where Tadhg Matheson sat on his horse, well in front of Katherine and her guard. "What is the meaning of this, Matheson? It isn't enough ye take my wife, and slaughtered her MacLennan guard, now ye hide behind her skirts?"

"Slaughtered? MacIan, ye have been woefully misinformed. Laird MacLennan was nowhere in sight, and the six knaves who were supposedly guarding her practically handed her to me without raising a blade. The most impressive resistance came from the lass herself. The worst I did to her guard was leave them trussed on the road, and steal their horses."

"Why are ye lying about this? I received a message from Malcolm yesterday saying most of his men were killed, and he himself was gravely injured."

"Laird, ye have been deceived and I suspect Laird MacLennan is behind it. If your army will stand down, I will let Katherine come forward and she can tell ye herself."

"*Ye* will let her come forward? She is *my wife*, ye bastard," Niall roared.

"And she is as stubborn as ye are, which is why she is here, against my better judgment. However, unlike the MacLennans, my guard have sworn to protect her with their lives, and until I am sure your hot temper is not going start a war in which she could be injured, she will stay where she is."

Niall could not believe what he was hearing. Matheson was protecting Katherine from him! "Fine," Niall ground out. He signaled for his men to stand down and dismounted. A very small part of him was grateful Tadhg appeared to be protecting her, but only a very small part.

Tadhg also signaled for his men to stand down, dismounted, and motioned for the guard to bring Katherine forward. Katherine flew off Eachann's back and into Niall's arms in a flash.

After the message he had received from Malcolm, Niall had imagined the worst. "Katherine, are ye all right? I swear I will kill him now if he hurt ye."

"I'm fine, Niall. Laird Matheson has treated me as a guest. But there is no time to waste. Ye must listen, love, what he said was true. Malcolm abandoned me, and my guard simply surrendered. It was as if they expected an ambush, and I suspect they did." As quickly as she could, Katherine explained what she and Tadhg had pieced together.

After hearing it all, Niall said, "Katherine, ye are accusing Malcolm of the unthinkable. He is a trusted friend and ally. Ye would have me believe these heinous accusations because Matheson, the man who kidnapped ye, said he didn't lead the raids on my land? He could have as easily made up the story of how he knew ye would be traveling to Brathanead."

In a gentler voice, he added, "Ye look for the best in people, sweetling, and are too willing to trust. That was my father's downfall—he trusted Eithne and she nearly ruined us. Why can't ye see Fingal is behind this? He is in league with this devil." Niall glared at Tadhg. "Matheson will see us both dead and Fingal as Laird MacIan."

"If that were the case, Niall, why would he have met ye here, in the open? He could have stayed behind the walls at Cnocreidh and let ye lay siege until he decimated your forces. I know as well as ye do ye would never have given up as long as ye thought ye had a chance to rescue me. As to killing me, he certainly didn't have to bring me here to see that done. Ye are as guilty of blind trust as ye say I am. Ye may believe all of the rest of this is conjecture, but here is a fact no one can deny. I witnessed it. The man ye trusted to guard me, the man ye believed to be your most faithful ally, abandoned me and apparently lied to ye about it."

"Why would he do that, Katherine?" Niall asked, sounding irritated. "What could he hope to gain?"

"Duncurra," she answered, exasperated. "I suspect he thought to fatally weaken ye with the raids last spring. Malcolm and Eithne are an unholy pair, and I wouldn't be surprised if the financial ruin she nearly achieved was part of the plan. If that had gone on unchecked, Malcolm could have taken Duncurra by now with an army of squires. Instead, he had to ensure ye would retaliate against Matheson with a sufficient enough force to leave Duncurra vulnerable. The raids have become increasingly more brutal, Malcolm was goading ye to do this."

"But Malcolm didn't kidnap ye."

"Nay, he just laid the groundwork for someone else to. Malcolm intended to draw ye and your army out of Duncurra. Niall, don't ye see, Duncurra can be held for quite a while with a small number of men, but not if the approaching army is expected to be there as reinforcement."

The realization hit Niall like a rock fall. Tadhg, who had been standing to one side, cautiously watching the exchange, said, "Niall, I swear to ye, by all the angels and saints, I led one raid on your holding last fall in retaliation for your many raids on mine, and I abducted your wife to force ye into negotiating a truce. I fear the man who is responsible for this may already be in control of Duncurra but, if ye are willing, I will lend ye the support of my army to reclaim it."

Niall considered the offer for a moment. This, too, could be a trick to ensure the Mathesons surrounded and destroyed his army. However, Katherine was right, Tadhg could have achieved that, with much less damage to his own army, if he had simply stayed at Cnocreidh. Finally, Niall extended his arm and said, "I would be grateful for your support." He added, "But make no mistake, Matheson, I haven't forgiven ye for abducting my wife."

Tadhg gripped his forearm, grinned, and said, "I didn't expect ye had. However, speaking of your wife, perhaps it would be best to send her back to Cnocreidh now until Duncurra is secured."

Niall agreed, but Katherine refused. "I will *not* go back to Cnocreidh. My place is with ye."

"Katherine, we are going into battle, it would be folly for ye to be there. Ye could be killed," he said as he pulled her into an embrace.

"Nay, Niall. Nay," she said, and beat her fists against his chest. "I didn't want ye to send me away to Brathanead, and look what happened. I will be safe with ye."

"Katherine, I was wrong to send ye away and I am sorry, but I will not allow ye to return to Duncurra until I am sure it is safe."

"Ye'll send an excessively large number of men to guard me, anyway. I can stay well to the rear of any battle, miles back if ye choose, but please don't send me away."

Niall considered her plea for a moment. Truthfully, he didn't want her out of his sight ever again, but this was just too dangerous. He had no idea what they would find when they reached Duncurra. "Nay, Katherine, I will come for ye as soon as it is safe. Ye will go back to Cnocreidh now." Although his voice was gentle, it brooked no further argument.

Angry and frustrated, Katherine once again had no choice. She mounted Eachann and headed back to the Matheson stronghold, accompanied by Tadhg's commander, Hamish, seven other Matheson warriors, and four of Niall's elite guard, Muir, Turcuil, Rab-the-red, and Keavy.

"Does she ever just do what she is told?" asked Tadhg.

"Gave ye trouble, did she?" responded Niall with a chuckle. "Good for her."

With Katherine headed to safety, Niall and Tadhg turned their armies toward Duncurra.

Chapter 29

"He's a romantic fool," said Malcolm sadly as he watched his son ride back to the Chisholm army.

"He's a lapdog," said Eithne with disdain. "Every time he's kicked, he slinks back to Niall."

Malcolm leveled an angry stare at her. "And yet ye have gotten in your fair share of kicks, but he doesn't show ye that same devotion. Perhaps he sees nothing in ye worth slinking back to."

Eithne sneered at him. "Well, that is at least one similarity he doesn't share with his father."

"Ye need to guard your tongue, woman. If things don't go well for us today, I suspect ye will be banished from Duncurra, and would therefore be well advised not to bite the only hand left to feed ye."

"If things don't go well? Have we not already failed?"

"Not entirely, my dear. Victory will be a bit more difficult, but it is still within our grasp." With that Malcolm turned his horse and headed back to his men.

Eithne followed him. "You are going to do battle with Chisholm?"

"Well, I have no intention of leading the charge, but aye, I have an army here, and I intend to take Duncurra very soon."

"Then what are you waiting for? Order the attack and let's get this over with."

"Eithne, my love, I believe in having contingencies. I had hoped it wouldn't be necessary to use them, but as soon as I realized the Chisholm army approached, I sent a large number of my men into the forest on the east side of Loch Craos. It was partially to prevent Chisholm from knowing just how large a force I brought. But also, if a battle became necessary, my men there could approach from the other side, effectively surrounding Chisholm. I can destroy him. I just need to give my men enough time to get into place."

"And what if Niall returns before they do?"

"That will not happen. Ye continue to underestimate me. I also sent Duncan with a contingent of men into position near Cnocreidh yesterday. Once Niall has had the chance to get there and lay siege, my men will move in and take up positions well behind him. If Niall appears to be making any gains, they will attack. If he retreats, they will do away with whatever is left of his army. Either way, my dear, before the end of the day, Niall will no longer be an obstacle."

"And what if Niall happens upon them himself before reaching Cnocreidh?"

"Naturally, he will think I sent them there to support him," Malcolm said with a malevolent sneer.

~ * ~

When Fingal returned, Fearghas asked, "What's wrong? Ye look defeated. What did they tell you, lad?"

"It is as we suspected. Malcolm intends to take Duncurra. He planned to stroll in as an ally and simply seize control."

"He admitted this to ye?" asked Fearghas, looking astonished.

"Aye. He told me the entire plan. Lady Chisholm was right; he and Eithne have been plotting this for some time. They mistakenly believed I would join them."

"Because Eithne is your mother? Are they daft? Do they not recognize your devotion to your brother?"

"It seems that Niall is not my brother."

Fearghas looked at Fingal askance.

"Apparently, Malcolm is my father. Eithne was already carrying when she married Laird MacIan. They did all of this for me," Fingal said bitterly. "Niall was right, it is my fault."

"Don't be an idiot! If anyone is to blame, it is I. I should have known that conniving bitch was up to something when she pushed me to arrange the marriage. But I'm not sorry I did. Ye are the man ye are now solely because Alastair MacIan raised ye. Make no mistake, lad, ye are his son, regardless of what man that tart spread her legs for first."

"But the destruction they have wrought was for me," said Fingal in anguish.

"If ye believe that, ye are the daft one. Ye had nothing to do with this. This is about what they want. If this was truly all for ye, Malcolm should be turning his army home now ye have refused to be a part of it. Greed is the only thing that drives him, not paternal devotion. Given the chance, he would run ye through today regardless of whose son ye are, if it was the only way to achieve his goal. I'm not sure why he waits to attack, but I have no doubt he will, and probably very soon."

~ * ~

Malcolm didn't wait much longer. Just before midday, he ordered the attack to begin. From the rear he watched the battle with some dismay. The Chisholm warriors were fierce and highly skilled. Although Malcolm had superior numbers, he was losing men quickly. Then he saw something which caused him to doubt his ability to win the day. The men he sent around the loch had arrived as planned. However, Niall's army, reinforced by Matheson, approached from the west. Now, not only were his opponents more skilled, his army was also seriously outnumbered.

Malcolm did not know what could have happened. Niall should have just been reaching Cnocreidh and yet here he was with Tadhg Matheson at his side. Now it seemed not only would he not be victorious, he stood to lose the entire force currently in battle. If he ordered a retreat now, Niall would pursue him. He risked not being able to make good his own escape.

~ * ~

Niall wasn't sure what he expected to find when he reached Duncurra, but perhaps the last thing he imagined was Laird Chisholm's army defending it.

"It looks like your baby brother has your back after all," Tadhg said, his face splitting into a grin.

"If ye would stop patting yourself on the shoulder for a moment, ye would realized they are about to be surrounded," Niall growled, pointing to the MacLennan men approaching from the east.

Once the Matheson and MacIan armies joined the fray, however, the battle ended quickly. A small number of MacLennans turned tail as soon as they realized their laird had retreated, but many others died or fell wounded. When the battle was over, Niall ordered Duncurra opened so the injured could receive treatment. Then he found Fingal and Fearghas Chisholm. Gripping Fearghas' forearm, he said, "Laird Chisholm, thank ye for defending Duncurra. I will never be able to repay ye."

"I trust ye will do the same for me if I ever need ye," Fearghas replied.

Then Niall turned to face Fingal. He had spent much of the ride back wondering what he would say to his brother. He felt he had no right even to ask for Fingal's forgiveness. Finding Fingal defending Duncurra in spite of everything was humbling.

"Fingal, I am sorry. Ye have never once given me a reason not to trust ye, and rather than rely on that fact, I have listened to barbs and innuendos from people whom I had good reasons not to trust. I fear in my blindness, I have lost something of great value—the love and respect of my brother. Please forgive me."

Fingal smiled, but there seemed to be a deep sadness behind the smile. He said, "There is nothing to forgive. Malcolm and Eithne have been practicing deceit for so long, they have become masters. I have only just learned the true depths of their treachery today. As fate would have it, I am not truly your brother after all."

"Fingal, of course ye are my brother. What are ye talking about?"

With a sad shake of his head, Fingal explained. "Apparently, Eithne was pregnant by Malcolm when she married your father. I am ashamed to say everything that has happened was their attempt to wrest control of Duncurra and Clan MacIan from ye. Malcolm's primary goal was to expand his own power, and ultimately to pass it all on to me as his heir. To make matters even worse, my father revealed the true depths of his cowardice by fleeing and leaving his men to die as he escaped."

"He is not among the dead?" asked Niall.

"He never entered the battle," replied Fingal in disgusted. "He held a position at the rear of his men, surrounded by a handful of guards. Shortly after ye and Matheson arrived, he escaped without ordering a retreat. I intended to follow him, but by the time I fought through, he was long gone."

Laird Chisholm said, "I think we should run the cur to ground and finish this today."

Niall answered, "There is nothing I would like more. It is not wise to let him reach Brathanead. Select the men ye wish to take and we will leave immediately."

As Fingal prepared to join them, Niall pulled him aside and said, "Fingal, I think ye should stay here." At the pained look on Fingal's face, Niall added, "It isn't what ye think. I will never again question your loyalty, and I know ye want vengeance. However, I don't think ye should be put into the position of possibly having to kill the man who sired ye."

"Niall, he deserves to die, even if only for abandoning his own men today."

"I agree, but still, no man should have to carry that on his conscience, justified or not. Let me do this. Stay and see to things here for me."

Fingal reluctantly agreed. Within minutes, Lairds MacIan, Chisholm, and Matheson, with warriors from all three clans, headed south toward the MacLennan border.

~ * ~

Katherine and her escort were only a few miles away from Cnocreidh when Hamish reined in on the edge of a clearing and motioned to Muir. After a quick discussion with Hamish, Muir came to her and said quietly, "My lady, I don't wish to worry ye; however, there appear to be a large number of men on horseback in the woods beyond the clearing. We can hear them, and Hamish doesn't know who they might be or why they are here. Until we know differently, we can only assume they are a threat, perhaps sent by Laird MacLennan, but we don't think they have seen us yet."

"We are going to backtrack with ye and avoid them by circling to the north. Stay as quiet as ye possibly can and, if we are attacked, ye must not leave my side unless I tell ye differently. Do ye understand?"

Katherine nodded.

They quietly retreated a safe distance, and skirted around the threat, reaching the edge of the forest on the northeast side of Cnocreidh.

Before they entered into the open land surrounding the castle, Muir said, "We think we have avoided them, but if we are attacked as we move into the open, ye ride with Hamish as hard as ye can toward the keep. He will see it opened to ye, and the rest of us will protect your back.

They had barely entered the open area when a group of at least two score and ten men swarmed out of the forest to the east of Cnocreidh. As Muir instructed, Katherine rode hard toward the keep with Hamish at her side. They had barely covered a quarter of the distance when Hamish's horse took an arrow to his chest and crumpled under him. Katherine stopped to reach a hand to Hamish, but he slapped Eachann's rump, forcing the horse back into a run toward the castle. However, that momentary pause was enough time for Duncan, who had separated himself from the battle, to reach her. He pulled her onto his horse and rode full speed toward the forest. Before he reached the forest with her, Katherine was able to twist in his arms enough to see her escorts were holding their own, joined by warriors pouring out of Cnocreidh. Duncan crushed her against his chest and pushed her forward, leaning low over the horse's neck to avoid the branches. He held her so tightly she could barely breathe. She wanted to fight, but knew if she fell from the horse at the breakneck speed they were riding, she could be seriously injured and possibly lose the baby. So she held on, praying someone would catch them.

As they rode, Duncan shouted orders to the others, telling them to cover his back and follow as soon as they were able.

"Duncan, there is no way ye can win this today. We know Malcolm was behind everything. Niall and Laird Matheson have joined forces and returned to Duncurra. Stop now, take me back, and Niall will reward ye."

"Ye are daft if ye think I believe that, my lady. Malcolm is my cousin and has been planning this for years. He is not only cunning and cautious, but he was also prepared to do whatever was necessary to achieve his goal."

"Ye are the daft one if ye believe he will prevail against their combined armies."

"I will admit that together Matheson and MacIan will present a challenge, but it is likely Malcolm controlled Duncurra well before they arrived. The fact is, my lady, if Malcolm holds Duncurra under siege, having Laird MacIan's wife as hostage could only be advantageous. Nevertheless, if ye are right and Malcolm fails, I still stand to gain control of Clan MacLennan. Having ye as a hostage won't hurt me, either. This is far from being over for me, and ye are too valuable a tool to just let ye go."

The ride was bone jarring and Katherine suspected Duncan pushed his mount as hard as he dared. She heard horsemen following them, but she didn't know if they were the other MacLennan warriors, her own guard, or more

Mathesons from the castle. Late in the afternoon, Katherine finally recognized her surroundings. They were just north of the mountain pass where Tadhg had kidnapped her only two days earlier, and she knew this was MacLennan land. However, rather than turning south, in the direction of Brathanead, Duncan turned north.

"Why are ye not riding toward Brathanead?"

"So ye know where ye are, do ye?"

"Aye, but why are ye riding north?"

"Because, my lady, it is unexpected. If the men following us are MacIans or Mathesons they will ride toward Brathanead. By heading north we will elude them. Besides, Laird MacLennan is likely to be at or near Duncurra, and we may have a better chance of reaching him there."

Duncan's ruse appeared to have worked, for as they travelled northward, there did not seem to be anyone in close pursuit. However, they had not been on their new course long before they heard horses approaching ahead of them. Duncan swore and turned his horse into the woods. Before Katherine realized what was happening, he clamped a hand viciously across her mouth. "Ye are more valuable to me alive than dead, Lady Katherine. Still, I will slit your throat if ye make a sound."

~ * ~

Malcolm was surprised to see Duncan leave the forest with Katherine.

"Well, what have we here, Duncan?"

"We waited, as ye said, for Niall's army to arrive, but they never did. Finally we saw Lady Katherine arrive under heavy guard. I knew something must have gone wrong, and I suspected ye might need her as a hostage."

Malcolm listened but his eyes didn't leave Katherine. She appeared calm and composed and she didn't look at him. The mask she assumed didn't fool him. She was afraid, and fear was an excellent motivator for cooperation. Pain was as well, and he would use it if he needed to.

"Indeed I do," Malcolm sneered. He moved his mount until he was within reach, grabbed her chin, and turned her head to face him. He laughed malevolently. "With Niall's bonny little wife in residence at Brathanead, we will have a delightful morsel with which to bargain. Well done, cousin."

She knocked his hand away and spat on him. He backhanded her. "Ye will pay for that, wench, and I can assure ye that ye will remember your uncle as gentle before I am through with ye."

To Duncan he said, "Bind and gag her, we need to keep moving."

Duncan did as Malcolm instructed, but said, "Laird MacLennan—I did not expect to find ye returning to Brathanead. Riders followed us from Cnocreidh, but I don't know how many. Some may have been my own men, but I suspect they were not alone. I turned north hoping to elude them all, but if we proceed southwards, we will put ourselves within their reach."

Malcolm looked irritated. "We can't stop here. I have no doubt vengeance is on our heels as well. We will ride up the mountain and hide in the caves until it is safe to proceed to Brathanead. Make sure that gag is secure, I don't want a sound out of her." Malcolm decided to take another precaution as well. "Eithne, dismount and give me your mantle." He switched Katherine's mantle for Eithne's and hoisted Katherine onto Eithne's palfrey.

"What are ye doing?" demanded Eithne. "Why are ye giving her my mount?"

"Ye'll ride with Duncan." Eithne protested, but Malcolm pacified her by explaining, "From a distance, anyone will assume ye are Katherine, and they will not risk harming ye." Besides, he might need a diversion, and as long as he secured his own safety, the consequences mattered little to him.

~ * ~

With her hands bound in front of her, Katherine knew once they began to move again, she would be unable to do anything but stay in the saddle. The wind sharpened and the clouds thickened in the late afternoon sky. It looked as if a snowstorm were brewing and, if it broke soon, the fresh snow would obliterate any trace of their trail. With her bound hands concealed by the mantle around her shoulders, Katherine unpinned the jeweled brooch that had been Niall's present to her on Epiphany. She hid it between her palms, and just before they left the trail to head up the mountain, she let it slip out of her hands to land in the track. She prayed no one noticed it, and, in their rush to escape, no one did.

Chapter 30

As the day wore on, Niall's frustration rose. Malcolm seemed to remain just out of reach. Late in the afternoon, dread filled him when they met Muir and Turcuil with a contingent of Matheson soldiers riding north.

Muir filled him in as quickly as possible. "As soon as the MacLennans poured from the woods, I knew we were badly outnumbered, but we thought we could hold them back long enough for Hamish to get Katherine inside the walls. Matheson reinforcements joined us immediately and we routed them."

"And Katherine is safe?"

"Nay, Laird. Hamish was unhorsed and she slowed to help him. He slapped Eachann back into a run, but it was too late. Duncan reached her and escaped."

"Dear God."

"Laird, I'm sorry. Rab was gravely injured as well. We left him at Cnocreidh, but Hamish, Keavy, Turcuil, and I pursued them with Matheson warriors. We reached the mountain pass leading to Brathanead less than an hour ago. Not knowing for sure which direction he would go, we split up. Hamish and Keavy led some of the Matheson warriors south, while Turcuil and I led the rest north."

"And ye met no one?"

"Nay, Laird."

Niall swore. How could he have underestimated the true depths of Malcolm's deception? He hadn't simply relied on drawing Niall away from Duncurra, he had men in place to assure his defeat at Cnocreidh as well. With every ounce of control he had, he tamped down his rage and focused on finding Katherine.

The leaders agreed it was unlikely Malcolm's party had been far enough ahead to have made it through the pass before the warriors riding from Cnocreidh had reached it. Muir and his men should have met Malcolm and his guard on the track. Since they didn't, it was likely that Duncan had indeed ridden north and met Malcolm's party. Once alerted, Malcolm had probably left the trail to hide in either the woods or the mountains.

They searched along the track for signs of Malcolm's trail, but because his army had ridden north the previous day, horses had trampled the snow on the track, making it impossible to distinguish a new trail from an older one. To make matters worse, the clouds thickened and before long, a light snow began to fall. If they didn't find some indication of where Malcolm had left the track soon, fresh snow would cover any evidence. They had nearly given up hope when one of the Chisholm warriors saw the jewels from Katherine's brooch glinting in the snow.

It appeared that Malcolm's party had headed for caves in the mountains, and once again Niall was in pursuit. It wasn't long before the fresh snow changed from a curse to a blessing. They found Malcolm's tracks.

~ * ~

Katherine tried to work her hands free, but only succeeded in causing the rope to chafe her wrists until they were raw, bloody, and burning. The gag Duncan had stuffed in her mouth tickled the back of her throat, requiring her to constantly fight the need to retch. On top of everything else, she was freezing.

While riding with Duncan, she had at least been warm. Now she had very little to protect her from the cold. Having removed the brooch holding it around her shoulders, Katherine's plaid slid down her back underneath the mantle and bunched around her waist. Furthermore, knowing why Malcolm had forced her to trade places with Eithne, she had shaken the mantle's hood off, exposing her kertch. Even from a distance, in the gathering darkness, Niall would know she was not Eithne. While she thought the plan was clever and no one seemed to notice or care that her hood had slipped off, her linen kertch provided no protection from the cold and snow.

~ * ~

Malcolm held up his hand, halting his men for a moment. In spite of the wind that whipped and moaned around him, he heard the unmistakable sound of horses approaching. If he could buy himself just a little time, he could disappear into the caves with Katherine.

"Duncan, stay here with Eithne and the rest of the guard. They will think it is Katherine with ye, and that will give me time to escape to the caves. When they approach, surrender."

"Aye, Laird," answered Duncan.

"Surrender? They'll kill us all when they realize ye still have the little bitch," screeched Eithne.

"Nay, they won't. Niall is nothing if not noble. He will accept your surrender and not harm ye. I will pay the ransom to get ye and my men released.

~ * ~

Niall and the men with him saw the small party stopped ahead of them and charged. As they drew closer, Niall noticed the pair riding away. Even in the heat of battle, Niall's brain registered the white covering on the woman's head and knew that Malcolm still had Katherine. He pulled back and skirted around the battle, riding hard to reach Katherine. As he did, he heard Eithne's blood curdling scream and Tadhg's anguished battle cry. Ignoring it, he continued to chase Malcolm and Katherine.

Niall saw Malcolm look over his shoulder, panicked. In horror, Niall watched as Malcolm drew his sword and raised it toward Katherine, but it wasn't Katherine for whom Malcolm aimed. He slashed at the flank of Katherine's mount. The mare screamed and reared. Unbridled fear gripped Niall's heart as he helplessly watched Katherine struggle to stay on her mount with bound wrists.

He tried to reach her as she clutched desperately at the edge of the saddle. The ground had become slippery with snow and the horse was sliding and stumbling. All thoughts of vengeance for Malcolm fled as Niall saw Katherine lose her struggle to stay in the saddle. She was thrown to the ground, but with her bound hands, she couldn't break her fall.

When he finally reached her side, he removed her gag. Relief flooded him when he found her unconscious but still alive. He cut her bonds and felt her limbs for signs of breaks. It looked as if her only injuries were the lump on her head, a bruise on her face, and abrasions on her wrists caused by her bonds. Vengeance would have to wait; he couldn't leave his wife.

Tadhg arrived at Niall's side just as Niall gathered Katherine's small limp body into his arms.

Enraged, Niall said, "The bastard caused the horse to throw her to save his own worthless skin."

"I'll take a few men and go after him. Get her to safety."

By this time, Laird Chisholm had joined them and said to Tadhg, "I'll go with ye."

"Nay, Fearghas," Tadhg said. "Malcolm has laid so many traps in the bid to win Duncurra, there is no telling what might await on the way back there. Niall needs as many men as possible riding escort."

"Aye, Fearghas. I have to get her home," Niall said as he wrapped his plaid around his unconscious wife and rose from the ground with her. "I cannot lose her," he said, his voice raw with emotion.

Chapter 31

Vaguely aware she finally felt warm, Katherine had trouble remembering why she had been so cold in the first place. As she struggled to emerge from oblivion, she also realized she had a terrible headache. She fought to open her eyes, but the light only intensified her pain, causing her to moan and retch. Gentle hands rolled her to her side, yet her retching brought nothing up.

She heard her husband's anxious voice say, "Effie, she is waking."

She tried again to open her eyes. For a moment, the light sent another wave of searing pain through her head, but she kept them open this time, and saw her husband's worried face. He was kneeling by her bed. Effie moved into view behind him. "Ye've come back to us, have ye? Do ye know where ye are?"

Katherine blinked and tried to look around. The movement caused her head to swim and she wanted to retch again, but she said, "Home."

"Aye, lass, ye're home," Niall said, his voice husky.

Katherine closed her eyes for a moment. *Why was the midwife here?* She opened her eyes again and managed to ask, "The baby?"

"Is fine," answered Effie. "But ye have a nasty bump on your head from the fall."

"I fell?" asked Katherine. She closed her eyes again, trying to remember. Images began to flood her mind as her memory returned. She moaned again. "Malcolm slashed my mount's side and the poor thing threw me."

"That's right, sweetling, but ye will be fine now," said Niall, with a hint of desperation in his voice.

Effie brought her a bowl with some broth in it. "Try to drink some of this, my lady."

Katherine swallowed a few sips before, overcome with exhaustion, she slipped back into oblivion.

~ * ~

When she awoke later, the room was dark save for the light from the fire. Niall held her in his arms, but he was not asleep. "Back again?" he asked, his voice still thick with concern.

"Aye," Katherine answered. Her head hurt less than it had earlier and she felt hungry. "Is there any more broth?"

Visibly relieved, Niall answered, "Aye, sweetling, there is." He helped her drink a little more, and she ate a few bites of bread as well before giving in once again to the powerful urge to sleep.

~ * ~

The next time she woke, sunlight streamed in through the window, and she felt considerably better. Niall slept beside her, but woke instantly as she stirred. "Good morning, love," he said, and kissed her gently.

"What happened?" she asked.

"Ye were thrown from a horse."

"I remember that. What happened here? What happened with Malcolm and Eithne? And how did I get back here?"

"Whoa, sweetling, there is plenty of time to tell ye everything. For now, I will tell ye Fingal arrived at the same conclusions ye and Matheson did. He brought Laird Chisholm here to defend Duncurra, and was holding Malcolm off when we arrived. Malcolm fled, as ye are aware, because he managed to get his clutches on ye. After ye were thrown from the horse, I brought ye back here. Ye slept for almost a full day, waking for the first time yesterday afternoon."

"But what about —"

"That is enough for now," he said firmly.

For the next couple of days, Niall refused to let Katherine leave their chamber and made certain she did little more than rest and eat. He gave her very sketchy details of events prior to her capture and none of what had happened since. Finally, on the third evening, she insisted on dining in the great hall. She wanted to hear the full story before she did, and, grudgingly, Niall agreed. He told her what Fingal had learned from Eithne and Malcolm.

"Sweet Mary," she said, "What a shock for Fingal."

"Aye. Apparently many MacLennans either knew or suspected Malcolm was his father. It is easy to see the similarities now we know, but no one here ever suspected."

"That doesn't surprise me, because he is so much like ye."

"Katherine, my sweet, other than our height, Fingal looks nothing like me. Everyone always assumed his looks came from Eithne."

"I didn't say he looked like ye, I said he *is* like ye. He is a strong, competent warrior, but he is also gentle and tolerant. He is fair and kind, and protects those who need him. He is proud, unfailingly loyal, and he would sacrifice his life for this clan. He is so much like ye that no one who truly knows ye both would ever deny he is your brother."

Her pronouncement took Niall aback. Everything she said about Fingal was true. He found it endearing that she also applied those traits to him. However, the fact that she believed others drew the same comparisons was, quite frankly, humbling. Furthermore, she had referred to Fingal as his brother in the present tense. He certainly still considered Fingal his brother, and was glad she did as well.

"How is he handling all of this?" Katherine asked after a moment.

"He is upset, as ye can imagine, but worse, he feels guilty."

"Over what?" Katherine demanded.

"Over the fact that Malcolm and Eithne told him they did all of this for him."

"What a load of nonsense. Malcolm and Eithne are the two most self-serving people I have ever met, even surpassing my Uncle Ambrose. Having Fingal as a son was a convenient excuse, but that is all."

"I'm sure ye are right, but Fingal is determined to return to Chisholm. It is one of the reasons I have kept ye secreted away up here. He will not leave until he has apologized to ye, and I keep telling him ye are too weak to have visitors." Niall added sheepishly, "I had hoped after a few days he would change his mind about leaving."

"What's the matter with ye? He has sworn fealty to ye, hasn't he?"

"Aye, he has, but—"

"But nothing, ye must simply refuse to release him. Ye have no problem commanding other people and expecting your commands to be followed without question."

By "other people," Niall assumed she referred not so subtly to herself, and he laughed for what felt like the first time in weeks. "As ye wish, my lady," he said, bowing to her. "Ye still haven't forgiven me for sending ye away—twice?"

"Well, I forgive ye for the first time. Had ye not done that, we never would have learned Tadhg wasn't behind the raids."

"True," Niall agreed.

"So have ye forgiven him for abducting me?"

He realized she had cornered him and glared at her. "I suppose I have," he acknowledged grudgingly.

"Good. Then, I will consider forgiving both of ye for sending me back to Cnocreidh."

"My lady, ye will do more than consider forgiving us. I command it," he said, capturing her in his arms and kissing all thoughts from her head.

Soon the memories of last few days fled and all that remained was their deep love and need for each other. Niall lowered her to the bed, intending to make sweet, unhurried love to her, but his good intentions fled as her passion fanned his desire for her. After they had reached a soul shattering release together, they lay in each other's arms, feeling sated and basking in the afterglow.

Before either of them was ready to leave this haven, a knock sounded at the door. Diarmad called, "Laird, I am sorry to bother ye, but I have just received word from the watch that Laird Matheson approaches."

Niall called, "I will be down shortly." Reluctantly he rose from bed and dressed. Katherine did as well.

"Ye didn't finish telling me all that happened," she said. "Where has Tadhg been?"

Niall sighed. "Ye remember Malcolm put ye on Eithne's palfrey wearing her mantle?"

"Aye, he was trying to buy time for his escape. He believed ye would not harm Eithne when ye discovered it was her."

"Aye, I wouldn't have, but evidently Eithne didn't believe that. As Malcolm's men surrendered, she stabbed Duncan in the gut and tried to push him off his horse. I think she intended to run, but as Duncan fell, she was pulled off the horse with him. In the confusion, they were both trampled."

"Poor Duncan, what a terrible way to die."

"Katherine, he was Malcolm's commander and clearly a big part of this whole plan."

"I know," she said sadly. "It is hard to feel much pity for Eithne—her death was the direct result of her own cowardice—but he had a wife and daughters who will have to go on without him."

"Tadhg suffered a moment of panic trying to save her, thinking it was ye. I knew ye were with Malcolm as soon as I saw him riding away; I saw your kertch."

"Well then, I guess it was worth freezing over," Katherine said, and confessed she had shaken her hood off on purpose. "So Eithne caused her own death, but what happened to Malcolm?"

"Malcolm's little trick worked. By causing your mount to throw ye, he bought enough time to elude us. Tadhg and his men followed him that night, but I am not sure what happened after that. Perhaps we'll learn more when he arrives."

"Then I suppose we should join our guests," said Katherine as she pulled a plaid around her shoulders.

"Ye might need this," Niall said, producing the brooch she had dropped in the snow.

"Ye did find it," she said, giving him the brilliant smile that made his knees weak.

"Aye," he said, pinning her plaid together at her neck. "I am going to have to keep ye firmly rooted by my side to make sure ye don't lose it again." He kissed her, and reluctantly breaking the kiss, he said, "Ye really need to stop distracting me."

~ * ~

When they reached the great hall, Tomas barreled toward her, throwing his arms around her waist yelling, "Mama, ye are all right!"

Everyone there greeted Katherine with nearly as much enthusiasm. It filled Niall with pride to see the firm place Katherine held in the hearts of his clan. Looking up at the front doors, he saw Tadhg and his men enter the hall just as Fingal approached Katherine and bowed. "My lady, please accept my apologies for everything that has happened."

Katherine looked him squarely in the eyes. "I will not."

Fingal appeared stunned and the room fell silent.

"Fingal, there is nothing to forgive. Ye are Niall's brother, and nothing that has happened is your fault. Well, nothing other than ye saving Duncurra by bringing Laird Chisholm here."

Fingal glanced at Niall, "Didn't ye tell her?"

"Aye, I told her."

"Then, my lady, ye know I am not Niall's brother."

"Fingal, I would have thought by now ye would know blood ties mean very little to me. Given enough time, my father's brother would probably have beaten me to death."

"That's different."

"Is it? Do ye think I could possibly love Tomas any more if I had given birth to him?"

Fingal didn't answer.

"Regardless of who your parents were, ye have been a better brother to Niall and to me than anyone could hope for. Ye are Fingal MacIan because Alastair MacIan was your father in the truest sense of the word." Then taking his hands in hers, she said earnestly, "Ye will always be my brother, and ye have my eternal gratitude for saving my home."

With that she kissed him on the cheek. Then breaking the silence in the room, clearly trying to imitate Niall's commanding voice, she said, "This discussion is over. I will hear no more of this nonsense."

Niall laughed until tears ran down his face to see his little wife render his brother speechless. "No more arguments, brother, I couldn't allow ye to return to Laird Chisholm now if I wanted to, and I don't."

Fingal grinned.

Tadhg also appeared to have trouble containing his amusement. He crossed the room to greet Niall and said with a smirk, "Ye deserve her, Niall. I, for one, intend on having a quiet life married to a sweet, biddable lass."

"Don't tempt fate, my friend," responded Niall, gripping his forearm. "I swore never to marry at all, but I will be eternally grateful to our king for this match. Join us for our evening meal. I will hear of your travels later." As much as Niall wanted to know what had happened with Malcolm, he did not want to risk upsetting Katherine before the meal.

Tadhg took the hint.

There was a festive feel to dinner that evening and Niall did not want to spoil it. However, after the meal was finished and they moved to sit by the hearth, he could delay no longer and finally asked, "What did ye find when ye searched for Malcolm?"

"Initially we found nothing. It was snowing heavily by then and we thought it must have covered his tracks completely. We took shelter in the caves until the storm blew out, assuming he'd done the same thing. Then we searched for several days but found no sign of him. We finally found him after we turned back. It looked as if his horse lost its footing and stumbled where the track skirted the edge of a deep gulley, not far beyond the place where we thought we lost his trail in the heavy snow. Both he and the horse were dead at the bottom of the gulley."

All was quiet for a moment, and finally Father Colm said, "Malcolm was responsible for his own destruction. I hope the poor horse didn't suffer."

Epilogue

It had been an unusually hot summer, or so Katherine thought. Perhaps she only felt it more keenly because she was heavy with child, but this August morning felt particularly stifling. Hot and edgy, she hadn't slept well that night, waking up often with her back aching. She must have worked too hard the previous day, she reasoned. After the fitful night, she woke earlier than usual, tired and with her back still sore. She tried to do the things she normally did, but had trouble focusing on even the simplest task. Finally, she gave up and walked out of the keep and across the courtyard. She reached the wall circling the steep crag and looked out across Loch Craos. The water glittered in the bright morning sun. It looked cool and refreshing, and right then she wanted nothing more than to take a swim in it, or at least to wade at its edge.

She decided she would find Niall and ask him to go with her when a pain gripped her, taking her breath away. She braced herself against the wall with one hand and put the other on her swollen belly. It felt rock hard. After a minute or so the pain receded. Maybe she wouldn't go swimming, she thought. Instead, she decided she would walk down to the village and find Effie. She hadn't walked very far when another pain gripped her, forcing her to stop once again and hold onto the wall of a nearby cottage.

After the second pain had receded, she decided it might be better to return to the keep and send someone for Effie. Before she made it all the way back, yet another pain struck. She bent over, clutching her abdomen. She felt sweat beading on her face. She saw Father Colm step out of the chapel. He was at her side in an instant. He lifted her in his arms, carried her into the keep, and began shouting orders.

Katherine smiled briefly, thinking the old priest sounded much like Niall at that moment. Her smile disappeared when yet another pain gripped her.

Within minutes, Edna had Katherine settled in bed and someone had gone to fetch Effie. When she arrived, Effie asked, "Why did ye not call me sooner, my lady?"

"The pains only just started a little while ago," said Katherine.

"Ye've had no other pain?" asked Effie, looking worried.

"Well, I wouldn't say I've had no other pain," snapped Katherine. "My back has hurt since last night, but I have only had a few birthing pains."

Effie relaxed and smiled. "My lady, it is likely ye have been in labor since last night. Birthing pains for some women begin as a back ache."

Even well into labor, several hours passed before the bairn made her appearance. When she did, Katherine suspected the whole castle could hear her lusty cries. Effie allowed Niall into the room after she had bathed the lady and tucked her into a clean bed, holding her sleeping baby in her arms. Clearly in awe of his tiny daughter, Niall looked almost frightened.

"Would ye like to hold her," asked Katherine, lifting the swaddled bundle to him.

"Nay, I might break her."

"Nonsense," said Katherine, "take her."

He gingerly took the bairn in his huge hands. She nearly fit in the palm of one hand and he cradled her head in the other. She began to squirm and fuss a little. He jiggled her gently and said, "Wheesht, lass." She settled and Niall grinned, looking overly pleased with himself.

He still held her some time later when a quiet knock came at the door. Katherine called, "Come in," and Tomas slipped into the room.

"Come see your new sister," Niall said. Tomas came cautiously forward and stood by Niall.

"She's just a wee thing," said Tomas, sounding surprised. "By the noise she was making, I thought she'd be bigger."

Katherine chuckled and Niall winked at her. "It's the wee ones ye have to be careful of, lad."

Tomas wasn't sure what his parents were laughing at, so he ignored it and asked, "Does she have a name?"

"Not yet," said Katherine.

"Can we name her Mab?"

"Mab is your pony's name," said Niall.

"I know," said Tomas. "I like that name."

"Well, maybe since ye have already given it to your pony, we can pick another name for your sister," said Katherine gently. "What do ye think about the name Beitris? It was your grandmother's name."

Tomas said the name a couple of times, then announced, "Well, it isn't as nice as Mab, but since Mab is taken, Beitris is pretty good."

"Beitris it is, then," said Niall, smiling. He leaned over and kissed Katherine on the cheek. He whispered, "I love ye verra much. Ye will never know how happy I am ye chose me instead of the convent."

About The Author

Ceci started her career as an oncology nurse at a leading research hospital, and eventually became a successful medical writer. In 1991 she married a young Irish carpenter who she met at a friend's wedding. They raised their family in central New Jersey but now live with their dogs and birds in paradise, also known as southwest Florida. With their youngest off to college, Ceci is breaking away from "primary efficacy endpoints" and writing a few "happily ever after's."

She is diligently working on Fingal MacIan's story, Highland Intrigue and hopes to release it in the Fall of 2014. Until then, enjoy getting to know Tadhg Matheson a bit better in Highland Courage. She is also thrilled to join with six other great authors of Scottish romance on a bundle of novellas due for release November 17, 2014.

Don't miss the second book in the Duncurra series,
Highland Courage.

Highland Courage - Chapter 1

Carraigile, The Western Highlands, Mid-September 1360

Her father looked bewildered. "Mairead, don't ye want to be married? Look at how happy yer sisters are. Ye love yer nieces and nephews. Don't ye want to be a mother?" Cathal MacKenzie had tried for years to make a match his youngest daughter would accept. Now she suspected his patience was at an end, and he would no longer wait for her approval. Her father had arranged strategically sound marriages for his six oldest children, and they all seemed to be very happy. "Da, I do love the children, but with eight living here and three more when Annag and Hogan visit, why does anything need to change? I'm happy with things the way they are."

Her mother, Brigid, tried reasoning with her. "Mairead, my sweet lass, things can't stay as they are forever. I know ye don't want to live the religious life. Ye would miss yer family too much, and I couldn't bear to think of ye locked up in a cloister. Please, dear one, it is time ye were married."

"Why, Mama? Why can't I just stay here?"

Mairead desperately wanted to avoid the discussion of marriage, but the look of pity in her mother's eyes spoke volumes. Mairead fought to hold back her tears. She hadn't cried in seven years, and she wouldn't start now. Mairead pleaded silently for her mother to intervene, to tell her she never had to marry or leave home if she chose not to. Perhaps sensing his wife's resolve waver, her father answered, "I'm sorry, Mairead, but that is not an option. Ye are well past the age when most lasses marry." Mairead started to argue, but her father put up his hand to stop her. "Nay, lass. No more.

We will arrange a betrothal for ye when we attend the Michaelmas Festival at the end of this month."

"Nay, Da, please..." Terrified, her voice broke, and she couldn't say more.

Her father's countenance softened. "Come with us, sweetling. Ye haven't been for years, and ye used to love it so. We will find ye a new instrument to conquer and ye can meet the young men we are considering. We'll take yer wishes into account if we can, love."

"I don't want to go, Da, and I don't want to get married yet!" Again, she had to blink rapidly to keep the tears from slipping freely down her cheeks.

"What are ye afraid of?" demanded her father.

"I'm not—afraid," she snapped, her voice catching with a sob.

Now her father's eyes mirrored the pity she had seen in her mother's. "The choice to go to the festival or not is yers, Mairead, but we will arrange a betrothal for ye and ye will be married. Soon."

"Aye, Da," she whispered and left her parents' solar. Mairead wanted to retreat unseen to her chamber, but escaping unnoticed was nearly impossible at Carraigile. All of her siblings and their families lived in the MacKenzie stronghold except her sister Annag, who was married to the laird of Clan MacBain, and her little brother Flan, who had just begun his training as squire for Laird Matheson. After leaving the solar, in order to reach the stairs leading to her chamber, she had to cross the great hall, and her siblings managed to corner her there.

Both Cathal and Brigid had lost their first spouses, and each had brought children to their marriage. Mairead was their first child together. She had been the baby of the family for years, until Flan was born, and in a way was the person who had firmly united both sets of children. They could all claim her as a sister. She grew up loved and adored by her siblings, but they could also overwhelm her.

"Mairead, go with us," Rowan said. "We're all going. It'll be fun."

"Ye aren't all going," countered Mairead. "Cullen and Marjean aren't going."

"That's because of our new baby," answered Cullen, "but everyone else is."

Mairead crossed her arms and did her best to look defiant. "Lily and Rose aren't going." She looked pointedly at their twin sisters, Lilias and Rhoswen.

"I want to," said Rhoswen, "but it is awfully hard to travel that far with a baby." Her youngest was only a year-old and quite a handful.

"I'm only staying to keep Rose company. Both of our husbands are going," said Lilias. Cullen rolled his eyes. Lily had given her an opening and Mairead seized it. "Then I will stay and keep ye both company."

Peadar's wife, Rhona, jumped to the rescue. "But then who will keep me company? I'll be the only woman going if ye stay here."

"That's not true. Naveen is going."

Gannon's wife, Naveen, shook her head, "I am only going as far as my parents' holding."

"Well, Mother is going, and yer mother will be joining ye as well, Rhona," countered Mairead.

Rhona pouted prettily. "That's not the same as a sister."

Mairead simply arched an eyebrow at her. Rhona had to know how weak that argument was; at least a score of other Chisholm clanswomen were going.

Mairead loved her family, but now they smothered her. She slowly edged away from them, saying, "Really, I'm sure it will be fun, but I want to stay here."

Gannon tried. "Laird Matheson is going, so Flan will be there, too. Ye were just saying how much ye miss him."

"Nay, Gannon. I can't go." She edged past him and rushed from the hall.

Peadar said, "Well that went well," just before she left.

By the time she reached her chamber, her emotions were a jumble, and once again she had to fight back the tears. This was awful. Clearly, her family didn't understand why this scared her so much. They couldn't possibly understand it. She had never given them the opportunity to understand because she had never been able to tell them why. Perhaps she should have, but she hadn't found the courage to tell them before and she wasn't about to tell them tonight. She had to take hold of herself and find the strength to face this.

She sat by the hearth in her chamber with her head in her hands when a knock sounded at the door. Completely exasperated with her siblings, she yelled through the door, "Go away."

Her brother Quinn ignored her and entered her bedchamber. "I can't, Mairead. We need to talk about this."

"Quinn, I know ye all mean well, but please leave me alone. I don't want to go to the fair."

"I know ye don't want to go." He leaned his back against the door, but his casual stance belied the serious expression on his face. "I want to know why."

"I just don't. Why can't ye all accept that?"

He ignored her question. "Mairead, I've never talked with ye about it and maybe I should have, but I know something happened the last time ye went."

She waved her hands in irritation. "Everyone knows something happened, Quinn. To quote Peadar, I was *colossally stupid* and wandered off with Flan."

"Yes, everyone knows that. What I want to know is what happened when ye wandered off?"

"Ye know that already too. I lost Flan, then I found him, and that priest walked us back to camp."

"Mairead, ye're lying to me. I knew it then, and I know it now."

Mairead couldn't meet his gaze. "Go away, Quinn."

"Ye changed seven years ago. Tell me what happened." The urgent note in his voice was unmistakable as he crossed the room and crouched in front of her.

"I don't know what ye are talking about. I didn't change." She slammed her fists against the arms of her chair in frustration.

"Ye did. I'm sure there are cloistered nuns who are more outgoing than ye are, Mairead."

"And ye know a lot of cloistered nuns?"

"That's not the point."

"Nay, but it's all nonsense anyway. I have always been...timid. MacKenzie's Mouse, remember? I just like being at home."

She hated the nickname "MacKenzie's Mouse" and no one within the family used it. However, many people outside the family and clan did, although it was her appearance and not her temperament that initially gave rise to the name. Da's children by his first wife were tall and blond with crystal blue eyes. Although her mother was petite, all Mama's children from her first marriage were also tall— frankly, Peadar and Rowan were huge—and they all had Mother's dark hair and dark brown eyes. Remarkably attractive, all eight of her older siblings turned heads. Even at four and ten, Flan was a head taller than most lads his age and already showed signs of having the dark good looks of Mama's family, but with Da's bright blue eyes. More like her mother, Mairead was smaller than her siblings, with light brown hair and pale grey eyes. She felt mousey in comparison. However, Quinn was right. She would never admit it to him, but something had changed seven years ago.

Quinn looked directly into her eyes. "Mairead, I know ye better than anyone. I know something bad happened to ye then, and ye have been hiding ever since. Da is getting ready to marry ye off, and I am worried for ye. For the love of God, lass, tell me what happened. No one can help ye if ye keep this locked away."

"Go away, Quinn," she whispered.

He sighed and shook his head in frustration. He rose and kissed the top of her head. "Ye can talk to me, Mairead. Ye can tell me when ye're ready." Then he turned and left her room.

She would never be ready. She couldn't tell him. She couldn't tell anyone. She wanted to keep it locked away.

Available now on Amazon and other online retailers

www.ingramcontent.com/pod-product-compliance
Lightning Source LLC
Chambersburg PA
CBHW032210190626
46810CB00019B/2430